DUBIOSITY

DUBIOSITY

Christy Barritt

Waterfall
PRESS

Text copyright © 2015 Christy Barritt

Published by Waterfall Press, Grand Haven, MI

www.brilliancepublishing.com

Amazon, the Amazon logo, and Waterfall Press are trademarks of Amazon.com, Inc., or its affiliates.

ISBN-13: 9781477826805
ISBN-10: 1477826807

Cover design by Marc Cohen

Library of Congress Control Number: 2014945740

Printed in the United States of America

This book is dedicated to anyone who feels unseen.

There's someone who sees every tear, acknowledges every whisper, and walks with you each moment.

Stop doubting and believe. ~ John 20:27

CHAPTER 1

In the depths of the forest, the rough bark of the pine tree scratched the skin of his back through the thin flannel of his shirt. The discomfort didn't dissuade him from his mission to watch the grand house situated down the lane.

Or rather, to watch the woman inside the grand house.

As he did nearly every evening, he crept through the woods at dusk until he reached his hiding spot. He'd searched for weeks for the perfect place—a nook where he couldn't be spotted from either the road or the bay. And in his fortress of trees, he settled back. He watched the lights in the windows flicker on and off. He watched the woman walk about unaware of his eyes soaking in her every move.

She didn't know what was coming, the great glorious things waiting in her future.

She couldn't know. Not yet.

He'd much rather convince her to agree to his plan of her own free will. But if she didn't, he had other ways to get her to come around to his way of thinking. Delighted prickles danced over his skin in anticipation.

He rubbed the penny in his pocket as he watched her move into her office, just as she did every evening. She sat at her desk, which faced the lane, and even though he couldn't see her clearly, he knew she was crying.

When he was nine years old, two neighborhood boys had goaded him into going to the train tracks that slashed across the landscape behind the neighborhood. They'd convinced him to put the change he'd been saving onto the metal there, promising something wonderful would happen. Instead, his coins had been flattened and were no good anymore. The money he'd saved was worthless.

The townspeople of Cape Thomas were just as naive as he'd been that day so long ago. They were like pennies on a railroad track. They thought they were valuable. Soon they'd realize they were worth nothing.

His childhood days—those days when he'd learned how to be a nobody—were now working to his advantage. He'd learned to show people the person they wanted him to be, all the while hiding his true self. He meandered from the daylight into the black shadows with the same ease that some people felt as they entered and left their homes.

The same way he could enter and leave people's homes, for that matter.

He'd never thought he could take another life. Not until six years ago anyway. And it had been so easy. So simple. And done with such a lack of regret.

Soon it would happen again.

He watched Savannah as she sat stoically by the window, caressing something in her hands. Finally he crept back through the woods. Tonight he had something else he had to do. Something else equally important.

He had a penny to smash.

CHAPTER 2

Solitary. Definition: *to exist alone.*

Savannah Harris sat at her desk with a glass of untouched wine, a box full of tissues, and a random definition that caused her soul to ache. The wine was to numb the pain; the tissues were for when the alcohol didn't work. Though she'd won her school's spelling bee with the word *solitary* in third grade, she would never have guessed the word would take on such a personal meaning later in life.

She twisted the baby rattle in her hands. A lone ball spun around and around inside the pink toy, its sound eerie, an echo of isolation.

Just like me. Alone. Going in circles with no one to hear me.

She used the back of her hand to wipe her eyes. She'd thought by now that the tears would quit coming, that they would have dried up right along with her soul.

No such luck.

Savannah placed the rattle back on her desk and stared out the window at the blackness of her front yard. She finally had the solitude she'd been craving. Out here, it was just her and several acres on the Chesapeake Bay. She felt a kindred spirit with the place.

She sighed and turned off the lamp atop her desk. Time to call it a night.

She was reaching for her wine when she heard the footsteps on her front porch. Quick, urgent steps.

Savannah's muscles tightened. Fight or flight?

She stood frozen.

The screen door screeched, jolting Savannah's already shaken nerves. Who would stop by at this time of the night? And why?

The area had had some break-ins lately. Plus, people always warned her about the dangers of a woman living out here alone . . . out here where there was no one to hear her scream for help. Her heart leapt into her throat.

The front door flew open and a mass of hair, limbs, and clothing tumbled onto the floor. Savannah sucked in a breath as she glimpsed the young woman's face.

"Lucia," Savannah whispered. She hurried to the teen and knelt beside her, brushing her black hair from her face. Tearful eyes looked up at her.

"Papa." Lucia's voice was raw as she whispered the word with life-and-death urgency.

Savannah's heart pounded erratically. "Papa? Señor Lopez? What happened?"

A string of unintelligible Spanish rushed from the girl. Savannah tried to follow but couldn't put the words together, couldn't make sense of anything—which made her heart pound even harder. "Slow down, sweetie. My Spanish isn't as good as it used to be."

Lucia locked eyes with her, and Savannah could see the desperation in their depths. "Come. *Por favor*. He needs you."

Me? Why would he need me? Savannah barely knew the man. She barely knew Lucia. Still, she nodded reluctantly and helped Lucia to her feet. "All right. Come on then. I'll drive us over there."

Lucia sobbed as she stood. Savannah had to keep an arm around her waist for fear she'd fall under the weight of her emotions. They hurried onto Savannah's porch and into the icy nighttime air. Each cell of Savannah's body tightened at the early autumn chill.

"What's happening with your papa?" Savannah asked as they jogged across the gravel driveway to her car.

Tears streamed down the young Mexican girl's face. "Death is close. I can feel it. Everyone can."

Savannah's throat tightened. "Did you call 911?"

"No, Papa wants you."

Savannah helped Lucia into her sedan before running around to the driver's seat. Had the teen run all the way here? The distance from her papa's place to Savannah's was at least a mile, maybe shorter if she'd cut through the woods. But it was dark outside and so cold already. Why would Lucia have run to Savannah of all people? Savannah barely knew the family. Lucia should have gone to Marti Stephenson, who worked at the migrant camp. Or sought out Landon Kavanagh, Señor Lopez's employer. Why Savannah?

Savannah shoved her questions aside and gunned the car down the road. Lucia sobbed beside her, using the edge of her sweater to wipe her tears. Savannah reached across the seat and squeezed Lucia's hand. Her palm felt calloused, probably from the many hours the girl spent working the fields here on the Eastern Shore.

Just one more turn and they'd be at the migrant camp. Savannah's hands began to shake. What would she say to Señor Lopez? She had no hope to offer him in his final minutes. Her days of being a pastor's wife were long gone, never to be resurrected. And she'd never been good at being a pastor's wife anyway.

They turned off the main highway into the migrant worker camp. A group of dilapidated buildings appeared on either side of the road. They were mostly small houses with broken siding, smashed windows, and strings of clothing on makeshift lines outside. Some homes were trailers with front porches made from scraps of wood and leftover lattice. Beer cans littered the flower beds, a fast-food wrapper blew in the wind like urban tumbleweed, and odd assortments of junk lay scattered across the patchy grass. Someone yelled in the distance, but otherwise the night was eerily silent.

Savannah knew the area was poor, but she'd seen worse. She'd toured a squatter camp in South Africa, visited shantytowns in Rio de Janeiro, and seen a garbage dump that people called home in Manila. Compared to these migrant workers, the people who'd lived there had nothing. Still, her heart ached for the hurting people here.

As they pulled up to Señor Lopez's home, Lucia sobbed again. "Por favor, we must hurry. There's not much time."

Lucia practically dragged Savannah from the car and up the creaky steps of the three-room house where eight people, including Señor Lopez, lived. Savannah heard weeping from inside the house before the front door even opened. The sound clutched her heart, tried to wrench her back in time to the night of the accident. She shook her head. She couldn't go there. Not now.

Alba, Papa's wife, stepped outside and reached for Savannah's hands. Savannah found herself pulling the woman into a hug. Alba melted in her arms, a wet mess of sobs. The scent of cumin and cheap air freshener saturated her gray hair.

Finally Alba stepped back and wiped her eyes with a dishcloth before waving it toward the door. "There's not much time."

Savannah gulped in a deep breath, nausea pooling in her gut. She wanted to run, to insist that they find someone else. But how could she turn away from a family in their time of need? She squeezed Alba's hand. "Please, take me to him."

Alba led her down the hallway to a bedroom at the end. With each step, pressure mounted on Savannah's shoulders, pressing down. She wanted to return to the safe confines of her home. Avoid anything that hinted of grief. Steer clear of hopeless situations like this.

Instead, Alba slowly opened the battered door. The scent of urine and body odor drifted out, and Savannah flinched. Inside, candlelight flickered. A cross hung over a threadbare bed.

"Savannah."

Papa's voice was barely audible. When his eyes met Savannah's, she went to his bedside and knelt beside him, her throat dry.

What were all those things people said to comfort others in their last moments? That they were going to a better place? No, Savannah had to speak the truth. But could she tell him that he'd reached the end of the road? That beyond tonight there was nothing? No one? No hope?

The realization still felt like a punch in the chest, still threatened to make tears cascade down her cheeks. She forced herself to cast aside those thoughts.

"Señor Lopez," she whispered, her voice cracking. "I'm so sorry."

Once a strong and robust man, he now looked like a mere skeleton clothed with skin.

"Señora . . . help." He struggled to speak, each syllable causing him to choke. His mouth hung open as he waited for her to respond.

"Whatever I can do."

The candlelight flickered across his bony face, sending eerie waves through Savannah. "I've . . . been . . . murdered."

Savannah sucked in a breath. "Murdered?"

Señor Lopez must be delusional in his final moments. Or she'd misunderstood. His accent was so thick.

His hollow eyes caught hers. "Must . . . pay."

Savannah's body tensed as questions, confusion, and doubts collided inside. "Who must pay? Must pay for what?"

"Justice."

What was he talking about? She shook her head. "Justice how? I don't understand."

Señor Lopez's grip on her hand tightened with surprising strength for a dying man. He tried to speak, but his voice was barely audible. She leaned closer, curious, concerned . . . afraid. "I can't understand you, Señor Lopez. What did you say?"

His lips moved. She leaned her ear toward him, so close that his breath brushed her cheek.

"Landon . . . Kavanagh."

She jerked her head back, a chill sinking all the way to her bones. "Landon?"

She searched his face, desperate for answers. What did Señor Lopez mean he'd been murdered? What did Landon have to do with it? Landon was a good man. Kind and generous to everyone. He took in rescue dogs even. Someone who took in rescue dogs wouldn't murder someone . . . would they? "What do you mean? Please, tell me more."

Savannah watched him, holding her breath, waiting for him to clarify the reason he'd said Landon's name. Not in accusation. Certainly not.

"Landon . . ." Señor Lopez's eyes froze.

The room grew still.

And Savannah knew he was gone.

CHAPTER 3

Sinister. Definition: *the impression that something evil is going to happen.*

If Savannah allowed herself, she might see conspiracy theories filling the town of Cape Thomas more quickly than the retirees who settled in the town's golf course communities. She might see something ominous and threatening going on.

And if she believed in fate, she might believe that was the reason she'd been summoned by Señor Lopez the night before. She might believe she was a pawn being played in the game of life or that she'd received some kind of call to action.

But Savannah believed none of that.

She'd lived long enough to know that theories rarely panned out to be reality. If in doubt, logic prevailed. Besides, small-town conspiracy theories were the thing of made-for-TV movies. In real life, danger didn't loom around every corner. People's motives, while often hidden, were rarely threatening.

And fate? Fate was just a theory people relied on to bring themselves comfort. Life happened as it wanted to happen.

She opened her eyes, her living room coming into focus. She'd been spacing out all day, her mind replaying the events from last night. The whole evening seemed surreal, like something that had happened in her dreams.

But Señor Lopez really had died. Why in the world had he said he'd been murdered? Why did he say Landon Kavanagh's name? It just didn't make sense.

It would take her a while to forget the moment of life leaving Señor Lopez as she'd held his hand, as she'd waited for an explanation about why he'd muttered Landon Kavanagh's name.

The rest of the night had been such a blur. Dr. Lawson had come to the camp and explained to Savannah that Señor Lopez had cancer, that he'd been diagnosed with it months earlier. Meanwhile the family had wept, and Savannah had been swept into a role she thought she'd left behind. She'd attempted to be a comforter to the family, a director to the emergency personnel on the scene, and a good neighbor to people whose language she didn't speak.

Death broke the hearts of innocent people. Wasn't that the cycle of life? The sooner she accepted the reality of death, the easier the future would be for her. No human could conquer dying, but people shouldn't be snatched away before their time. That's what she had a problem with.

With a sigh, she rose from the sofa, where she'd been trying to edit a social studies textbook. The project was due soon, and she couldn't wait to have it off her plate. Editing textbooks paid the bills, but it was never something she'd aspired to do. Which made it the perfect job for her now.

She wasn't sure if the world condemned her or not, but she certainly condemned herself for the actions that had led to the death of her husband and baby girl. She'd created a prison of her own out here in the middle of nowhere, isolated for the most part from any hint of a social life, busy with a career that left her feeling unfulfilled.

She lived on what was called the Eastern Shore, a peninsula of land shared by Virginia, Maryland, and Delaware, that was bordered on one side by the Chesapeake Bay and on the other by the Atlantic Ocean. The small town of Cape Thomas, nestled between historic Cape Charles and Eastville, had a population of less than six thousand. Train tracks divided the landscape, running parallel to the coast. The trains were especially busy during harvest season, carrying produce from the Eastern Shore's many farms to distributors.

Savannah's feet echoed on the wooden floor as she paced. She'd used every penny she had after selling her old place and nearly everything else that had belonged to her to buy these five acres with this run-down old house here in Virginia. It needed a paint job. The floors needed refinishing. The bathrooms needed updating.

One day, she'd told herself. Maybe restoring this house would in some way help her to restore her soul. And maybe that was one of the reasons she hadn't started the makeover process yet. Her soul wasn't ready to feel new.

She shook her head and went into her office, which was located across the entrance hall from the living room. The leftover wine from last night remained on her desk. She reached for the goblet and took a sip as monster-sized emotions began to creep up on her . . . again.

With another shake of her head, she dumped the rest of the wine into the plant beside her desk and swallowed hard. She stared at the piles of papers on her desk, reaching for the project at the top of her list. At least the job kept her connected with the writing world, something she'd walked away from five years ago when she'd met Reid.

Reid. She paused, papers in hand, at the thought of him.

She'd been a journalist covering a story in Afghanistan when she'd met him. He was an army chaplain, and she, by all definitions, was a "worldly" girl, bent on success and materialism and the pursuit of pleasure. But she'd also had a heart for people and justice and exposing the wrongs of those with power. How ironic that they'd fallen in love. She'd accepted Jesus into her life. Reid had gotten out of the army shortly thereafter and taken a pastorate at an eight-hundred-member congregation outside Raleigh, North Carolina. A year later they'd married.

She'd tried her best to be a good pastor's wife, even if it meant being fake—and most of the time, for Savannah, that's exactly what it meant: keeping her mouth closed when she'd wanted to tell someone what she really thought, smiling politely as people offered up their judgmental leanings, shoving down her emotions as church politics took precedent over living lives of transformation.

Maybe she'd just accepted Jesus to appease Reid. Had that been it? Because lately it sometimes felt as if Jesus was the biggest conspiracy theory of them all. No loving God—no God of Justice—would have allowed her life to be filled with this much grief. If God were real, He obviously didn't care.

She sat at her desk and glanced at the pink rattle she always kept there. Every time she saw it, hurt washed over her. *Just work. Work, Savannah.*

Mother Nature was the one who'd killed Señor Lopez. In the time between talking to Señor Lopez and Dr. Lawson, she'd come up with some crazy theories and ideas about how he could have been murdered. She was starting to sound like her friend Marti, a conspiracy theory buff. Señor Lopez had probably let some of Marti's crazy superstitions take hold of him. Or perhaps Landon had given him what many of the migrant workers called the "evil eye" and cursed him. It wouldn't be a stretch for Señor Lopez to think that a curse had caused his death.

She nodded and pulled the keyboard toward her. A piece of white paper tucked under it caught her attention. What was that? She didn't remember leaving something there.

She pulled the paper out, her heart rate quickening as she unfolded the crisp squares.

Her eyes widened as she read the words scratched across the paper.

It wasn't cancer.

CHAPTER 4

Savannah grabbed a sweater from the coat rack in the corner of the kitchen, convincing herself she was chilled because her house was drafty, not because of the note.

It wasn't cancer.

What concerned her more than the authenticity of the note were the questions she kept asking herself: Who had been in her house? Who had left the message? And why did someone want to bring Savannah, of all people, into the middle of this mystery?

She scanned the kitchen as a shudder raced over her skin. Was everything the same here, or had someone invaded this room also? Her gut told her something was off. She'd trusted her gut to keep her alive before.

Her cell phone beeped. Marti.

Savannah's heart sank. She'd intended to call Marti earlier but hadn't. She wasn't prepared to answer her friend's questions, to hear the ache in her voice from both the loss of Señor Lopez and his summons of Savannah instead of her during his final moments. Marti was sensitive and might feel hurt when she found out.

Savannah paused and forced some light into her voice as she answered. "Hey, Marti. What's going on?"

"Savannah, is it okay if I come over for a few minutes? I really need to talk to you." Her voice came out high-pitched, her words colliding into each other.

"Of course."

"Good, because I just pulled up in your driveway."

Moments later, the screen door at the front of the house screeched open. Funny how Savannah used to like that noise. It reminded her of summers at her grandmother's place. But after last night, when Lucia had tumbled through her front door in panic and pain, she knew the sound would haunt her.

Tall, lanky Marti rushed into the house. She always seemed to be going a hundred miles a minute. If it weren't for the red streaks in Marti's otherwise black hair, her nose ring, and slightly crooked teeth, she could have been a model. Instead, she'd chosen a life of service by starting a nonprofit for Eastern Shore migrant workers. She called it La Tierra Prometida, Spanish for "The Promised Land."

"Hey, sweetie. How are you?" Savannah kissed her friend's cheek, which was wet with tears. Marti's eyes were red. She'd always been prone to highs and lows, but Savannah knew the cause of today's sadness. The migrant workers were like family to Marti. They were her reason for living.

"I've been better." Marti wiped her cheeks with the back of her hand before laughing self-consciously and sniffling. "Can I have some coffee?"

"Of course. Let me fix some." Savannah led her to the kitchen table and busied herself making coffee, grateful for the chance to look away.

"I heard Señor Lopez asked for you last night before he passed. Why?"

Savannah paused and pressed her palms against the chipped countertop. "I have no idea why he asked for me instead of you," she said without looking up. "I've asked myself that same question." She turned around. "I'm sorry, Marti."

Marti shrugged, but her lips were pulled down in a frown. "Don't apologize. You didn't do anything wrong. I'm glad you were there for them."

Savannah wiped her hands on a dish towel, trying to choose her next words carefully. The last thing she wanted was to hurt her friend any further. "How's the family doing today?"

"Okay, I guess. We're planning the wake. I know Señor Lopez had been getting thinner, frailer lately, but I didn't know he had cancer."

Did he?

Yes, of course Señor Lopez had had cancer. Dr. Lawson had been treating him for it.

"Didn't he once work on a tobacco farm?" Savannah asked.

"At least Landon didn't grow the tobacco." Marti scowled and plucked a crumb off the table.

Savannah grabbed a mug and filled it with the steaming coffee. Marti and Landon had never seen eye to eye. Since Landon employed most of the migrant workers in the area, he was prone to be the target of Marti's criticism. It wasn't a secret that many of the migrant workers lived in less than desirable conditions. They provided cheap labor, which helped the farms turn a profit. The scenario wasn't perfect, but it was what it was. At least Landon did more than most, paying eight dollars an hour plus a bonus for every basket of produce collected.

Savannah placed the coffee before Marti, then grabbed a mug for herself.

Marti eyed her dubiously. "I thought you hated coffee. You're so confusing sometimes, my friend."

For the same reason I leave my doors unlocked and play golf even though I hate it, Savannah thought. She didn't share, though. No one, not even her best friend, would understand her need to make things right. Some might call it punishment. Savannah called it justice.

"Are you still glad you moved out here, Savannah?" Marti took a sip of coffee and looked at her with big, round eyes. They seemed to have this conversation at least once a month. Marti worried about Savannah way more than she should.

"Of course. I needed a change, and Cape Thomas is definitely a change."

Marti smiled. "I'm glad you're here."

Savannah's fingers tightened around her coffee mug. A remnant from the previous owners, it was decorated with a chipped yellow smiley face. "You're the only person who keeps me sane. You're the only one who can put up with me anyway, and that's only because you're a saint."

"That's ridiculous. You're perfectly lovable. Besides, Landon would love to put up with you, if you'd let him. Maybe you should give him a chance."

"You don't even like Landon."

"If he made you happy, I might change my mind about him."

"Nothing will make me happy, Marti. It's an empty pursuit." The words seemed to slam against Savannah's heart. She used to naively think she could achieve at least some measure of happiness. Now she was simply in survival mode.

"You know that's not true."

Savannah lowered herself into the opposite chair. She carefully set her mug on the wobbly table, another gift the previous owner had left, and cleared her throat. "What did you need to talk to me about? Is everything okay?"

That look of anguish gripped Marti's features again. "Something's going on with the migrant workers, Savannah. I need your help."

"What can I do?"

Marti looked off into the distance, her gaze filled with hope and grief. "You used to be a reporter. You have good instincts about stuff like this."

Savannah's curiosity perked. "Stuff like what? Why do you think something's going on?"

Marti rubbed the edge of her mug. "A couple of people from the camp are missing. They've just disappeared. Since there's no sign of foul play, a lot of the other field workers are speculating that they disappeared on purpose before immigration could grab them."

"Do you think that's true?"

Marti swung her head back and forth. "Absolutely not. These guys aren't the type who would just leave without telling someone. Besides, these field workers are the perfect crime victims. No one sees them. There's no justice for them. No one cares about them except . . ."

"You. Except you," Savannah finished. She leaned back, her investigative instincts rearing up. "Tell me about the people who are missing."

Marti drew in a shaky breath. "One is Felipe. He's probably only nineteen. Nobody's seen him for three weeks now. Even some of the migrant workers are saying he's run off with a gringa, some girl he met on the beach. But I know Felipe better than that. He wouldn't do that. Then there's Jorge. He's in his late twenties. He's . . . he's prone to drinking and causing trouble. But he just got married and loves his wife so much. She's in Mexico, and he sends her most of his money."

"When did he disappear?"

"Last week." Marti's tear-filled eyes met Savannah's. "Will you help?"

Savannah raised her hands, palms up, not wanting to let her friend down, but . . . "I don't know what I can do."

"You were the best, Savannah. The best. You know that. You didn't fear anyone. Not your editors, your colleagues, dictators even. You were nominated for a Pulitzer, for goodness sake."

"That's not who I am anymore." That familiar pressure tugged at her heart, feeling as if it might rip her in two. She'd had to leave that part of her behind, yet journalism seemed to be in her blood, something she could never cleanse from herself.

Marti reached across the table and touched Savannah's hand. "It was terrible what happened to Reid and Ella, Savannah. But you've got to forgive yourself. You've got to go on with your life—"

A loud knock on the front door interrupted her. Savannah was more than happy for the excuse to abandon this conversation.

"Excuse me a minute," she said.

When Savannah opened the door, she had to blink twice. The man standing on her doorstep was a stranger. He was tall, broad-shouldered, and wore a five-o'clock shadow, a flannel shirt, and work boots. His hands were casually stuffed into the pockets of his jeans, but his eyes were intense. Not especially friendly, but not hostile either.

Or were they?

"Savannah Harris?" His deep baritone voice seemed to reach all the way down to her bones.

"Yes?"

"I'm Clive Miller. We talked last week on the phone."

Clive Miller? Last week? All she could remember was Señor Lopez and *it wasn't cancer*. "We talked about . . . ?"

"About renting a room."

Their conversation flooded back. Was that just last week? It seemed like months ago. "That. I'm sorry . . . what did you say it was? Clyde? But I called you back and left a message that I changed my mind. The idea was a crazy whim."

"It's Clive. I switched cell phones right after you called me. I never got the message."

"I'm sorry to hear that."

He shifted, his eyes no friendlier than before. "I hope you'll reconsider. I've just driven four hours, and I really need a place to stay."

Savannah could have kicked herself. Marti had been the one to suggest that she rent the carriage house behind her property when Savannah admitted she needed money. For one day, Savannah had not only entertained the idea, she'd immediately posted an online ad, had a bite within an hour, checked out Clive and his reference, and then just as impulsively changed her mind. She'd thought it was over and done, a hasty mistake quickly remedied with a phone call.

Only she'd been mistaken, and now her impulsivity was here to haunt her in the flesh-and-blood form of Clive Miller. Savannah didn't know who she'd pictured showing up after their initial conversation. She'd imagined he would be a studious nerd, not this man. He was too young, too rugged, too . . . unnerving. She needed a way out.

"What brings you to this area, Mr. Miller?"

He shifted his weight. "I need a change of scenery."

A change of scenery? That wasn't enough to convince her to abandon her privacy. She didn't know what would have been enough. Probably nothing.

"There are some apartments in town that are rented on a monthly basis. I'm sure you can find something there." She softened her voice. "I hope you understand."

She started to close the door, but his hand quickly blocked it. She stared at him until he lowered his arm to his side. Just what kind of game was this man playing?

"Please. I can pay you in cash for six months in advance. I'm quiet and like to mind my own business. You won't even know I'm here." His gaze, though still edgy, seemed to implore her.

There was more to his story—Savannah was sure of it. What she wasn't sure about was whether or not his intentions in being here were honorable. She had to be careful with her waterfront property. The bay was an ideal place for smuggling operations. She didn't want to be the unsuspecting homeowner who rented her property to a criminal.

"I'm not interested in a boarder. I'm sorry for the misunderstanding. I truly am."

Before he could argue, she closed the door and locked it. When she turned, she saw Marti behind her, shaking her head with her arms crossed over her chest. "The apartments downtown are full, Savannah."

Savannah raised a brow. "How do you know?"

"It's harvest time. All the extra migrant workers have filled everything up, even the campgrounds."

Savannah swiped the hair out of her eyes, determined not to worry about it. "I'm sure he'll find something."

"What could it hurt to rent him the place out back? It's not a bad idea to have someone else around. You're so alone out here. I worry about you. If anything happened . . ."

Savannah started back toward the kitchen, toward her coffee. Why was everyone suddenly so worried about safety? A few break-ins in the area and suddenly it was dangerous to be by herself? No one had been harmed in any of the burglaries. And while Savannah certainly didn't want someone to invade her home, her stuff was just that—stuff. If someone was desperate enough to steal it and possibly go to jail for doing so, then let them.

"He's nice to look at, if nothing else." Marti trailed behind her.

Savannah shook her head, wishing she had something to throw at Marti. "The last thing I want is someone nice to look at. I like being out here alone. I only regret that the guy drove so far for nothing."

"He could be a nice distraction."

A distraction? She had enough of those in her life. Starting with Señor Lopez and the note.

She was going to forget she ever got that note, Savannah decided. She was going to leave it to the authorities to find Felipe and Jorge. She was going to go on with her self-imposed prison sentence of a life, continue on like a lone bead in an old baby rattle.

CHAPTER 5

Savannah took one look at Marti and knew her friend wasn't ready to drop this subject. As she skirted past her to get to the kitchen table, she braced herself.

"Savannah, you know I love you, right?" Marti followed her.

Savannah leaned against the table and crossed her arms over her chest. Her defenses were going up, whether she wanted them to or not. "Of course."

"Then you know I'm saying this in a loving way." Marti stood in front of her. "You are your own worst enemy right now. What happened was tragic, but you've got to move on. The Savannah I knew wasn't afraid to take risks."

"The Savannah you knew destroyed lives."

"You *saved* lives. The fault was in other people. Not you. You were always a fighter."

Savannah shrugged. "I'm not that person anymore."

"You are. Deep down inside, you are. You're a world changer, Savannah."

"My world was changed. That's for sure." She shook her head. "Part of my problem was that I didn't know when to quit."

Marti raised her chin. "Maybe part of your problem now is that you don't know when to start."

Marti stared at her another moment, challenge in her gaze, before grabbing her purse and heading toward the front door. She cast one more disapproving look at Savannah.

Excuses flooded Savannah's mind. Outrage coursed through her.

Marti didn't understand. She couldn't. No one could.

"I'm meeting with Landon today about donating to La Tierra Prometida," Savannah called.

Marti threw a glance over her shoulder, said nothing else, and shut the door behind her.

How dare she give her this guilt trip. Savannah had gone out of her way to help her friend. Wasn't that the only reason she'd agreed to play a ridiculous golf game today?

Marti made it sound as if she never did anything. That wasn't true. She worked. She helped out with La Tierra Prometida.

She was doing things that would keep her out of trouble, things that would prevent her from making the mistakes she'd made before. She'd been blinded by her ambition, by her causes, and her family had paid the ultimate price. She couldn't let that happen again. And that meant she was done investigating. Done reporting. Done with her old life.

Maybe her penance was that she had to give up the one thing she felt she'd been created to do.

. . .

"You're up, Savannah."

Savannah swung her head toward the voice, and Landon Kavanagh came into focus. He leaned against his golf club with a sparkle in his eyes, as if he knew her mind was in another world.

His lean, wiry figure looked like it was made for the golf course. His clothing was neat and perfectly pressed, and the shirt was carefully tucked in. He was deeply tanned, supposedly from working outside on his farm, but Savannah had suspicions that he had a tanning bed tucked away somewhere in his house.

She'd thought about cancelling this outing, but the immature part of her wanted to prove Marti wrong, to show that she still had some fight left in her.

"Time to show you who the boss of this golf course is." She frowned at the forced cheerfulness in her voice before gripping her club and stepping up to the tee.

It was a beautiful, crisp autumn day and the perfect weather to play golf. Too bad it was such a miserable game. Her parents had insisted she learn to play so she could be a country club kind of girl. She'd never wanted to be one of those society gals, though. She'd always preferred getting her hands dirty exposing the greedy and those who liked to prey on the less powerful. As soon as she'd graduated high school, she'd vowed to put the game of golf behind her, but Landon had made it clear that the only time he would discuss donating to Marti's charity was on the green.

Marti was the only reason Savannah was plastering on this smile and drawing on her severely underutilized social skills right now. La Tierra Prometida needed the money. Landon seemed to know that and used it to his advantage.

As Savannah centered her club, Señor Lopez's face flashed through her mind. She tried to push away the image, but it kept returning. His desperate eyes. His raw voice. His ominous accusation.

"Savannah?"

Landon's voice pulled her back to the present. "Sorry," she mumbled.

25

She glanced toward the hole a few hills and sand traps over and swung. The ball sailed through the air, white plastic colliding with blue sky. The sphere rose like a bird before free-falling and landing mere feet from the target.

"Nice swing. But I'm not ready to give up my title here yet."

"You may not have a choice in that, Mr. Kavanagh." Savannah raised an eyebrow. Inwardly she groaned. How much more of this facade would she have to endure? She longed to be back at the house alone. Brooding. Attacking herself for all of her failures. Allowing her despair to grow deeper and darker.

Landon chuckled and put his hand on the small of her back. She resisted, flinching at his touch. He directed Savannah toward the golf cart parked a few feet away. They climbed inside and started across the lush green turf. The crisp air blew over Savannah's face as they rolled down the path.

Landon casually draped one hand over the steering wheel and the other across the back of the seat. He wasn't a large man—only five foot eight, three inches taller than Savannah—but he carried himself like a giant and had enough confidence to fill this entire golf course.

Last night slammed into Savannah's mind again.

Murdered. Justice. Landon Kavanagh.

As if he could read her thoughts, Landon said, "So I heard you were there when Señor Lopez passed."

Savannah cringed. Why would Señor Lopez have muttered Landon's name? Despite her best logic and reasoning, Savannah suddenly felt chilled by Landon's nearness. It was ridiculous. Sure, the man had used his power to convince Savannah to play golf. But despite his self-centeredness, he wasn't capable of murder. Savannah had always had good instincts about people, and she felt certain Landon was innocent.

"Lucia came and got me."

He raised a brow, glancing away from the golf course for only a moment. "I didn't realize you were close to the family."

"I'm not. I'm not really sure why they wanted me there."

Ask him.

No, she couldn't ask Landon if he'd had a part in Señor Lopez's death. Landon was a good man, not capable of harming a flea.

Ask him, then.

The words wouldn't leave Savannah's mouth. In her mind, they sounded ludicrous. To voice them aloud would only make her feel loony.

She cleared her throat and steadied herself against the side of the golf cart as they bounced across the green. "Do you know the family that well, Landon?"

"The Lopezes?" He shrugged. "Can't say I do. They've been working for me . . . I don't know . . . three years maybe? Hard workers."

Ask him.

She pushed a wavy strand of brown hair out of her eyes. Dr. Lawson had told her about Señor Lopez's cancer, but she wanted to find out what Landon knew. "Have you heard how he died?"

He glanced at her, clearly confused. "How he died? He was old, Savannah. That's how he died."

Some of the pride she used to wear like a designer jacket seemed to pull at her frame, causing her shoulders to straighten and her chin to rise. She was no idiot. She had awards that showed just how bright some people had thought she was. "I know that, Landon. I just mean that even seventy-six-year-olds die from something."

His grip on the steering wheel seemed to loosen as they veered right, and bright sunshine lit his face. "I heard he had cancer."

"So did I," Savannah admitted.

"There were no signs of foul play, right?"

"Right."

"Then it sounds like you have your answer."

They climbed from the cart and found their balls. Landon practiced his swing for a moment, looking as casual and laid-back as ever in his khakis and polo shirt. He made the answers sound so easy. Maybe they were. Maybe Savannah just needed to let this go.

"Any plans for this evening?" Landon asked.

"Same old, same old." Savannah gripped her golf club, twisting it in the grass and wishing it was anything but a golf club—a baton, a baseball bat, anything.

Landon swung at the air again. Golfing was one punishment; golfing with a perfectionist who took his game way too seriously took it up to the next level. "Being alone, in other words."

She shrugged and gripped her golf club like a lifeline. "I like being alone." Even as she said the words, her heart thudded with sadness. She hadn't always been like this.

"I don't think you do."

"Maybe you don't know me that well then."

"I've been trying."

She couldn't deny that. Six months ago, her car had broken down on the side of the road, and Landon had been the one who'd stopped to help. From the start, he'd asked her to dinner and to charity events and even to church. She'd always said no. Somehow, one thing had led to another, and now she was here. Coerced. Her arm twisted. Her soul in a bind. "You've been very kind, Landon."

His eyes connected with hers, imploring. "Have dinner tonight with me then."

"I can't, Landon."

Landon wasn't used to people saying no to him. Savannah sometimes wondered if that's why he liked her—because she was a challenging conquest, someone unreachable. Nearly every single woman in the area seemed to be dying for the chance to date the man, and instead he focused on Savannah—the one woman with no interest in a relationship.

"Why not?"

"I'm . . ." *Why not, Savannah?* "I'm . . . not ready."

He turned toward her and placed his hands over hers. His crystal-blue eyes implored her. "I'm not asking you to marry me. I'm asking you to dinner—a meal. You have to eat. Why not eat with me? You already play golf with me. Why is dinner such a big deal?"

"I'm sorry, Landon." He'd never understand. He couldn't. Sometimes Savannah didn't even understand her reasoning—probably because her emotions entirely outweighed logic. She didn't want to feel sorry for herself, but at the same time, she didn't know how to move on. Every time happiness appeared in the distance, an army of guilty thoughts closed in, reminding her that she'd lost her right to be happy. Forever.

His hand dropped, and he turned back to the game. His gaze flickered at her from the corner of his eye. "I'm not giving up."

"I'd expect no less."

He swung his club, and his ball escaped through the air. Savannah wanted to be that ball—she wanted a quick way out of this conversation.

"Do me one favor though, will you?" Landon said.

"Perhaps."

"Lock your doors tonight. There have been some break-ins in the area. I'd feel a lot better if you'd do that for me."

"I'll think about it."

He cut a sharp glance at her. "I still don't understand why a city girl like you is so trusting. Cape Thomas may seem safe, but in this day and age, everyone should lock their doors. At least take one of my dogs, for goodness sake. He'll offer you some protection out there all alone."

He wouldn't understand, Savannah mused. "You sound like my dad."

"Someone's got to watch out for you. And never say I'm like your dad again."

Savannah smiled reluctantly. "Let's just play golf. I've been dying to show you up. Again."

CHAPTER 6

After golf, Savannah climbed into her beat-up old Volvo and started down the country road. She needed to swing by the grocery store before heading home.

The good news was that Landon had agreed to donate ten thousand dollars to Marti's nonprofit. The bad news was that Savannah had had to suffer through a game of golf in order to make it happen.

As much as she tried to put the events of the last twenty-four hours out of her mind, they wouldn't evaporate. Last night played over and over like the reel of an old movie. The note was now burning a hole in her back pocket. The handsome but pushy stranger who'd shown up at her door kept staring her down.

Life was different now. Ten years ago, a day like today would have gotten her blood pumping. She would have wanted to dig, to ask questions, to not leave well enough alone. Of course, ten years ago she would have never wanted to be living by herself, absent of nights out with her girlfriends, trips abroad, heart-pounding assignments, and an overall investment in people and world affairs.

She missed her old life—both of them. There was life before she met Reid and after she met Reid. She was now on her third life.

Her mom had told her when she was breaching adulthood that her thirties would bring some of the best times she'd ever experience. It was the age when you became sure of yourself, when many of your insecurities disappeared, and you knew where you were headed for the future. Funny how circumstances had turned Savannah's thirties into the most heart-wrenching period of her life.

She pulled into the parking lot of a local grocery store. She'd made her list and just needed to pick up a few things. With any luck, she wouldn't run into anyone she knew.

As she got out of her car, she glanced over at an older-model Jeep parked at the back of the lot. She did a double take at the sight of the man leaning against the side, drinking a bottle of water and staring into the distance. Her heart pounded.

Clive Miller.

Marti's words echoed in her mind. Maybe she was right. Maybe Savannah was too rigid; maybe she'd become too set in her ways. Maybe she should consider taking on a boarder. With a touch of hesitation, she started toward him, unsure of what she would say.

"Ms. Harris." Clive leaned forward, one arm still casually resting on the door of his Jeep. The autumn sun highlighted his strong face, made his hair glint. "Fancy seeing you here."

Savannah wiped an imaginary piece of lint from her sweater with one hand and grasped her purse with the other.

She cleared her throat. "Did you find a place in town?"

He continued looking into the distance. "Nope. Not one. Everything's full. Harvest season and all."

"Maybe something will open up in a few days. I'm sorry it didn't work out at my place." She couldn't bring herself to let the words leave her mouth, to extend the invitation to him.

He nodded slowly, not saying anything, even though his actions said plenty. He knew good and well nothing would open up. So did Savannah.

She wrestled with her decision. She so valued her privacy, her isolated little life. Could she really give that up?

The extra money would be nice. Cash flow had been tight. This would be a great way to bring in some extra income. And to prove Marti wrong.

"I'll let you stay until harvest season is over . . . if you give me one good reason why you're in town." As soon as she said the words, she wanted to snatch them back.

It was too late.

His gaze seared hers. "One good reason? I need closure on my wife's death. She loved it here."

Savannah's breath caught. She swiped a hair behind her ear and swallowed. "Your wife?"

He nodded, some of the edge leaving his eyes. "She's been dead six years."

"I see. I'm sorry about her passing."

He raised his head in a half nod. "Me too."

She looked away, realizing she was staring at the man with complete sympathy and curiosity. Maybe it was Señor Lopez's passing, or maybe it was the passing of her own spouse. She wasn't sure. Still, she muttered, "Come by in an hour. You can stay at the carriage house for a few weeks, until the harvest is over and something in town opens up."

He smiled, though only thinly. "Thank you, Ms. Harris. You won't regret it."

Too late again. She already did.

• • •

As she shopped and then drove home, Savannah questioned her decision to let Clive Miller stay in the carriage house. Why had she changed her mind? Because of his sob story? Had she fallen for some act?

Or had she changed her mind because of the look in his eyes? She could relate.

She put the thought aside as she hurried toward her house. The hour she'd given Clive to stop by was nearly over. She wouldn't even have time to air out the carriage house before he arrived. Not that she cared. It was simply that some old habits were difficult to forget. Her mom had always insisted that Savannah be proper and polite. Though Savannah had fought those instructions, they'd spited her by embedding themselves in her psyche anyway.

On the top step, balancing two bags of groceries on her hips, Savannah paused. Apprehension crept up her spine. Something seemed off.

She turned and scanned the landscape around her. The country lane that stretched from her home. The tranquil bay in the distance. The woods across the street.

Nothing.

Why did she feel like someone was watching her? The note she'd found under her keyboard came to mind, and her throat went dry. Someone had been in her home once before. Were they back again? This time with more sinister intentions?

She shook her head and opened her front door. She placed her keys on the walnut table in the foyer and paused. What looked different about the table? The old milk bottle with a dozen roses inside—compliments of Landon—was just where she'd left it. A jar candle stood a respectable distance from the flowers. A wood-framed mirror hung lopsided above it all. Everything appeared in place.

Savannah squinted. No, something was wrong.

She leaned closer. A faint line ran across the dust on the table, almost as if someone had taken a finger and dragged it over the wood there. Had Savannah done that?

She shook her head. She couldn't be sure. Why had she even noticed such a small detail?

She tried to shake it off as she straightened, but she couldn't get the line out of her mind. How had it gotten there?

Just then she heard a vehicle rumbling down the road.

Clive.

He'd arrived right on time. She'd have to worry over that line in the dust later. She waited for him to stop and get out of his vehicle.

"Can I help?" he called, pointing to the open trunk of her car.

"Sure." She watched as he grabbed the remaining three bags. He balanced them in his strong, well-defined arms as he strode across the grass and up the porch. Savannah held the door open with her heel. "Just put them in the kitchen."

He followed her inside and placed the bags on the kitchen table. He surveyed the interior of the house for a moment before nodding. "Nice place."

Savannah looked up. His gaze contained . . . satisfaction? Curiosity? What was that emotion lurking there? Whatever it was, it made her pause, wondering if this strange man should be in her house.

She cleared her throat and turned from him, trying to get a grip. "I like it. It needs some work. Maybe one day." She grabbed the milk from her bag, already uncomfortable with how imposing Clive's broad-shouldered frame felt in her home. She needed a way to get him out of her space. "Let me just put a few things away. Why don't you go on out back? I'll be there in a second."

"Sure thing." He stepped outside.

Savannah pressed her hands on the countertop and closed her eyes, composing herself. Why was Clive having this effect on her?

What was it about him that had her frazzled? She didn't have time to examine it now. She quickly put away the orange juice, eggs, and butter and then headed for the back door. She might as well get this over with. Maybe he'd see the place and hate it, change his mind.

As she approached the carriage house where Clive Miller stood waiting for her with his hands thrust in the pockets of his jeans, she soaked him in again. Most women would consider him handsome, even with the slight scar she now noticed running across his jawline.

But there was something about his eyes that made Savannah curious. She couldn't put her finger on exactly what it was. A hardness? Determination? She couldn't be sure, but she made a note to keep her eyes open for an answer.

She forced a smile as she approached. His smile looked equally forced.

Savannah dangled the key. "Let me show you the place. Follow me."

He fell into step beside her, their feet trampling the brittle grass.

She searched her mind, trying to remember all the small talk she'd been taught to use in awkward social situations. "So, Clive, huh? Unique name."

"I was named after my mom's favorite author." He slid a glance her way.

"C. S. Lewis?" Savannah asked.

Clive's eyebrows inched up in surprise. "Not many people know that. You a fan?"

She shrugged. "Used to be. Where did you say you were from?"

"The DC area."

"Busy up there."

"You can say that again."

"Cape Thomas will be quite the change of pace."

They reached the dainty white clapboard house, and Savannah twisted the key in the lock. As the door opened, the musty odor of a space that had been closed up for too long drifted out. She hurried across the wood floor, sneakers padding, and opened a window. Cool air flooded in.

She turned to Clive, folding her arms over her chest to ward off the cold. "This is it. As you can see, the house is small but ample. There's an efficiency kitchen and a bathroom. The living room and bedroom are the same. The couch pulls out into a bed."

His gaze scanned the room before nodding. "It's different than what I expected."

"This used to be a carriage house. That's how old the property is. The previous owner fixed this place up, hoping to use it as a guesthouse for out-of-towners looking for a relaxing getaway vacation. They didn't quite make it around to fixing up the main house."

"What happened?"

"They were an older couple. The wife had a stroke, so they sold this place and moved to a retirement community."

"It's a shame they couldn't enjoy their hard work. This place is beautiful."

"It is. The property goes to the Chesapeake Bay to the west, the cornfield to the east, and the woods on either side of the drive." She strode across the room to the linen closet. "Here's all the towels and sheet—"

She opened the door and gasped.

Blood soaked every one of her white linens. Even worse—it still looked wet.

CHAPTER 7

Clive Miller closed the carriage house door after Chief Lockwood bid them farewell and headed back to his cruiser. He glanced over at his pretty new landlord and saw that her face still looked pale. Her arms were crossed over her chest, and a strange, almost vacant look had appeared in her eyes.

"Sorry about that welcome," she finally said. Her voice wavered, and her entire body looked tense.

"Don't worry about it. It wasn't your fault."

"Who would have thought hunters were using this place? I think I would have noticed something like that." She looked so uneasy, so uncomfortable and conflicted.

He didn't dare offer her any consolation. Nothing other than the obligatory words of encouragement. He had a feeling if he even laid a hand on her arm she'd snap.

In a woodpile behind the carriage house, the chief had found some tangled fishing line and other evidence indicating that some local sportsmen had used this place between hunts. Apparently they'd cleaned up here, used the towels, and then placed them back in the cabinet.

Just in case, the chief had taken the linens back to the station to be tested. He'd said he was 99 percent sure it was animal blood.

Now Clive reached into his pocket and pulled out a bank envelope. He handed it to Savannah. "Two months rent plus a deposit. I appreciate you doing this so, whether I stay a few weeks or a couple of months, the money is yours."

She took it, casting a pensive glance at him before stepping toward the door. "Great. I'll leave you to get settled in."

"Thanks again, Savannah. I appreciate this."

She scrutinized him another moment before nodding and walking out.

Clive stood there a moment, listening to her steps tapping across the porch. From the window, he watched as she crossed the sweeping lawn back to her house.

Savannah wasn't what he'd expected, and that realization made him both anxious and curious. He'd figured someone living out here in such a large house would have a horde of kids or be the grandmotherly type who'd stayed on the property because of tradition and routine. Too bad. Kids would have distracted her. Kids would have kept her from asking too many questions. Being a grandmother would have prevented her from being too mobile, too nosy.

Instead, Savannah appeared to be single. Not only single, but easy on the eyes. She had a slim figure, porcelain skin, full lips, and big eyes framed with thick lashes. Her hair was dark, on the luscious side, with easy waves and natural gloss. She was probably in her early thirties, if he had to guess.

None of that mattered, though. He was here because he had a mission to accomplish. No one would get in his way. Not even Savannah Harris.

He'd keep to himself, mind his own business, try not to get people asking too many questions.

He pulled out his cell phone and dialed his friend Wheaton's number. Wheaton answered on the first ring. "You there?"

"I am. No problems so far." Clive glanced around the carriage house, noting how casual and cozy it seemed—a direct contrast to what he felt inside.

"Anyone suspect you?" Wheaton asked.

"Not yet. I'll be careful."

"You know you don't have much time. I'll keep you updated on things here."

"I appreciate it, Wheat. More than you'll ever know."

He hung up and closed his eyes a moment. He didn't have any time to lose. Because once people discovered who he really was, his job here would become a hundred times harder.

That meant he needed to get started. Now.

• • •

Savannah couldn't get Marti's speech out of her mind.

Marti's words had led Savannah to another term: squander. Definition: *to waste recklessly.*

Was Savannah squandering her life away? Was there a way to punish herself while still making a difference? And even more, would jumping back into her old way of doing things somehow atone for her past sins?

She'd tried to bury every aspect of her old life right along with her husband and daughter. Maybe she had somehow in the process become self-centered, self-focused, self-everything.

At once she made a decision. Before she lost her determination, she hurried down to the kitchen. She put together a quick cream cheese dip, added some crackers, and covered the tray with plastic wrap.

She'd stop by and pay her respects to Alba, she decided. It was the least she could do. It didn't mean she was getting involved or investigating or anything. She was just being neighborly. Withdrawing from her self-seclusion. Trying to tap back into the parts of her that had been good and decent.

She couldn't deny a slight twinge of excitement as she drove down the road toward the camp. Emotions and motivations could be so complex at times. She decided not to analyze her feelings. She had to do this. Maybe take baby steps out of her seclusion. If it didn't work out, she could return to her life of solitude. She wasn't making any commitments.

Her hands trembled as she climbed the steps to Alba's weathered, neglected house. She shivered as she remembered Señor Lopez's final words.

Landon Kavanagh.

Something shiny on the porch caught her eye, and she stooped to pick it up. She smiled at what she saw.

A flattened penny, most likely made that way after being left on the train tracks. Her dad used to say they were good luck. She slipped it into her pocket, taking it as a sign that she should be here.

Voices drifted from the open windows, but Savannah couldn't understand anything they were saying. There was weeping, some laughter, some quickly spoken words.

She knocked at the door. Lucia answered. As soon as she spotted Savannah, she pulled her into a long hug. "You came."

Savannah smiled at her. "I wanted to check on everything."

"You just missed Señora Marti. She ran to the store for some sodas and chips." Lucia hooked her arm through Savannah's. Her English was considerably better when she wasn't emotional and frazzled. "Come on in. They'll be happy to see you."

She addressed everyone in Spanish and then pointed to Savannah. Savannah smiled softly and set her tray on the kitchen table beside some crème-filled cookies, sliced tomatoes, chips and salsa, beans and rice, and some other food she couldn't identify.

Lucia led her around and introduced her to everyone, saying more words that Savannah couldn't understand. Every time the instinct to flee arose, she pushed it down. She wasn't used to being around so many people since her self-imposed exile.

When the introductions were over, Savannah hoped she could take a breather for a moment. Instead, Lucia pulled her into a corner.

She was really a pretty girl, with curly black hair that fell halfway down her back. She had bright, intelligent eyes, soft features, and a slim build.

"He told you," she whispered.

Savannah's throat tightened. "Papa? He said all kinds of things before he died."

"His death wasn't natural, Señora Harris. Someone murdered him. You've got to believe me."

Savannah looked from side to side, making sure no one could overhear them. "Why would you think that?"

"Did you hear about Felipe? Jorge?"

"Marti mentioned them. But—"

"Someone snatched them," she whispered.

"Did you tell the police?"

"The police won't do anything. They never take us seriously."

"They might. They can do far more than I can—"

"I know who you are, Señora Harris." She leveled her gaze.

Savannah blanched, uncertain if she'd heard correctly. "What was that?"

Lucia nodded. "It's true. I went to the library. I know. Señora Marti let it slip once that you were a writer. I saw all those articles."

Savannah took a step back. "Lucia, that part of me is in my past."

Lucia grabbed her arm. "Please. We have no one else."

One look into Lucia's eyes, one look at the desperation there, made Savannah question her resolve.

Marti's words haunted her. *Now you don't know when to start.*

Maybe Savannah could take a chance. Maybe she could just dip her toe in the water.

Maybe somehow she could move past her past.

"I'll think about it," she promised. "Right now I need to go. We'll talk more, though. Okay?"

Lucia nodded, her eyes glimmering with tears. "Okay."

CHAPTER 8

Savannah had found the gift he left. At best, he'd thought Señor Lopez's family would find it and shrug it off as a coincidence.

But having Savannah not only find it but touch it, keep it—that was more than he could have hoped for, more than he could have dreamed.

Soon the police would realize what was going on, even though they'd failed to see any of the signs so far. Even the dim-witted PD in Cape Thomas would eventually catch on. But their blindness and stupidity was what made this the perfect place to carry out his scheme.

Because by the time they put it all together, it would be too late.

Despite his delight, an equal amount of agitation churned in his gut.

The last thing he'd expected Savannah to do was to show up at the migrant camp. It didn't fit her MO. She was lonely and secluded, not one to mix and mingle. So why had she gone there? What was going through that brilliant mind of hers?

He rubbed the bark of the tree, watching her now as she sat at her desk. He imagined what her skin felt like. Not rough and dry like this tree. No, he imagined her to be soft, silky.

She was probably cold, though. She was always pulling on sweaters and jackets, drinking warm drinks, trying to thaw not only her body but her soul. She needed someone to keep her warm, to hold her when she felt scared.

What he wouldn't do to reach out to her, to smooth her hair, to wipe away her tears.

He couldn't do that, though. Not yet. But maybe one day.

It was time for him to go, he realized. He'd seen all he needed to see. Now he had other demands pulling at him. He had more work to do.

He flipped a penny in the air and slithered back into the dark woods, whistling "I've Been Working on the Railroad" as he went.

CHAPTER 9

Savannah tossed and turned all night, unable to clear her head. Marti's words. Señor Lopez's proclamation. Savannah's past life versus her current one.

Finally morning dawned and she threw back the covers and got out of bed. Normally she'd get right to work editing. But today things were different.

She dressed, grabbed her purse, and headed out the door.

Ten minutes later, she pulled up to the police station.

Again, she wasn't committing herself to anything. She just wanted to ask a few questions.

She smiled at the officer at the counter. In typical small-town fashion, she'd seen him around before, yet she didn't know him well. He had prominent teeth that were slightly crooked, large ears, and an unflattering buzz cut.

"Tennyson. Is the chief in?" She'd always marveled that he had such a proper name for such a backwoods persona.

He nodded slowly. "Yup. Let me see if he can talk."

Savannah tried not to let her annoyance show. This routine was obviously a little game they played here, because Savannah could clearly see the chief sitting at his desk in the back room, staring into space, toothpick bobbing up and down in his mouth.

Tennyson picked up the phone and mumbled something into the receiver. Then he hung up and looked at Savannah. "Go on back."

She appeased him with a polite nod, skirted the desk, and stepped into the chief's office.

"Ms. Harris. What can I do for you?" Chief Lockwood leaned back in his chair, his hands perched atop his ample belly.

He was a tall man with a large gut, a white mustache that completely hid his upper lip, and a neck in constant need of a shave. A coffee stain had formed a brown ring on some papers on his desk, and a calendar featuring hunters hung behind him.

In addition to that call to her carriage house two days ago, she'd encountered the chief a few times on the golf course, and he'd seemed kind enough, always quick to make a joke. He and Landon were buddies and, from what she'd heard, often met for drinks. Apparently Landon was instrumental in getting him elected four years ago when the town's former chief, who'd been on the job for twenty years, had retired to Florida.

Savannah had never been to the police station before, but she wondered now if she should question this department's competence. She lowered herself into the faded brown chair across from Chief Lockwood.

"Any updates on the blood found in my guesthouse?"

He shook his head. "I had to send the samples to the state police for testing. It'll be a few days. You're not worried about that, are you? I'm sure it's animal blood. Nothing to be concerned about."

"Until I know for sure, how can I help but be concerned?"

"You've lived here long enough to know that crime is practically nonexistent."

"But is it?"

"I've been chief here for four years. I can say with confidence that this is one of the safest areas to live."

Savannah had never been one to accept easy answers. Growing up, she'd even questioned her parents' choices, much to their dismay. If there was one thing she'd learned as a journalist, it was that people very rarely laid it all out there. Life was more complicated than that. The stakes were often too high, too complex. Sometimes people didn't even realize their own agendas.

"How about the break-ins?" she ventured.

He scoffed. "Those things? If that's what you want to call them. Nothing's been taken and no one's been hurt. Probably just some kids pulling pranks. I still consider our town to be safe."

Savannah leaned forward. "What about the missing migrant workers?"

The chief's eyebrows twitched, a subtle action that she almost didn't notice. "Missing migrant workers?"

Savannah frowned, realizing with clarity that the chief didn't take those crimes nearly seriously enough. "That's right. At least two disappeared weeks ago and haven't been seen since."

"Now Ms. Savannah, I've been around the block a few times. I've seen all of this before. Every year, a few migrant workers 'disappear' when they fear the INS might come around. It's nothing new. I'm sure they're just fine."

The condescension in his tone riled her up. "Chief, no one wants to report it because that's exactly what the workers think you're going to say. They think you don't care."

He frowned. "I care about all of the residents here. It's my job to care."

Savannah leaned toward him, careful not to break her gaze. "Then you'll look into it?"

"Of course."

Savannah smiled, though the action was forced and tight. "Great. Thank you, Chief."

She left, her duty done. The responsible thing was to put this in the hands of the proper authorities. No one could fault her for that.

Now she had to get ready for Señor Lopez's funeral.

. . .

Savannah stood at the back of the crowd and pulled her gray cardigan closer as a brisk autumn wind swept over the cemetery. Being here was surreal, like something out of a nightmare.

Señor Lopez was really dead. She kept telling herself it was from natural causes. But doubt lingered.

Of course, ever since her husband and daughter had died, every funeral brought back terrible memories. The memories played with her logic, preyed on her emotions. She wasn't even sure why she was here, what had compelled her to come.

Most of the people at the graveside service were migrant workers. Landon had given them the day off to attend. Marti and Savannah took their places at the back of the crowd as Pastor Tom, a man who volunteered with Marti's nonprofit, gave the eulogy in Spanish beside the coffin up front.

As he spoke, Savannah scanned the crowd and spotted Landon at the front. She cringed.

I shouldn't feel this way, she chided herself. Landon was a good man.

Then why had Señor Lopez mentioned his name? She shook her head. Certainly it was a misunderstanding. Maybe Landon wasn't the *problem*, as she'd first assumed. Perhaps he'd said Landon's name because Landon was the one who held the *answer*. That made more sense. Savannah had only ever seen Landon treat the immigrants kindly. Marti even said that Landon had chipped in for Señor Lopez's funeral.

"You should go stand with Landon," Marti whispered.

Tension still stretched tightly between them. Marti was obviously still aggravated because Savannah hadn't jumped at the chance to help her find those two missing migrant workers. In return, Savannah hadn't let down the walls that had come up when she realized Marti was disappointed in her.

The two hardly ever fought. They'd known each other since high school and felt more like sisters. Savannah still talked to her mother about once a week, but other than that, neither she nor Marti had a family to speak of. The members who were still around weren't active parts of their lives. That meant that in some ways Marti and Savannah just had each other.

That made their fight even harder to swallow.

Savannah shook her head. "No, I'll stay here. I don't want to make a scene." *Among other reasons.*

She tried to concentrate on the funeral. Lucia stood in front of her, four children under the age of five around her. They were her brother's kids, not hers.

Savannah's heart ached for them. She'd seen the conditions they lived in. Those houses were no place to raise a child. Had their circumstances really been that deplorable in Mexico? Could this really be a better life? Savannah found it hard to believe.

The pallbearers lowered the coffin into the ground. People around her wept. Minutes ticked by until the service ended.

As everyone dispersed, Lucia grabbed her arm. Savannah knew from the look in her eyes where the conversation would go. She stepped to the side so no one would overhear.

"Señora, are you going to help us?"

Savannah's throat went dry. She glanced at those passing, hoping they weren't listening. Finally her gaze settled on Lucia. "I'm so sorry for your loss, Lucia. I know it must be very difficult for you. Your father was a great man."

Lucia lowered her voice. "He was murdered."

The tightness returned to Savannah's chest. "I don't know what I can do, Lucia. I talked to the chief today, and he promised to look into it."

Lucia's face hardened, starting in her eyes and rippling all the way down to her taut lips. "They'll never listen. They don't care about us." Her fingers dug into Savannah's arm enough to make her flinch. "Señora, I know you're a good person. I know you're the one who sent the toys and diapers and food for my niece and nephews."

Savannah remained silent.

Lucia's eyes flashed with . . . something. "I know about your past. About your family."

Savannah jerked her arm back, too many emotions flooding her. Pain. Fear. Sorrow. The beginning of anger. "Again, I'm sorry for your loss, Lucia, but if I wanted you to know my story, I would have told you." Before her anger emerged further, she walked away.

Marti, who'd been standing nearby talking to Landon, fell into step beside her. "What was that about?"

Savannah shook her head, afraid she might spark another argument. "Nothing."

"What's going on, Savannah? And don't tell me 'nothing.' I've known you since high school. I know when something's wrong."

Savannah sucked in her cheeks before exhaling slowly. "Lucia thinks her papa was murdered." Savannah flinched at the bluntness of her voice.

Marti's face distorted in confusion. "It's like you said—he had cancer."

"I know. It doesn't make sense. He wasn't murdered. Couldn't have been."

"What if he was?"

Savannah stopped where she was, and her lips parted in surprise. "How could he have been murdered, Marti? Is there something I'm missing?"

Marti shrugged, and Savannah could see the defiance on her face. "Maybe someone poisoned him and made it look like cancer."

"Why would they do that? It doesn't make sense, Marti."

"Maybe he knew something he wasn't supposed to know."

"You think there's a conspiracy going on?"

Marti was a conspiracy theorist through and through and had been ever since Savannah had met her. Savannah loved her friend, but the truth was that evil plots weren't lurking around every corner.

"I really thought more of you, Savannah," Marti muttered.

"Maybe that was your first mistake." As soon as the words left Savannah's mouth, she wanted nothing more than to take them back.

But something stopped her. Pride? Fear?

She didn't know. She only knew that for some reason she was pushing away the only person who'd been there for her through thick and thin.

CHAPTER 10

"I'm going to head over to Lucia's," Marti said. Her lips were set in a tight line.

Savannah started to speak but stopped herself. The stubborn part of her wanted Marti to apologize. The logical part knew that Marti had spoken the truth. To make any progress, she needed to merge those two parts of herself into one.

She nodded and watched Marti walk over to her beat-up old Toyota.

Her friend was inspirational on so many levels. She did so much for others without complaining. Her heart truly was for the migrant workers, and she didn't think of herself.

Savannah would make things right. Their friendship was more important than this, but as Marti pulled away, she realized that conversation would have to wait until later.

A hand warmed her lower back. She looked up and saw Landon standing there. He smiled. "Hey there. I didn't expect to see you here."

"Just wanted to pay my respects."

He nodded. "How are you?"

"I'm hanging in. How about you?" They started walking across the grass toward Savannah's car.

"It's harvest season."

"Enough said, right?" Savannah knew just how busy this time of year was.

"You want to have dinner sometime?"

Savannah glanced at him, no longer surprised at his forthrightness. "Didn't you just ask me that yesterday?"

"I've learned that persistence can pay off." He stood there, a wry grin on his face. "My mom always said my determination would get me far in life."

She smiled. "I'll think about it."

"You're always noncommittal, aren't you?"

"I played golf." How many times was she going to use that excuse as proof that she wasn't totally rigid?

"I'll take what I can get." They stopped by her car, and Landon crossed his arms. "Did I hear you're considering getting a boarder?"

"News travels fast around town."

"Marti mentioned it to me just now."

"I see." She nodded slowly.

"Did you check him out?"

Savannah shrugged. "He paid in cash. No need to do a credit check."

Landon's eyebrows pushed together. "Paid in cash? How much in advance?"

"Just two months, plus a deposit."

"Only criminals pay in cash."

She tilted her head and half rolled her eyes. "Landon . . ."

He shrugged. "That's what I hear, at least. Even aside from the money, how about a character reference? Is he safe?"

"I called one of his past employers, who's a Navy SEAL. He said he could recommend him without a doubt."

"That's good to hear. Still, keep your eyes open. You just never know about some people."

"That's the truth," Savannah mumbled.

Landon squeezed her arm. "So think about that dinner, okay? And the harvest festival I host at the end of the season. I'd love to have you join me. Think about it?"

She managed a nod. "I will, Landon."

He nodded, squeezed her arm again, and hurried back to his professional-grade luxury truck, one that was perfect for work on the farm. It was too bad the vehicle never got dirty, though. Every time Savannah saw it, it shined like it was brand new.

CHAPTER 11

His car crept behind the red Volvo. From his vantage point, he saw Savannah's head bobbing in the front seat. He could only imagine her thoughts.

He eased his foot from the accelerator, not wanting to draw attention to himself. He had to stay a safe distance behind Savannah so she wouldn't spot him.

He'd seen her at the funeral. So pretty. So sad.

He wanted to reach out to her. To offer her comfort. But he couldn't do that. Not yet.

His knuckles turned white as he gripped the steering wheel. He knew about Savannah Harris's background. Knew she'd won awards for her investigative journalism.

Just today, someone had told him that a migrant worker had fetched Savannah on the night that Lopez man had died. He could only imagine what lies he'd told her. The last thing he needed was for Savannah to stick her nose where she shouldn't.

Sweat beaded across his forehead, and he reminded himself to slow down again. He'd keep watching Savannah. And if she started discovering information she shouldn't, then he'd take action.

As she turned off the highway onto the road leading her home, he continued straight. He had to get back to work. But as soon as he was off, he'd come back and watch her again from his perch in the woods.

CHAPTER 12

In her bedroom, Savannah changed from her heels into black flip-flops. She left on the flowing black dress from the graveside service but ditched the cardigan in favor of a denim jacket before starting across the field behind her house. She passed her guesthouse and Clive's Jeep parked outside and continued past the tree line until she reached the bay. The beautiful Chesapeake Bay.

It was almost enough to distract her from her uneasy thoughts about Clive. She'd checked him out, and he'd gotten a glowing review. So why did worry still nag at her?

Was she reading too much into his presence here? Or was she so desperate for solitude that she would reject anyone who wanted to "intrude" in her life?

She didn't know, and today wasn't the day to figure it out. Why did it seem like her every thought revolved around Señor Lopez? Why couldn't she stop thinking about Lucia? Why couldn't she prevent the smell of sickness and poverty in Señor Lopez's house from flooding back to her?

She stopped before the sand began and let the stiff breeze smack her in the face. The fresh air off the bay never failed to bring her senses to life. She knew why so many people wanted to call the seaside home. Something about the waves and the tides helped life make sense.

Closing her eyes, she absorbed the saltwater scent. She listened to the seagulls crying overhead. She felt the wind carrying the sand aloft, the soft grains hitting her bare legs.

She desperately needed some peace right now. She'd needed peace for a long time but had nearly given up believing she'd ever obtain it again. Was peace even possible after all she'd been through?

One of her first assignments with the Associated Press had been a piece about a woman who'd lost her husband and three children in a tornado in Oklahoma. She still remembered when, halfway through the interview, the woman began singing "It Is Well with My Soul." The words were sung with passion and absolute faith, knowing that peace could come from God in the harshest of circumstances. Even as tears rolled down the woman's face, an inner sense of calm seemed to radiate from her. She was like a rock, unmovable even in the fiercest storm.

Savannah would give anything to have the faith of that woman.

A branch snapped behind her. Her heart raced as she whirled around.

Clive Miller walked toward her, his hands deep in the pockets of his dark-wash jeans. He stopped in his tracks when he saw her. Regret registered on his face, and Savannah knew he'd come out here expecting to be alone.

"Ms. Harris." He raised his chin to acknowledge her. "I'll leave you alone. I didn't realize you were here."

He started to turn around.

"You're not disturbing me." She waved him over. "Please, enjoy the bay. It's the sole reason I bought this property. You don't get views like this just anywhere."

He moved to her side, towering over her. He jangled some change in his pocket. "That's the truth. I loved exploring the woods when I was a kid. This place brings out my childhood ambitions, I suppose. I can't help but find a sense of adventure here on this property."

She turned away from the breeze, and her hair invaded her face. She pushed it out of the way and looked at Clive through a few rebellious strands. "Have you settled into the house okay?" she asked.

He nodded, the action clipped and quick. "I have. The place is just what I needed. Perfect."

Landon's words rolled over in her mind. *Only criminals pay in cash.* Landon was just being overprotective. She couldn't fault him for that.

She tried to think of what to say next. She was out of practice. But certainly she hadn't lost all of her ability to make conversation.

She cleared her throat. "You have everything you need for your stay? Is the thermostat working okay?"

"Everything's great. Thank you."

Relief washed over her when she realized that his short, clipped answers meant he didn't want to talk.

"Good." She turned toward the house. "If you need anything while you're here, please let me know. I'm going back."

As she started to walk away, a loud screech came from the tree line. Savannah paused, searching the underbrush.

Nothing.

She glanced at Clive. "Did you hear that?"

"I thought it might be a seagull." Clive joined her, looking equally concerned.

"I don't think so. That was a cry of pain."

Something rustled in the bushes. Savannah pushed through the vines, thorns grabbing at her exposed ankles. A ball of orange fur wrestled in the prickly briars. Fishing line encircled its legs and body.

"Poor thing." Savannah reached for the cat.

"Let me." Clive stepped forward and reached into the bush while Savannah slipped off her jacket and draped it over her arm. The cat hissed as Clive bent down to grab it.

"Come here, boy. It's okay." Clive's words and tone sounded so calm and soothing that Savannah nearly forgot about questioning his intent. As Clive reached for the cat, it lunged and sank its teeth into his arm.

Clive jerked back. Savannah held her breath, waiting for him to curse.

Instead, he said, "Poor thing's in a world of pain."

Blood dripped down his arm. The cat had gotten him good.

"Are you okay?" She started to reach for him but stopped.

He brushed off her concern. "I'll be fine."

Savannah's eyes widened when he reached down and grabbed the cat again, this time successfully nabbing it. Savannah held out her jacket, and Clive placed the cat inside. It looked as if it hadn't eaten in days.

"Let's get you some food." Cradling the squirming bundle, she walked quickly toward the house. "You come too," she called over her shoulder to Clive. "I need to put some medicine on that bite."

"Don't worry about me. I'll be okay."

"Don't be ridiculous. It can get infected. What about rabies?"

He shook his head. "A kitten that age wouldn't survive a bite from a rabid animal. I'm not worried about it."

"Still, come in for a moment." She looked over her shoulder. "I'm putting something on that bite. It's the least I can do."

His steps sounded behind her as they climbed onto the back porch. *He just saved a cat; he can't be that bad*, she told herself.

"Let me get the antiseptic and a bandage."

"Get some scissors first. There's still fishing line around him. My arm can wait."

"You sure?"

He nodded. "Absolutely."

She grabbed some shears from a drawer. As Clive held the cat, she carefully began cutting the binds around his legs. Her hands brushed Clive's, and something shot through her.

Not electricity, she told herself. It's just the closeness of someone unfamiliar. That was the only possible reason her throat felt tight, that she was entirely too aware of how near he was.

"Based on the fishing line found on the beach, it looks like someone's been using your property," Clive said.

"Apparently they have. I've always considered myself observant, but maybe I should rethink that."

"You can't see the shore from your house, so don't beat yourself up about it."

"It's probably just some retirees who've been out boating for the day. They probably saw the stretch of sand and figured the beach was uninhabited. This property was abandoned for a year or so before I purchased it, so their assumption wouldn't be without logic."

She pulled some briars out of the cat's fur, hoping that would help her reach the fishing line better. "Apparently they've helped themselves to my carriage house as well." She frowned.

"If that's the worst crime that happens around here, I guess you're doing okay."

Images of Señor Lopez flashed back to her, but she pushed them away. Finally the cat's legs were free. She pulled the fishing line away and threw it in the trash. The cat jumped from Clive's arms and stretched.

Clive and Savannah exchanged a smile.

"I think he's going to be okay," Clive said, standing.

"Let me give him some food. Then I'll get the hydrogen peroxide. In the meantime"—she tore off a paper towel and handed it to him—"put this over the bite."

She pulled down two bowls from her cabinet.

"How long have you lived here?" Clive asked, slipping off his jacket and placing it over the back of the chair.

"Two years." Had it really been that long? Sometimes it felt like decades; other times like mere weeks.

She grabbed a can of tuna and pulled a half-gallon of milk from the fridge. She filled the bowls and placed them on the floor. The cat wasted no time eating.

Savannah turned to Clive. "I'm sorry. Let me get the antiseptic, and I won't keep you any longer."

She was back downstairs in less than a minute and led him to the kitchen sink.

"He got you good." Savannah grasped his hand, appreciating— no, observing—the calluses, the firmness. She poured some hydrogen peroxide over the wound and watched it bubble on the skin's surface.

"So, Savannah, do you work?"

She waited for the peroxide to finish sizzling before dabbing on some ointment. "As a matter of fact, I edit. Textbooks."

"Interesting."

"Not really." She wrapped a bandage around his hand and taped it firmly. "There you go. All better."

Clive smiled. "Thanks."

She looked at the door, hoping he'd get the hint that it was time to go. The last thing she wanted was to have him asking more questions.

• • •

Clive took one last glance at Savannah before closing the back door.

While she'd been upstairs, he'd taken a moment to walk quickly around the downstairs rooms. He'd seen the dozen roses sitting on the outdated table by the front door. The card sticking out of the bouquet was what really caught his attention and made his pulse quicken.

Thinking of you. With affection, Landon Kavanagh.

Landon Kavanagh? Could luck really be on his side? Had fate led him to the residence of someone connected with *the* Landon Kavanagh?

He smiled. Maybe this would be easier than he'd originally thought.

That was good. Because nothing about the past six years had been easy.

He knew there were still people who were desperate to track him down, desperate to carry out what they considered justice.

But Clive had other plans. There were things he had to do. Wrongs he needed to right.

He walked back to his temporary home, glancing over at the bay as he did so. Just standing on the shore a little while ago had reminded him of his freedom, freedom he'd taken for granted for too long.

No more.

He had to work fast, but carefully. He had to stay under the radar. But most of all, he had to find the person who'd ripped his life apart.

CHAPTER 13

Fury burned inside him.

Who did that man think he was, sweeping into Savannah's life like that?

He had to find out his name. Had to find out where he was from. Why he was here.

He wasn't sure how he'd do that. But he would. Somehow. He had his ways.

He crouched in the woods, watching as the man hurried back to the guest cottage behind the house.

He'd had to use that place once. Just this week, actually. He couldn't have someone's blood on his hands, and he'd had to get rid of the evidence.

No one had even missed the homeless derelict. The man had caught him out here. He'd had no choice but to plunge a knife into his stomach. He couldn't take any chances. If the wrong person found out what he was doing, his life would be ruined.

He'd almost taken the towels with him. Then he thought about Savannah finding them. The idea had delighted him.

She would be scared when she saw the blood.

If she were scared, she'd be more likely to turn to him. To want someone in her life. Someone to protect her. Women were like that. They wanted knights in shining armor to sweep in and save the day.

His mom had been like that. She was a wounded soul. She'd been rejected by her family, rejected by two spouses. He was all she had.

He'd been her savior.

He was still her savior, sending her money. Making sure she was taken care of. Giving her only the best.

He'd learned a lot throughout his childhood. He'd learned how much he enjoyed holding that power over someone.

He'd seen that same loneliness in Savannah's eyes. He knew what had really happened to turn her life upside down, to lead her here.

One day she would see that he was her savior.

In the meantime, he'd have to keep his eye on Savannah's new boarder. The man could ruin everything. And he did mean everything.

CHAPTER 14

After eating breakfast the next morning, Savannah started to put her cereal bowl in the sink but then thought better of it. Instead, she placed the leftover milk on the floor and let the cat lap it up.

She smiled as she looked down at the skinny orange fur ball. He'd hardly left her side all night, even going as far as to purr on the rug beside her bed while she tried to sleep. He was probably infested with fleas, and she'd probably regret it later. But she couldn't bring herself to leave him alone after the ordeal he'd been through.

She rubbed Tiger's head. She'd decided as she was lying in bed that the cat looked like a tiger. So that's what she'd named him.

With one final pat, she hurried upstairs to get dressed. She was taking Tiger to the vet to be checked out. Her appointment was at nine.

When she turned to head up the stairs, something caught her eye.

Clive's jacket.

In their haste to take care of Tiger, he'd left it here. She picked it up, brought it to her nose, and inhaled Clive's leathery scent.

The aroma made her pulse quicken.

She quickly put it down.

She was not attracted to Clive Miller. She couldn't be. She never wanted to fall in love again. Especially after her marriage to Reid.

Reid had proven that romance was nothing but fiction, a fairy tale. What had started with fireworks had not only fizzled—it had crashed and burned. She'd disappointed him; he'd disappointed her. They were two different people and should have known better than to think true love could conquer all. Her mom had tried to warn her. Her colleagues had laughed at her. But her heart had told her differently.

Her heart had been wrong.

She pushed those thoughts aside and grabbed the jacket. She glanced out the window only to see Clive's Jeep rumbling down the driveway. She'd have to return it when he came home.

She hung the jacket back over the chair. A piece of paper sticking out of the pocket caught her eye. She shouldn't. She knew that. But the man was so mysterious.

After a moment of contemplation, she pulled it out. An address was written there.

156 Planation Lane.

She blinked. She knew that address.

It was Landon Kavanagh's. Why in the world would Clive have Landon's address in his pocket?

The mystery around the man deepened.

• • •

Clive Miller stopped in front of Landon Kavanagh's home. He pulled his hat down low over his eyes and rubbed his chin. He'd let his beard grow, not even an inch, but enough that it might cover pieces of his past. He had to tread carefully.

He stared at the man's house for a moment. The place was massive yet understated. In the background, the bay glimmered. A huge barn stood to the right, horses grazed in a pasture to his left. Clive knew enough about Landon Kavanagh to know that the acres and acres of crops he'd passed on his way down the lane belonged to him. Workers were in the fields picking corn and collards and apples.

Clive had thought a lot about Landon Kavanagh over the past few years. He'd never met the man before, but he'd certainly heard a lot about him.

He was wealthy, successful, and single. He was a mover and shaker in the community and sat on several boards, one of which was the Save the Bay campaign. He had a good name in Cape Thomas, a long list of women who'd like to marry him, and some strange connection to Savannah Harris.

That realization both fascinated and worried him.

One look into Savannah's eyes, and he'd known she was a good person. She was strong, capable, and . . . hurting. He didn't want to see another woman get mixed up with a scumbag like Landon. As far as Clive was concerned, the man was a wolf in sheep's clothing.

Dear Lord, what am I doing right now? He prayed silently. *Measure my words. Direct my steps. Guard my thoughts.*

Even as he prayed for God to guard his thoughts, he knew that some of them had fought viciously to grow without any kind of filter or restraints; thoughts that had spread like lava from a savage volcano, destroying everything in its path.

Thoughts of vengeance and retaliation and wrath.

A verse from Deuteronomy rushed into his mind. *It is mine to avenge; I will repay. In due time their foot will slip; their day of disaster is near and their doom rushes upon them.*

Clive balled his hands into fists. He burned for vengeance to be his own right now. A battle between his desires and God's desires warred inside him day after day.

He had to have patience and set aside his emotions.

One wrong move could ruin his whole plan.

"Mr. Miller?"

He looked up, his pulse quickening. It wasn't Landon Kavanagh approaching the Jeep, however. It was, if Clive had to guess, Ernie Davis. The man was tall, painfully thin, probably in his mid-fifties with only a wisp of light brown hair atop his head. His eyes behind his gold-rimmed glasses seemed perceptive and competent.

Clive smiled and extended his hand. "Mr. Davis. Pleasure to meet you."

"You're here about a job? It's only part time, a few days a week, and the pay is nominal."

"So you said on the phone. I'll take what I can get."

"You'll be in charge of driving the van to pick up workers as well as supervising a section of the fields."

"I think I can handle that."

Ernie nodded. "Great. Then let me show you around the property."

•   •   •

Savannah tried to get the slip of paper with Landon's address out of her mind. She rubbed Tiger's head, glad that he'd checked out okay at the vet, and sat down at her desk to check her e-mail. She'd gotten behind on her work yesterday, and she'd need to work extra hard today to meet her deadlines.

Tiger jumped on the desk and began pawing the baby rattle. She shook her head and pulled the cat into her lap. "No, no," she whispered. "We don't play with that."

She rubbed his soft head instead and stared at her computer screen.

She'd hoped Marti would call her last night, but she hadn't. Savannah had left her a message, asking if they could talk. She still hadn't heard back.

Sinister.

Savannah shook her head. The word still lingered in her mind, and she didn't know why.

Back when she'd actually believed God cared, she'd always felt He spoke to her simply, hammering her with one word over and over until she got the message. For six months, the word had been "surrender." She'd realized she needed to surrender her own desires.

She supposed if she still believed God cared, she might believe that He was putting the word "sinister" in her head, trying to show her something. Maybe even "squander."

She wavered back and forth in her thoughts about God, sometimes believing He was nothing more than an apathetic being watching from the realms and other times holding firm to the idea that God didn't exist at all. She'd yet to gather enough evidence to definitively prove that one of those beliefs was right. Either way, God was no longer a part of her life.

She turned on her computer and pulled up her e-mail account, going through her e-mails quickly and deleting most of them. She paused when she saw an e-mail from Marti.

"Marti, you're e-mailing now?" Savannah mumbled. "What happened to picking up the phone and calling?"

Her friend was notorious for calling to share brief snippets of news. Sometimes she called up to six or seven times a day, just to share something like, "Dr. Lawson winked at me. What do you think that means?" Remembering the conversation, Savannah smiled.

Because Marti loved conspiracy theories, she feared the government might be tracking e-mails, keeping some kind of log on every US citizen. She claimed she was going to be smarter than Big Brother by only using the computer when she absolutely had to.

Savannah clicked on the e-mail.

Savannah Banana,

Savannah smiled. Marti always began any correspondence, even text messages, with some kind of goofy nickname for Savannah.

Look, I'm sorry about the other day. Maybe I shouldn't have been so blunt. I just don't want to see you waste your life. Anyway, I tried to call earlier, but you didn't answer, so I left a message. I have a flat tire or I would have driven over. We've GOT to talk. Señor Lopez may not have been delusional after all. Scary stuff. Call me as soon as you get this e-mail, or I might lose my mind!
Love,
Marti Who's Smarti

The hairs rose on Savannah's neck. What had Marti discovered? Was her unsettling e-mail an exaggeration? Or was there some truth to Señor Lopez's claim?

She needed to call her.

Where had she left her cell phone? She tried to remember. She'd used it last night to call the vet and left it . . . on her dresser.

She rushed into her bedroom and pushed aside the city of cosmetics atop the dresser. Not there.

She placed a hand on her hip. Where else could she have left it?

She closed her eyes, replaying the events of last night. She felt sure she'd left it on her dresser. So why wasn't it here?

Maybe she'd left it downstairs on the kitchen table. She rushed to the first floor and turned the kitchen and then the rest of the house upside down looking for the phone. It was nowhere to be found.

"You've got to be kidding me." She closed her eyes and leaned against the kitchen table. Where had she left it? She never placed it very far away, especially since she didn't have a landline.

She hurried back to her desk to send Marti a reply. Her eyes widened when she saw another e-mail from her. Quickly she clicked on it.

I sent my previous e-mail in haste. Ignore it. Been working too hard. I'm going out of town for a few days to clear my head. I'll call you when I return.

Savannah stared at the e-mail. There was something about the way it was written, about the rhythm of the words, that just didn't sound right. Besides, Marti hated traveling. She relaxed by jogging or windsurfing or taking a long swim.

She would never—ever—leave town during harvest season when there was so much needed, especially if she suspected something was going on with Señor Lopez.

Savannah leaned back in her chair and pinched the bridge of her nose, trying to keep her rising panic at bay. It was no use.

Something was wrong.

She had to call Marti.

Now.

Clive's Jeep rumbled down the driveway. Savannah ran out the back door and waved her hands to get his attention. He braked beside the house.

As he rolled down the window, she leaned against the door, panting from the sprint over. "Clive, do you have a cell phone?"

He unclipped it from his belt and handed it to her. "Everything okay?"

She dialed Marti's number before answering. "I hope so."

The phone rang. And rang. And rang.

"Pick up, Marti." She tapped her foot on the ground, waiting. Voice mail kicked in.

Savannah hit "end" and dialed again. Her hands shook so badly that she nearly dropped the phone.

Just like before, it went to voice mail. Savannah raked a hand through her hair, trying to get a grip, trying to think things through.

All she could hear were the alarms sounding in her head. Something was wrong. She knew it.

A crease appeared between Clive's brows. "What's going on?"

She glanced at her car in front of the house, realizing her only option. She had to check on Marti. Now.

"I think something's wrong with my friend." Her words came out fast, jumbled. "I'm going to drive to her house and see if she's there."

Clive leaned over and opened the passenger door. "I'll take you."

"You don't have to do that."

"For the sake of everyone else on the road, I'd say I do."

She didn't argue. Her thoughts were too scattered, and she knew she wasn't in the right mind-set to drive. She ran around the vehicle and climbed in. "Thanks."

Clive turned around and started toward the road. "Just tell me where to go."

"Go to the highway and take a right." Savannah's hands trembled as she pulled the seat belt over her lap.

Clive glanced at her, measured curiosity in his eyes. "Want to give me an idea of what's going on?"

"My friend Marti sent me an e-mail. Something's wrong. Said she's left me voice mails, but I can't find my phone." She looked across the seat at Clive and saw his expression. "I'm not paranoid, Clive. My gut tells me something's wrong. Marti always has her phone with her. And she never e-mails."

"How far away does she live?"

"Ten minutes."

"I'll get there in five."

Savannah's mind raced as they sped down the streets. It was probably nothing, she told herself. She was just overreacting. After what had happened in her life, no one could fault her for overreacting. And even though her gut instincts were usually right, this time she hoped they weren't. She hoped she'd show up at Marti's and find everything normal. That she'd be there watching TV or playing her Nintendo DS.

But the e-mail had said Marti was going out of town. That just didn't sound like her. She wouldn't leave her ministry without arranging for Savannah to pick up some slack while she was gone.

Savannah pointed ahead. "One more turn and we'll be there. It's just up ahead. A little yellow house on the left."

Clive pulled into the driveway. Savannah noted that Marti's car was there, the front left tire flat, just as her e-mail had said.

How had she gotten out of town with no car?

More red flags.

As soon as Clive braked, Savannah pulled her seat belt off. Quickly she opened the door and ran up the sidewalk. Clive was right behind her as she hurried up the porch steps and pounded on the door. "Marti? Are you there?"

She jiggled the doorknob. It was locked.

But Savannah had a key.

She reached for her pocket and flinched. She'd left without anything—wallet, keys, not to mention her lost cell phone.

"I'll check the back door." Clive jumped from the porch and jogged around the house.

Savannah peered into one of the windows. An empty living room stared back at her. She hurried to the next window and scanned the dining room. No sign of Marti.

Everything looked normal.

Maybe she was just being paranoid.

Clive came around the side of the house. "The back door's locked. The only thing I could see was the mudroom, no one in sight."

Savannah couldn't leave yet, not without knowing beyond a doubt that her friend was okay. "I've gotta check the rest of the house." She scrambled off the porch and looked for something to stand on so she could peer into the rest of the windows. Finally she spotted the five-gallon bucket that Marti used to collect rainwater for her garden.

"Sorry, Marti," she mumbled as she dumped it out, the water splashing on her jeans.

Savannah shoved the bucket upside down beneath the kitchen window. She pulled herself up, her fingers clawing the wooden windowsill for balance.

Savannah saw the sink, the countertop. Dirty dishes were piled high.

Leaving without doing the dishes? Savannah doubted Marti would do that, but maybe she had.

Her gaze moved down the counter, where a package of chicken was thawing. If Marti were going out of town, why would she leave that out?

Marti didn't believe in wasting things. She turned trash into art. She saved food scraps for her compost pile. Something wasn't fitting.

Her gaze went to the floor, and Savannah gasped.

What was that? It couldn't be . . .

Her fist connected with the window. Pounded on it with enough force to break the glass.

"Marti! Marti! Marti!" she screamed.

"What is it, Savannah?" Clive appeared beside her.

"We've got to get inside, Clive. Marti's on the floor. I'm not sure if she's alive!"

.   .   .

Before Savannah could even step down from the bucket, Clive took off toward the front door. Savannah followed after him and got there in time to see him knock it down. Taking the steps by two, she leapt onto the porch and burst into Marti's house. Clive tossed her his cell phone. "Call an ambulance."

Savannah's hands trembled as she punched in the numbers. As she talked to the operator, she watched Clive kneel down beside Marti, who was sprawled out on the floor between the kitchen and TV room. Savannah froze. There beside her friend's hand was . . . a bottle of pills? Pills? Marti didn't take any medicine. Did she?

"Oh Marti . . ." she whispered.

Savannah rattled off Marti's address to the 911 dispatcher, fixated on Clive as he shook her friend's limp body, shouted her name, patted her face.

"I need your help, Savannah!"

Savannah dropped the phone.

"We've got to get her in the shower. She has a pulse, but it's faint. We need to wake her up."

Savannah nodded, numb. Clive gathered up Marti in his arms. Savannah hurried down the hall and turned on the shower.

"Cold water," Clive ordered.

Savannah climbed in the shower, and Clive lowered Marti after her, both women fully clothed. Savannah supported Marti's weight. Dead weight.

The cold water blasted them, tensing and prickling Savannah's skin. Clive stood outside the shower, still shaking Marti, trying to wake her up.

"How long's she been treated for depression?" Clive shouted over the water.

Savannah's eyes widened. "She's not. She's not depressed."

He patted Marti's face again. "Those pills were prescribed to her."

"No, they couldn't have been. She wasn't depressed." Savannah stared at her friend's expressionless face. "Come on, Marti. I can't lose you. You know I can't lose you."

Her words turned into a cry. This couldn't be happening. Not Marti, too.

CHAPTER 15

Clive handed her a steaming Styrofoam cup. "Here, have some coffee."

Savannah carefully took it from him, grateful for something warm, even if she hated coffee. Her clothes were still damp from Marti's house. Yet she dared not leave the hospital, not until she heard an update.

Marti. Her dear, sweet friend. The only person in the world who hadn't given up on her.

Before she sank into the despair that desperately wanted to close in on her, she mumbled, "Thank you."

She took a sip, and the coffee was so bitter she nearly spit it out.

Clive offered an apologetic smile. "It's from the cafeteria downstairs. It was all I could find."

"Please don't apologize. You've done so much. I really appreciate everything, Clive."

Two doctors pushed through the ER doors. Savannah rushed to her feet, sloshing some coffee on her shirt. She didn't care. She held her breath, waiting for news, but the doctors kept walking. She felt weary, quivery, and spent as she dropped back into her seat.

"She's lucky to have a friend like you, you know."

Savannah pressed her lips into a firm line, remembering the bottle of pills on the floor at Marti's house. "She never even told me she was depressed."

"That's not something people like to talk about." His voice sounded firm yet soft.

"But I've been friends with Marti for fifteen years. I thought she told me everything."

"Do you tell her everything?"

"Yes—"

"No, I mean everything. Everything. Your deepest, darkest secrets?"

She took another sip of coffee and stared into the distance. No, Savannah hadn't told Marti everything, not if she was honest about it. There were some things Savannah didn't think she could ever talk about. She cleared her throat.

"So how did you learn to knock a door down like that?" She couldn't resist the question. The way he'd brought the door down and handled the entire situation made Savannah think there was more to Clive Miller than he'd probably admit.

"It's just male instinct."

Plausible explanation. But she didn't believe him. Perhaps he knew how to handle an overdose because he was a drug dealer? Maybe he'd been around uncountable people who'd OD'd, and he'd had to save them. If she believed that, then she had to face the question: What was he doing in Cape Thomas? And what would he be doing while he lived on her property?

"Don't think too hard, Savannah."

She broke her locked gaze on the vending machine across the room. Were her thoughts that obvious? She couldn't give him that satisfaction so easily. "Think too hard about what?"

"About me."

She quirked an eyebrow before looking away. "A little egocentric, don't you think? Maybe I was thinking about Marti."

"I'm pretty good at reading people."

"Well, don't read me. I'm a closed book."

His jaw twitched. "Understood."

She knew she should apologize. But she couldn't. Didn't.

Clive stood. "I'm going to take a walk. I'll check back here in a while."

"I don't want to keep you. If you need to go, please do."

"You have a ride home?"

She glanced at her hands. No, she didn't. And she had no one to call. The only person she could possibly ask was . . . Landon. He'd come right away. But she couldn't bring herself to dial his number.

"Call me when you're ready to go home." Clive jotted down his phone number, handed it to her, and walked away.

Savannah slumped against the vinyl-covered cushions of the hospital chair.

Apparently she'd perfected the art of pushing people away.

．　．　．

Clive was almost at the exit to the parking lot when he stopped.

He remembered the sadness on Savannah's face. He remembered how alone she looked.

He remembered what it was like to feel alone in his darkest hour.

He paused and leaned against the wall for a moment.

There was so much he needed to do. As soon as someone here recognized him, his investigation would get that much harder. He'd be an outcast. He didn't have any time to waste.

Yet despite that logic, he turned around. Something outside of himself seemed to be leading him as he walked back to the waiting room and sat beside Savannah. She looked up, her eyes widening.

"Did you forget something?"

He shook his head. "No, I just thought you could use a friend."

She let out a sigh, long and heavy. "Please, don't stay out of pity."

"It's not pity. It's compassion. It's understanding."

She scrutinized him a moment, and he felt sure she would reject his offer. Surprisingly, she leaned back and said nothing.

He wished he knew her better. If he did, he might offer her a shoulder to cry on. He might put an arm around her. But he didn't, so he didn't. It seemed a shame that someone in her position didn't have anyone to give her a hug, though. She looked so alone right now.

"How do you and Marti know each other?" he finally asked.

She seemed to snap out of her spell. "We met in high school. I started a school newspaper, and she was the only one brave enough to sign up as a reporter. We were inseparable after that."

"It's unusual to see a friendship that lasts so long."

She nodded, her eyes misting. "We've been there for each other through a lot."

"When you have a friendship like that, you hold on to it."

She squeezed the skin between her eyes. "Except we had a fight. We both said some things that were unkind. To be honest, it was mostly me. She spoke the truth; I reacted with anger. We hadn't smoothed things over."

"I had a friend once who was an art collector," Clive started. "He said you could tell the real thing from the fakes because of the imperfections. Imitations often looked too perfect. It's like that in relationships, too, isn't it?"

It certainly had been with him and Lauren. Their problem was that neither of them had learned to appreciate the imperfections in each other until it was too late.

A smile—ever so slight—finally cracked Savannah's face. "I like that. I suppose there can be beauty in imperfections."

"That's what can make a masterpiece."

That seemed to break the ice somewhat with Savannah. She leaned back, her shoulders a little more relaxed. "Are you working while you're here in Cape Thomas, Clive?"

He shook his head. "I'm taking on odd jobs right now."

"What *did* you do?"

He opened his mouth, started to speak the truth. But the truth could lead to too many questions. "I've held various positions in my lifetime. Most recently, a handyman."

It was true. As a teenager, he'd delivered newspapers, worked the fields, and done construction. He'd worked as a waiter to helped pay his way through college. And in the two weeks before he came here, he'd helped his friend Wheaton do some handyman work around his property.

Savannah raised her eyebrows. "A handyman? Really? Not what I would have guessed."

"If you need help with your house, let me know. I noticed one of your front steps seemed to be sagging. You buy the supplies, and I won't even charge you."

"I'll keep that in mind." She glanced at him again. Her eyes narrowed, her gaze seeming to churn with unspoken thoughts. "I found Landon's address in your pocket."

He raised an eyebrow. "You went through my things?"

"I picked up your jacket to give it back to you. That's when I found the paper."

He nodded slowly, thoughtfully. "I had a job interview there today."

"I thought you weren't working."

"I'm not really working. I took a part-time gig at the farm to earn a little spending money. That's why I had his address."

"I know they need a lot of extra hands this time of year." She released him from her gaze and leaned back.

"My wife used to love to come here whenever she could. She said it made her soul feel peaceful. There's something about working the earth and getting your hands dirty that's immensely rewarding."

"I can understand that," Savannah said.

"How about you? You from this area?"

She shook her head. "No, I actually came here because of Marti. I was living in the Raleigh area, but I needed a . . . a change of pace."

"I'd say this was a change of pace."

She shrugged, her eyes misting again. "I wanted to go somewhere boring, where there was absolutely nothing to spark my interest. With all of this farmland out here and the sparse population, I figured this would be perfect."

"Were you right?"

"I'm not sure anymore."

Just then the doctor walked into the waiting room. Clive hoped for Savannah's sake that he had good news.

CHAPTER 16

Savannah looked up at Dr. Lawson with a mixture of hope and fear. She hardly noticed Clive slipping away to give her some privacy. She rose to address the doctor.

He was a tall man, lean with blond hair and classic features. He wore dark-framed glasses and came across as reserved and studious, quiet. Marti had told Savannah that she thought he was the most beautiful man she'd ever met.

Savannah crossed her arms, bracing herself. "Dr. Lawson. How is she?"

His somber expression doused any hope she felt.

"She's still unconscious." He pushed his glasses up on his nose and peered at her, an unreadable expression on his face. "I'm sorry, Savannah. She's . . . she's in a coma."

Savannah's leg muscles gave out on her. Dr. Lawson caught her elbow before she hit the floor. They both sat down in sync.

He pushed his glasses up on his nose again. "It's a good thing you found her when you did, Savannah. You may have saved her life."

"Living in a coma isn't living." Savannah felt numb. The room seemed to blur. A coma? No, she was supposed to make up with

Marti. They would laugh and fix dinner together and go on with life as normal.

"I'm sorry. I know this is hard news to comprehend." His voice sounded soft, compassionate. But Savannah wasn't ready to accept what he had to say.

"Dr. Lawson, this isn't like Marti. Antidepressant medication? Tell me it's a mistake."

He shook his head slightly. "You know I can't talk about it with you, Savannah."

"She's my best friend. I just don't understand." Tears stung her eyes.

Dr. Lawson subtly glanced around and then lowered his voice. "I'm only telling you this because I know what good friends you and Marti are. You're practically family." He paused. "I prescribed the depression medicine to her back in August. I was worried about her mental state."

"Why didn't I notice? I should have noticed." Had she really been that wrapped up in herself? She'd just seemed like the same old Marti to her: talkative, imaginative, caring.

"You've had a lot on your mind, Savannah. Marti knew that."

What exactly had Marti shared with him about her life that would lead him to say that? This wasn't the time to think about it. Right now she had to concentrate on Marti.

Savannah swallowed, dreading her next question. She had to ask it, though. Certainly someone else would be on her side. If anyone, Dr. Lawson would be her ally. Savannah knew his relationship with Marti may not have been romantic, but it went beyond professional. "Do you really think she was suicidal?"

He frowned. "What else would it be? The police found a note."

Savannah's heart sped. "A note? What note?" She'd been so concerned with Marti that she hadn't searched the house for any clues as to what had happened.

"Marti left a note. It was a suicide attempt, Savannah."

"What did it say?"

Dr. Lawson shook his head. "You'll have to ask the police that."

I will, Savannah thought. But first she had more important things to do.

She rubbed her hands against her jeans and looked at Dr. Lawson. "Can I see Marti?"

.   .   .

Subdued. Definition: *quiet, reflective, depressed.*

That's how Savannah felt on the silent ride home. Savannah didn't mind the quiet. In fact, she appreciated it. Clive seemed to sense that. He'd slipped away, given her privacy at the hospital, and then waited to drive her back. He'd gone above and beyond, and she didn't know how to thank him.

She replayed her conversation with Dr. Lawson. His assertion couldn't be true. How could Savannah have been so clueless?

Savannah's gut clenched as they turned down the driveway toward her place. What now? The thought of sitting at home alone made her feel restless.

Of course, she had work to do.

But Marti remained at the forefront of her mind.

Clive braked and put the vehicle in park in front of her house.

"Thank you," she started. "You've gone out of your way to help me today, and I really can't say thank you enough."

"It's no problem." He paused, observing her for a moment. "You going to be okay?"

She didn't even try to force a smile. Her soul felt too numb. "I don't know."

"Do you want me to call someone for you?"

She shook her head. "No."

Clive reached behind the front seat to grab something and shoved a small plastic bag into her lap.

She looked at him quizzically. "What's this?"

"A prepaid cell phone. Since you can't find yours, I thought you could use one. Besides, I don't think it's good to be without a phone close by, in case of an emergency."

She took the bag, guilt pressing on her. She hadn't gone out of her way to show him kindness, yet he'd been considerate enough to do this.

"Thanks. That's very thoughtful of you, especially after the way I treated you earlier."

"You're in a stressful situation. It's understandable." He shrugged. "Besides, I've been treated worse."

"Thanks again." She climbed out of the car and walked toward her house.

Her clothes were now dry, but they still felt crinkly and gross. Savannah took a moment to rub Tiger's head and then went straight to the shower. As the water beat against her, she ran through the events of the day.

What had Marti figured out? Savannah had to find her cell phone and check her messages. This couldn't all be a coincidence . . . could it?

As soon as she dried off and dressed, she plugged in the new phone Clive had purchased for her. She'd reimburse him for it later. The gesture had been kind, which only continued to build the dichotomy of the person Clive Miller was. At times he seemed so gruff and aloof, and others, like when he'd saved Tiger, he seemed like a genuinely kind person. There was no need for her to try and figure him out. He'd be gone in a couple of months and she could return to her secluded existence.

She picked up the cell phone. When had Clive bought this? A receipt in the bag showed it had been purchased in Arlington last week. But Clive already had a cell phone. And he said he'd recently switched to a new one. That's why he hadn't gotten her original message saying she'd changed her mind about renting out her property. What kind of man changed cell phones the way most people changed clothes?

She didn't have time to think about it now. She went through all the steps to set the phone up, thankful she had enough charge to make a couple of calls. Then she punched in her old cell phone number. She waited to hear a ring. Nothing.

Strange. She knew her phone was charged, and since she used it in place of a landline, she'd left the ring volume on loud. Why didn't her voice mail pick up? She should be able to check her voice mail from another phone, for that matter. Why hadn't she thought of that earlier? How had they told her she could do that again?

After trying unsuccessfully to reach her voice mail several times, she finally called her cell phone carrier and explained the situation.

"We're not getting a signal from your number. Not even a ping. Did you drop the phone recently, ma'am?" a woman with controlled, even tones asked her on the other line.

"Drop my phone? What do you mean?"

"If the battery isn't in the phone, it becomes untraceable. You can retrieve your voice mail, however, without your phone."

She explained to Savannah the process for doing so. Savannah hung up and called the number, typed in her pass code, and waited.

"You have no voice mail messages," an automated voice told her.

What? That couldn't be right. Marti had said she'd left her messages. What was going on? Had someone stolen her phone from her house?

No, that was ridiculous. The events of the day were taking a toll on her emotions, her logic, causing them to be off-balance.

But what other reason could there be?

CHAPTER 17

An uneasy feeling remained in Savannah's gut as she stared at her new cell phone. Her mind was still racing, replaying everything that had happened but coming up with no solutions.

But the familiar inkling that someone had been in her house made her skin crawl. Obviously someone had been in here before. They'd left that note reading *It wasn't cancer.*

What if someone had come in here to steal her cell phone? What had been in Marti's voice mail that someone didn't want her to hear?

She went down to the kitchen to make some tea but paused at the island. She squinted, unsure if she was seeing correctly. Slowly she picked up the flattened penny.

Was this the one she'd found at Lucia's house? Had she taken it out of her pocket and left it here?

She shook her head. So much had happened that she couldn't even remember. She'd go back upstairs and check her pocket sometime. Right now she needed to clear her head.

Although it was already dark outside, she started across the lawn toward the beach. As she trudged across the grass, she glanced at the guesthouse. The lights were on, but she didn't see anyone moving around inside.

What is Clive doing? she wondered. He'd surprised her today. He'd been sensitive and helpful. Maybe she'd been wrong about him.

She cut through the patch of woods leading to the bay. Her throat tightened. Even though she'd done this a million times before, she was on edge tonight, anxious.

She froze when she saw a lone figure on the shore.

Clive.

He sat there on a blanket, staring at the water.

She intended to turn around and go back, but instead she kept walking toward him.

"Hey there," she called.

Clive looked up, surprise in his gaze. "Savannah."

"We keep running into each other like this."

He smiled and patted the space beside him. "Would you like to join me?"

Normally she'd refuse, but this time she didn't.

"What a day, huh?" she started.

"Yeah, what a day."

"You must like to come out here as much as I do."

"It's one of my favorite spots," he admitted. "Yours too, apparently."

She reached up and pulled something from his hair. "A leaf. You haven't been wandering through the woods, have you?"

A strange expression crossed his face, but only for a moment. It was quickly replaced with a wry grin. "Not lately."

"Listen, you haven't seen anyone lurking around my house, have you?"

He cast her a sharp glance. "I can't say I have. Why? Everything okay?"

She nodded. "Just wondering."

"I'll keep my eyes open for you, if you like."

"A second set of eyes is always good. Thank you."

"You are secluded out here."

"It's not as secluded as you might think. Through the woods that way is the migrant camp. If you go the opposite way, you reach another friend's place."

"Landon Kavanagh?"

Savannah nodded. "That's right. He's your new boss."

She shivered, the wind a little stronger than she'd thought it would be out here.

Clive slipped his jacket off—a different one from the one left at her house—and put it over her shoulders. "You're cold."

The warmth of the coat instantly enveloped her, as did the scent of leather. Her head was telling her she should refuse, but her spirit resisted. "Thank you."

"Listen, I was thinking . . . does Marti have family?"

Savannah shook her head. "They're estranged. She hasn't seen her dad since she was a kid, and her mom kicked Marti out as soon as she graduated high school."

"No brothers or sisters?"

"No. Why?"

"Do you know who has durable power of attorney?"

Savannah hadn't even thought about that. "I have no idea. Knowing Marti, no one."

"Eventually someone might have to make some decisions about your friend's care. It would be good to know who can legally do that."

"You're pretty smart for a handyman. Thanks for the advice. I'll look into it."

"No problem." He looked at Savannah, something softening in his gaze. "Look, I meant to tell you thank you. I know you didn't exactly want to rent out your space. Thank you for reconsidering."

She felt her cheeks heat, both at his compliment and his closeness. She chided herself. She hadn't blushed in years. Years. Probably since she'd first met Reid. So why was Clive having this effect on her?

Sure, he was handsome and mysterious, and he'd practically been a knight in shining armor today. Still, she felt unbalanced.

"You're welcome," she finally said.

The moment spooked her enough that she stood and wiped the sand off her clothes. "I should probably be going."

Clive stood. "Can I walk you up? Seems like a good idea, especially if you suspect someone may have been lurking outside your house."

Normally she'd refuse. But for some reason, she nodded. "That sounds nice. Thank you."

Silently they walked through the patch of woods, across the lawn, and to Savannah's back door. She slipped Clive's coat off and handed it to him. "Thanks again."

He nodded, a strange look in his eyes. "Any time, Savannah."

As Savannah stepped inside, she realized her heart was racing.

• • •

First thing in the morning, Savannah went to visit Chief Lockwood again.

"Ms. Harris." He must have just walked in because he slid his coat off and then placed his metal lunch pail on the shelf behind his desk. "What can I do for you today, young lady?"

"I think you know why I'm here, Chief."

His expression grew sober. "I'm sorry about your friend, Marti. I'm sure it's been a tough couple of days for you. It would be tough for anyone to find their friend like that."

Savannah lowered her voice. "Do you have any idea what might have happened?"

"What might have happened?" His eyebrows shot in the air. "Ms. Harris, there was a suicide note."

She took a deep breath, reminding herself not to become shrill. She'd accomplish a lot more by remaining even-keeled. "You're just going to assume the note was legit?"

The chief sighed, so slightly that Savannah might have missed it had his mustache hairs not moved. "We don't have reason to believe the note was *not* legit."

"I don't think she tried to commit suicide, Chief. I know my friend."

"According to Dr. Lawson, she's been suffering from depression for quite some time now. Suicide attempts are not unusual in people with her state of mind."

"Did you look for any other evidence that might show there was foul play involved? Maybe there were fingerprints? Broken furniture?"

"There were signs of forced entry—by you and your friend," he said, annoyance evident in his tone. "Any physical evidence or fibers would have been washed away in the shower."

The way he said the words made Savannah feel like the bad guy. Maybe she was responsible for the lack of evidence. But her friend's life had been more important at the time than disturbing the scene.

"So that's it? Your duty is done?"

He scowled at her before taking in a deep breath. "I can send a crew to fingerprint her place, if that would make you feel better. But there's nothing to indicate foul play was involved." He raised an eyebrow. "Unless you know something."

Savannah only had to think a moment before sharing. "I got an e-mail from Marti before she OD'd. She hates e-mails and never sends them. The fact that she would send an e-mail raises a red flag. The pieces just aren't fitting for me, Chief."

He shifted his weight and sat down, motioning for Savannah to have a seat also. "Tell me about the e-mail."

Savannah sat across from him and rubbed her hands on her jeans. She explained the e-mails, the voice mails, and her missing phone.

The chief leaned back in his chair. Savannah held her breath, waiting for his reaction. He nodded and rubbed his mustache a moment before looking at her.

"I think you're reading more into this than is there, Ms. Harris. I hate to say it. Have you considered that maybe your friend was losing it? Maybe it was a desperate cry for help before she took those pills?"

Savannah's gaze didn't waver. "No, I haven't considered that. It's not a possibility."

He nodded slowly. "Then what do you think happened?"

Savannah drew in a breath so deep it felt like a burden. "I don't know really. Maybe someone forced her to take those pills, to write that suicide note. Maybe she discovered something she wasn't supposed to. I don't know. I just know she didn't try and commit suicide."

"I admire your faith in your friend."

"But you don't believe me." Savannah stated the obvious. "May I see the suicide note, Chief? Maybe there's something there I'll see that will offer a clue."

He steepled his fingers in front of him and tapped his index fingers together. Finally he leaned forward. "Let me go retrieve it."

As he walked from his office, she noted the mud on his shoes.

She wondered if the town's police chief had been traipsing through the woods recently.

CHAPTER 18

Savannah was surprised to see that the note was typed. It was her first clue that something was off. Marti loved to handwrite things. It was part of her artistic side, the side of her that liked to make things beautiful, the side that fought conformity, even against things as simple as typing.

Savannah carefully fingered the note, four brief paragraphs on a printed sheet with her signature below. Her eyes went to the signature first. Yes, that was definitely Marti's signature, loopy and bold. But did the lines look easy and flowing as usual? Or were those loops more controlled, done under the watchful eye of someone making her sign it?

She read the note.

I know this will come as a surprise to many of you who thought I was living out my dream here, helping the migrant workers. I toiled for them day and night, until my bones were weary. I do hope someone else will step up and finish the task that I've started.

You wonder why I'm writing this note? My life is hopeless. I can't deny the overwhelming sadness that this has caused me.

Outwardly, I like to pretend that everything is good, that I'm happy and fulfilled. Inside, I'm a mess. I hate who I am.

I've felt like this for months now and can no longer take it. That's why I'm choosing to end it all. Death is the only solution to my misery.

Please forgive me for the pain this act will cause.

All my love.

Savannah put the note on the desk, her heart heavy and conflicted. "She didn't write this."

"How do you know that?"

"It doesn't sound like Marti. I can't put my finger on it, but this isn't something she would write. I just know it." She looked at the note. "For instance, she said 'migrant workers.' She never called them that. She calls them field workers or Mexicans or friends. Not migrant workers. And she'd never use the word 'toil.' It's way too stuffy for Marti. She hates pretenses."

The chief didn't say anything. What did she expect him to say?

Savannah stood. "Will you just do one thing for me?"

"What's that?"

"Test the paper. See if it was really printed at Marti's house."

"Or if someone else brought it and forced her to sign it?" the chief finished.

"Exactly. You should be able to prove if it was printed at her house on her printer."

He remained silent a moment before nodding. "We'll test the paper and printer for you, if for no other reason than to put your mind at ease."

"Thank you, Chief. I appreciate it." She took a step toward the door. "Any results on those towels?"

"Not yet. The crime lab is backed up, and unfortunately this isn't top priority for them. I wouldn't worry about it. I'm certain that blood was from an animal."

She nodded, not feeling nearly as confident about anything at the moment.

"Savannah?"

She stopped and looked at the chief.

"Don't get your hopes up that this will turn up anything."

. . .

Clive had spent the past six years thinking about the murder of his wife.

He'd replayed the events leading up to her death. He'd replayed their fights, their estrangement, their heated exchanges.

Now he replayed their conversations, the ones where he'd pleaded with her to stay. Where he'd tried to convince her that they could work things out.

He squeezed his eyes shut when he remembered her adamant refusal.

She'd been preoccupied with her work. Slowly, she'd begun to shut him out. What had started as a happy marriage crumbled into one with two strangers living in the same house.

And now she was dead.

He intended to figure out what had happened.

The killer was still walking free, and that wasn't okay.

From his Jeep, he stared at the building in front of him. The Eastern Shore Marine Wildlife and Ecology Center. It was where his wife had spent all of her time.

A sad smile crossed his lips when he remembered the day she'd rushed home and told him the news that she'd gotten the job out here. As a marine biologist, this had been her dream career.

But that one life event had changed everything.

He'd begged her to talk to him. To tell him what was going on.

But she'd shut down, and he'd dealt with it by pouring himself into his job as well. At least he'd felt affirmation there. At least he'd felt like a success.

Looking back, there were so many things he'd do differently now. But there was no going back; he could only face the consequences of his decisions.

A familiar figure stepped out of the building.

Lauren's best friend, Bobbi Matthews. They'd worked together at the center, went diving together on weekends, and shared dinner often. Because Clive was engrossed in his own job, he'd skipped out on those dates, insisting he had to work. He could tell that Lauren was relieved, that she really didn't want him there anyway.

Right now, that worked to his advantage. Bobbi might recognize him from photographs, but they had never met. Besides, he'd changed. He'd worked out, bulked up. Stubble covered his once clean-shaven face. The sun had darkened his skin. He'd begun to harden.

Sometimes he looked in the mirror and still didn't recognize himself.

Loss and grief could do that to a person.

He watched Bobbi as she walked to her car. She reminded him of Lauren, only about two decades older. Lauren's skin had always looked sun-kissed. Her hair, naturally blond, was even more bleached from the hours she'd spent outside. She'd loved being in a wetsuit more than any other outfit. She'd smelled like salt water and sun and the beach.

She had a smile that could light a room, a gaze that was determined, and a will that couldn't be broken.

Was that ironclad will of hers what had gotten her killed?

As Bobbi drove out of the parking lot, he started his vehicle. Slowly, carefully, he pulled out behind her.

He might have dismissed Bobbi altogether. But as he was sitting by the bay, he'd noticed an unusual amount of boats coming and going from the wooded area around Savannah's house. Something was going on out there. Something secret and hidden.

As a marine biologist, Bobbi would know what was happening on these waters. She checked water temperatures and pollution levels and the state of the wildlife. She monitored what was going on, not always in an official capacity. But people who loved this bay did whatever they could to preserve it.

And besides, Bobbi might—*might*—even know who had killed his wife.

That's why she was worth keeping an eye on.

• • •

Savannah had stopped to see Marti at the hospital after talking to Chief Lockwood. There was no change in her condition. Her friend, once so full of life, simply lay there unmoving. Machines beeped and dripped and hummed. But there was no sign of life from Marti.

"I still don't believe it, Marti. You would never try to commit suicide. Never. You had too much to live for."

Savannah stayed for a while before deciding she couldn't take the smell of antiseptic and rubbing alcohol. Instead of going home, she drove to Marti's house. She sat in her car outside the place for a while, staring at it. She turned off the radio, where the news reported something about the rising cost of produce, a body found in the Chesapeake Bay, and a reminder about a local farmer's market.

Finally Savannah gathered enough strength to climb out. This time, she had her key with her. She twisted it in the lock and stepped inside.

Overwhelming sadness pressed on her as she wandered through her friend's home. The place so screamed Marti, from the brightly colored walls, to the paintings she'd created herself, to the potted plants that desperately needed to be watered.

Savannah filled a pitcher and made the rounds, moistening the dirt of all the plants.

Back in the kitchen, she placed the pitcher on the counter and looked around. The dinette chairs were still strewn across the floor where Marti had fallen. Savannah studied the angles. Did she fall or was there a struggle?

If there was a struggle, how did the person get inside? There were no signs of forced entry, other than those Clive and Savannah had left.

That would mean Marti knew the person who'd attacked her.

Had he or she come to her door and been invited inside to discuss something only to turn on her?

Most importantly, why would someone want to kill Marti? She'd given up everything in her life to help the poor. She made the community a better place. Did she really have any enemies?

And what message had she left for Savannah?

Savannah could feel her hackles rise. She went to Marti's office and glanced around the room. She sat at her desk and searched for a sign, a clue. A desk calendar lay under the keyboard. She flipped back to August. Frowning faces were scribbled on the edges of the sheet. What had happened?

Savannah continued to skip through the months, looking for a telltale note. Nothing.

Until she reached October. There at the top left of the sheet was an unfamiliar name, Leonard Griffith, and a phone number. Below it was written: *The Madden Society.*

Curious. Savannah had never heard of the society or the name Leonard Griffith.

She grabbed the phone, figuring she had nothing to lose. She punched in the numbers and listened to it ring. Finally a man said hello.

"I'm trying to reach Leonard Griffith."

"Speaking."

Savannah cleared her throat, wishing she'd taken more time to gather her thoughts. "Leonard, my name is Savannah Harris, and I'm a friend of Marti Stephenson."

"Yes, Marti." His voice softened. "How's she doing? I haven't heard from her in a few days."

Savannah's curiosity was piqued. "Oh, were you friends?"

He laughed. "You could say that. Although I prefer to say she's my soul mate."

"Soul mate?"

"Yeah, we've been dating for the last two months."

Savannah knew she'd been wrapped up in herself, but how could she not have seen the signs that her friend was in love? She thought Marti had a crush on Dr. Lawson, for goodness sake.

She snapped from those thoughts and focused on the present. She dreaded what she had to say next. "Leonard, I don't know how to tell you this."

"Is something wrong?" All the lightness had disappeared from his voice.

Savannah swallowed. "Leonard, Marti's in the hospital. She's in a coma. The police are saying she tried to commit suicide."

"Commit suicide? Not Marti. No, not Marti. Never." His voice cracked. "Oh my gosh. When did this happen?"

"Yesterday." It was hard to believe. It already felt like a week had passed.

"I've got to get down there to see her."

"How soon can you be here?"

"I'm at a conference out in Colorado. It's going to take me a while to finagle my schedule. I'll be there as soon as I can, though."

· · ·

Savannah left Marti's house and decided to stop by La Tierra Prometida headquarters. Since high school, it had been Marti's dream to help migrant workers. She and Savannah had gone to the same church in Richmond, Virginia. Each summer, their youth group took a trip to Cape Thomas to volunteer. Marti had fallen in love with the work and vowed to come back here one day. One college education and one failed marriage later, she'd fulfilled her dream.

Savannah pulled to a stop on the gravel driveway that led to an old four-room house that Marti now called headquarters. Inside was a food pantry, a room for tutoring, an office, and a library with Internet access that Marti allowed the migrant workers to use.

Marti had done well with it. Had Savannah told her that? She should have, should have encouraged her more.

Stepping from her car onto grass that needed to be cut two inches ago, Savannah followed a worn path to the front door. She pulled out the key Marti had given her to the place and stuck it in the lock. Savannah had helped raise money, organize finances, and solicit support for the nonprofit. A huge part of what Marti did in her interactions with the migrant workers was an effort to lead them to Jesus. Savannah couldn't do that, couldn't sign the statement of faith that the volunteers had to. Instead, she played a supportive role.

She shoved those thoughts aside and pushed the door open.

She wasn't quite sure what she was doing here. But something had drawn her here, almost like a magnet.

Walking through the kitchen, she ran her hand along the wooden countertop. The pantry would need to be restocked soon and the food distributed. Savannah could do that. She moved from the kitchen into the tutoring room. She'd need to post a sign, letting everyone know that tutoring was postponed until further notice. Finally she reached Marti's office. She hesitated before turning the knob. With a rush of willpower, she went inside.

It took a moment for her heart to slow down. It just didn't seem right that Marti wasn't here, smiling, spouting some kind of hidden agenda she felt sure the government was aiming at sticking to the little guy. Even—especially—the migrant workers were a target. Marti had called the Eastern Shore's fields the modern equivalent of sweatshops, for the most part unregulated by the government, sold out to gain profits for agribusiness. She said that officials turned a blind eye to the plight of the migrant workers and that people were so quick to judge the workers as illegal immigrants that they didn't see them as people.

Savannah knew many of them were in the country legally with work permits. She knew most were hard workers. Landon treated them fairly, but other migrant workers were paid a slave's wage, forced to work in harsh conditions, and treated worse than the livestock animals.

What she wouldn't do to hear one of Marti's rants right now.

Bittersweet. Definition: *sweet with a bitter aftertaste.*

That's what memories were like sometimes.

She glanced at the to-do list on Marti's desk. Medical clinics, shoe drives, canned food collections. She hadn't realized just how much her friend did. Savannah was going to have to call some board members to help.

She went to the desk and began flipping through Marti's address book. She found the phone number of Bobbi Matthews, one of the board members for La Tierra Prometida. Savannah had met Bobbi several times. The fifty-something marine biologist worked part-time for a marine center on the Eastern Shore. Having no children at home anymore, Bobbi was also one of the most active volunteers Marti had. Bobbi's husband, Tom, was a local pastor who held services for the migrant workers as well as working full-time for a small local congregation.

Savannah dialed the phone number, relief filling her when Bobbi picked up on the first ring. Savannah knew that Marti admired the woman and that the two had a good relationship. Savannah felt she could trust her.

"Bobbi, this is Savannah Harris."

"Savannah, great to hear from you." Her voice twanged gently, warmly. "It's been awhile."

"Bobbi, you heard about Marti, didn't you?" Savannah paused, hoping her words would come out right.

"I've been trying to call her today. What's going on?"

Weight pressed on Savannah's chest. "It's a long story, Bobbi. She's in the hospital. I was hoping that we might be able to get together so I could explain some things to you."

She gasped. "The hospital? Oh no. Is she okay?"

"Not really. I'd like to meet face-to-face, if you don't mind."

"Definitely. Anything for Marti."

They arranged to meet at Savannah's house the next day. Savannah hung up. Turning around, she noticed a shadow in the doorway. Slowly she drew her gaze up to see an imposing man standing there, an ax in his hands and a glare in his eyes.

CHAPTER 19

Outside, a child squealed. Savannah's eyes darted from the man to the window. In the field beside the house she saw Lucia's nieces and nephews running around, playing chase. She released the breath she held. The man in the doorway was Jose, Lucia's brother.

"Jose, how are you?" Just to be safe, she kept the desk between herself and the ax.

He spoke in rapid-fire Spanish. Savannah tried to pick out key words, but her Spanish was rusty. When Jose pointed outside, Savannah finally understood.

Marti was supposed to watch his children today. Jose probably needed to work. Many workers took their kids with them to the fields, but Marti always said that was no place for children.

"I'll watch them," Savannah said.

He stared at her a moment, a hard look in his eyes. Finally his gaze seemed to soften. He nodded and pointed to the clock.

"*Seis.*" He'd return at six o'clock.

He stomped out of the office, his work boots dirty and heavy, got into a run-down car, and tore down the road, dust kicking up behind him.

Savannah stepped outside and watched the four children running around like they didn't have a worry in the world. The oldest, probably five years old, toted around the youngest, probably eight months old.

Savannah crossed the grass and took the baby in her arms, noting her dirty face and soiled diaper. Despite that, the feeling of the baby's soft skin and silky hair made Savannah's heart pang.

"Penelope," the oldest child said.

"Penelope," Savannah repeated, bouncing the baby in her arms. "What a beautiful name."

Sorrow began to fill her, but she pushed it down. She had other things to think about right now. Four children, for that matter.

She clapped her hands to get their attention. "Good morning."

They turned and looked at her with blank expressions.

Reality settled on her chest. How was she going to watch the children today when she couldn't communicate with them? None of them spoke English, and she didn't speak Spanish. It had been so long since she'd had to entertain children.

She glanced at her watch again. Seven hours until Jose returned? It might as well be a month. She'd have to come up with some sort of plan, maybe do some art projects or play games.

A sound in the distance caused her to pause on the porch. She glanced across the field to a road that stretched by the migrant workers' homes.

A familiar Jeep was just disappearing around the dusty bend. Clive.

Just what was he doing here in the migrant worker camp? Was this part of his job with Landon? Or did he have other reasons?

She bit the inside of her lip. She had a feeling there was much more to Clive Miller than he let on.

. . .

Savannah wasn't sure how it happened, but after she finished baby-sitting and drove away from the camp, she found herself wandering the country roads of Cape Thomas and stopping in front of Landon Kavanagh's house. She sat in the driveway a moment, staring at the massive structure. The farmhouse style diminished the impos-ing nature of the house slightly, but no one could deny how huge it was. The tidy eaves, the dark green siding, the attractive shutters gave a false appearance of a cozy home. The effect was enhanced by the people whom Landon paid to plant cheerful flowers in his manicured beds and to artfully arrange the patio and sidewalks with paver stones and rock walls.

If she were to crack her car windows, she'd hear the waves crash-ing in the distant bay. She might also hear the horses in the stable across the field and the crickets in the woods beyond that. Landon had made a business of farming, yet to see him, you wouldn't think he was the typical farmer type at all. He had a wiry build and walked with fast-paced steps. His hair, receding, was always precisely groomed, his clothes neat, his house spotless. Premature wrinkles creased his forehead, evidence of the hours he spent out in the sun overseeing operations. Despite that, he still seemed more the type of man who'd head for New York City than Cape Thomas.

Apparently he'd developed some types of hybrid tomatoes and apples that had made him money and put his name on the map. He'd even gone so far as to name the apple hybrid after himself.

Those hybrids had allowed him to become the owner/operator of the farm, but his employees did most of his work for him, freeing him up for philanthropic endeavors—many of which involved golf somehow.

Anyone in town would say that he was a respected member of the community, contributing to charities and fund-raisers and serving on boards. There was nothing to not like about Landon Kavanagh. The fact that he'd gone out of his way to give Savannah special attention should be flattering. Perhaps she was still reeling from . . . life.

She stared at his house so long, trying to decide if she should go in or not, that finally he stepped onto the porch. He squinted into her headlights a moment before striding toward her.

"Savannah?"

She rolled down her window and offered a measly smile. "Sorry. I'm not stalking you. I promise."

He walked toward her, grinning and showing perfect white teeth as he leaned into her car. "No, please, tell me you're stalking me. It would make my day. Why don't you come in for a minute?"

"I hate to disturb you."

"You never disturb me, Savannah." He nodded behind him, indicating that he was inviting her in.

After a moment of hesitation, she turned off her car and opened the door. As she stepped out, Landon quickly found a place for his arm around her waist as he walked her toward the house. Why he gave her attention when there were dozens of other women in town who'd love his company still boggled Savannah's mind.

"I heard about Marti. I'm so sorry, Savannah. How are you holding up?"

Savannah shrugged, picturing her friend in the hospital. "Better than Marti."

"I can't imagine how you're feeling right now, finding her like that." He paused at the door. "How about if I make some tea and we can sit out here on the porch and talk for a while? You couldn't ask for better weather than this. We should enjoy it before winter hits."

"That sounds nice."

She settled into a white rocking chair, one that looked out over the bay. The full moon looked orange tonight and hung proudly in the crisp, black sky. Its reflection rippled in the inky water. The air had just the right amount of chill to it.

Landon returned to the porch and sat down in the rocker beside her. "The kettle's on." He followed her gaze. "That's some moon, huh?"

"It's beautiful." At one time, she would have said it reminded her of God's greatness. The thoughts still popped into her head sometimes, but she quickly brushed them aside. She'd waste no more time with those foolish fancies.

"I tried calling today to check on you."

Savannah pulled her arms over her chest as she steadily rocked back and forth. "I can't find my phone. I've looked everywhere, but it's gone."

"That doesn't sound like you, losing your phone. It's usually attached to you."

"I know. I have no clue what happened to it." *Unless someone stole it and deleted Marti's messages.*

"Savannah?"

She shook her head, breaking free from her thoughts. "Sorry. Enough about me. How are you doing, Landon? I know this is a busy season for you. Is everything going smoothly for the harvest?"

"I can't complain. The crops have almost doubled since last year. Technology is amazing." A whistle sounded inside and he stood. "A teaspoon of honey, right?"

Savannah nodded and watched him walk back into the house. Why was she here? What had prompted her to pay this unexpected visit to Landon? She knew he didn't mind, that he welcomed her company whether invited or not. But what did she expect to accomplish? Should she share her theories about Marti? Ask about Señor Lopez? No easy answers came to mind.

The front door swung open, and Landon emerged with a tray topped with two mugs of tea. He set it on the table between them and handed her some green tea with honey. She took a sip and let the drink's warmth soothe her for a moment.

"Need to talk about anything, Savannah?"

She drew in a deep breath, making a quick decision. "The things I need to talk about are also the things I don't want to talk about. I was hoping for a lighthearted conversation that would take my mind off all of those other things."

He smiled. "I can do that."

They filled the next hour with talk of small-town life, the latest Save the Bay movements, and a new restaurant that had opened in the neighboring town of Cape Charles. Finally Savannah stood. It was getting late. "Thank you, Landon. I just needed someone to take my mind off things. You helped me do exactly that."

"Any time, Savannah."

They walked side by side to her car. At the door, he grabbed her hand and kissed it gently. "Have a good evening. And I meant what I said. Any time you need to talk, about anything, I'm here."

Savannah climbed into her car. Could she ever talk to him? Or was the doubt forever planted in her mind that he just might be a killer?

CHAPTER 20

Oh, Savannah.

She shouldn't worry her pretty little head so much. It might ruin that flawless skin, cause her to gray too early.

He hadn't expected her to want to help. In the past, she'd been so withdrawn, so sullen. It was as if something was igniting inside her. He needed to figure out a way to extinguish that flame.

He left the property. He needed to return to his hideout so he could keep an eye on his projects there.

The stakes were rising.

His ears perked at a sound in the distance.

A smile tugged at his lips, starting small before turning into a full-out grin. The chuckle that escaped quickly transformed into billowing laughter.

The train was coming.

He could hear it in the distance, getting closer and closer.

The force of the mighty locomotive would be enough to shake nearby houses, enough for people from miles around to hear it. It was a force that couldn't be stopped.

Just like he was.

Getting closer and closer.

Making people aware of his presence slowly.
When he fully arrived, no one would know what had hit them.

CHAPTER 21

Desolate. Definition: *state of bleak and dismal emptiness.*

That was the word lingering on Savannah's mind the next morning as she pulled into the hospital's parking lot.

The day was rainy and gloomy, which fit Savannah's mood perfectly. She carried her umbrella over her head as the rain battered the landscape and everything else it could find.

When she walked into Marti's room, Savannah discovered that her condition hadn't changed. A tube still ran down her throat, helping her breathe. An IV dripped nourishment into her body. Her eyes remained closed.

Marti had always hated going to the doctor. She thought they ran batteries of tests just to inflate their paychecks. She thought medical insurance was a scam. She'd griped that doctors were overpaid and that none of them really cared.

None of them except Dr. Lawson.

She'd always liked talking about the man, usually with stars in her eyes. He could do no wrong in her book. He provided medical care to the migrant workers without ever charging them a dime. He worked endless hours, lived in a modest house, and at one time had said he stayed single because it fit his profession better. A spouse should never play second fiddle to his career.

Marti had hoped to change his mind.

Which was why Leonard was so surprising. Wasn't it just last week that Marti was talking about Dr. Lawson? Could Marti have been dating one man and pining for another?

Savannah took her hand. "Oh, Marti. I wish you could tell me what happened."

There was no response, just a steady beat from the heart monitor beside the bed.

"Why didn't you tell me what you were going through? I would have helped. I would have tried to help." She paused. "I thought we told each other everything."

Savannah remembered Clive's words to her that first day in the hospital. *Do you really tell her everything? Everything?*

No, she supposed there were things she hadn't told Marti. There were things she'd never tell anyone, though. The secrets were too dark, too shameful.

How could she not have seen the signs? Marti had always been the artistic type, prone to highs and lows. But despite that, Marti was grounded. She never went off the deep end.

"Savannah," a male voice said behind her.

She turned and saw Dr. Lawson standing in the doorway, looking as slick and debonair as always. "Doctor. How's Marti this morning? Any changes?"

He sat down on a stool across from her. "No, no changes. She's still stable, but unresponsive. Those pills did a number on her. Although we pumped her stomach and removed as many as we could, there's no telling what damage had already been done."

"Doctor, is there any evidence that . . ." She sucked in a breath, gathering her courage. "Any evidence that maybe she was forced to swallow the pills?"

He blinked several times, as if her question had thrown him off guard. "I'm not sure I understand what you're getting at."

"I mean is there anything about Marti that would make you think someone made her do this against her will?"

He stared a moment. "You think someone did this to her? Savannah, I've heard some wild stories in my life, but this . . ." He shook his head. "I know this is hard news to handle, but—"

"I'm not claiming anything. I'm just asking the question."

Finally he said, "No, I haven't seen anything that's raised suspicions."

"Is it too late to do tests?"

He shifted again. "I don't know what to say, Savannah. I suppose there might be bruises if someone forced her to do this. I haven't seen any."

She stood. "If you see anything, will you let me know?"

Dr. Lawson nodded. "Of course."

. . .

"Thank you for meeting with me." Savannah sat across the kitchen table from Bobbi and Pastor Tom, warm drinks in front of each of them.

Savannah had picked up some apple cider at the farmer's market earlier. She had heated it with a touch of caramel and a dollop of whipped cream. It was one of her favorite autumn drinks.

Pastor Tom had always seemed like a good man to her. He came across as honest, earnest, and hardworking. He had a quick grin and kind eyes, and he fit the image that Savannah had always had of a small-town pastor.

Physically he had an oversized stomach and a round tan face. What he lacked for in hair on top of his head, he made up for in the salt-and-pepper beard that filled out his face. She knew that behind the jolly look in his eyes, he was compassionate and didn't mind getting dirty.

A fire crackled in the fireplace in the living room, but the flames were visible from where they sat. The whole atmosphere seemed calming, too calming, especially considering what Savannah was about to say.

She cleared her throat and leaned forward. "I don't want to waste time with small talk. Marti's not doing well. The doctor and police are saying she tried to commit suicide by swallowing too many pills."

Bobbi gasped, her hand reaching toward her heart as if the news had stopped it from beating. "Suicide? Marti? That's not possible."

"I know. I feel the same way. But there was . . . there was a note."

Bobbi's eyes widened. Savannah explained what the note had said and that it had been typewritten. She ended with her opinion that Marti hadn't actually authored the note at all.

Tom leaned forward. "Savannah, are you saying you think someone wrote the note, forced Marti to sign it, and then tried to kill her?"

Savannah hesitated a moment, then nodded. "That's exactly what I'm thinking. I know it might sound crazy. I know it *does* sound crazy. But I just can't believe she tried to commit suicide." She paused. "Am I crazy?"

"I don't think you're crazy, Savannah, but why do you think someone would try to kill Marti?" Bobbi's intense gaze was fixed on Savannah.

Here goes nothing. "Some of the migrant workers think that Señor Lopez was murdered. I didn't give the idea too much thought, but Marti was looking into it. She was also suspicious about the disappearance of two other workers. That's the only possible reason I can think of—that someone might have felt threatened. Maybe she discovered something that this person didn't want discovered."

"Señor Lopez had a tendency to be very superstitious," Tom said thoughtfully. "I find it hard to believe that someone murdered him, especially considering how sick he was."

Savannah shook her head, her fingers gripping her mug of apple cider like a lifeline. "I just don't know what to think. My gut tells me there's more to this than meets the eye. And Dr. Lawson told me that Marti's been on antidepressants. Why didn't I know that? I'm her best friend. I should have known that."

Tom and Bobbi glanced at each other.

"She didn't want people to know," Bobbi whispered.

Savannah sucked in a breath before running her hand across her brow and through her hair. "You mean it's true? Marti told you she was depressed?"

Bobbi nodded, lines creasing around her eyes and across her forehead. "I'm sorry, Savannah. She felt ashamed of the fact that she couldn't control her emotions. She somehow felt it was a spiritual issue, that she'd let God down. I told her she had nothing to feel guilty about, but she didn't listen."

Savannah sat back hard in her chair. "I still can't believe it. I thought Marti told me everything." What else didn't she know about her friend?

Tom fidgeted before locking gazes with Savannah. "I think Marti feared you'd count her condition as another strike against God. She didn't want to do anything else to push you away from a Savior she loves immensely."

Savannah ignored the God reference, her mind still on Marti. "Why? Why was she depressed?"

The couple exchanged another glance. Tom finally spoke, his voice low, serious. "Savannah, we suspect that Marti was assaulted this summer."

"Assaulted?"

"Beaten up," Bobbi said.

"By who? Where? How?" Her questions seemed to blur along with the world around her.

"We think it was one of the migrant workers," Tom said. "She would never say, though. I speculated that she may have been trying to protect someone, though for what reason I'm not sure."

"So nobody was ever sent to jail for it? Why wouldn't she press charges? Whoever did that should pay for what they put her through!"

Bobbi took her hand. "We don't know, Savannah. She didn't want to talk about it. She just stuffed it inside and said she'd deal with it. We tried to help her, but she didn't seem to want help."

Savannah's world continued to spin. "How could I not know that? Why didn't she tell me? I don't understand."

"You were out of town when it happened. Visiting your mom, I think. She made us promise not to tell you—or anyone, for that matter."

"She thinks I'm that fragile?"

"She knows you're mad at God. She didn't want to add fuel to that."

"You can't be mad at someone who doesn't exist."

Silence stretched, heavy in the air. She hadn't meant to voice her thoughts so strongly, but her doubts had risen to the surface and burst out before she could stop them.

"I know this is a lot to comprehend, Savannah." Tom smiled sympathetically.

Savannah stood, needing to busy herself with something. "Anyone want more apple cider? Tea?"

"I think it's time for us to go." Bobbi stood as well. "Unless you want to talk. We can stay for as long as you need."

"I don't even know what to say."

Pastor Tom patted her hand. "We're just a phone call away if you need us. Any time of the day or night, we're there."

She nodded. "Thanks."

"You look like you need to be alone, Savannah." Bobbi stepped toward the door, her hand on Pastor Tom's elbow.

Savannah suddenly remembered she'd called them here to talk about something else as well. "La Tierra Prometida," she mumbled.

The couple paused at the door. "We'll make sure everything is taken care of, Savannah," Pastor Tom said. He stared at her a moment. "Can we pray with you before we go?"

"Don't take this personally, Pastor, but I think I'll pass. I don't want to waste my time or yours."

CHAPTER 22

Clive slowed as he pulled up the lane. He recognized the car at Savannah's house.

Bobbi Matthews.

What was Bobbi doing at Savannah's place? He wished he could charge up to the door, ask Bobbi the questions that pressed on him. But it was too soon. He had to plot each of his moves carefully. Otherwise his whole plan would crumble.

Tomorrow he'd launch that plan on Landon Kavanagh's farm. He wanted to talk to some of the workers, find out if any of them might have been employed by Landon six years ago when his wife was in this area. He wanted to find out what they knew.

Her death had ties to the farm. He felt certain of that.

As he stepped inside his temporary home, his cell phone rang. It was Wheaton.

"Anything?" his friend asked.

"Not yet."

"You doing okay on cash?"

"For now," Clive said.

"You have the other cell phone, right? Just in case someone tries to trace this one? In case you need to ditch the one you have?"

Clive frowned. "I had to let someone else use it."

"Really?" His friend's voice rose in surprise.

"It's a long story."

"They're on you like a hound dog after a rabbit during hunting season. You know that, don't you?"

"I'm doing all I can. Thank you for all your help. For believing in me." Wheaton was one of the few who had.

"I know you're above all that. I'll be in touch."

Clive hung up and stared out the window at Savannah's house. He had to find answers.

Because time wasn't on his side.

. . .

Marti had been attacked? How was that possible?

Savannah sat on the couch, her knees pulled to her chest. The firelight flickered on her face, and the flames warmed her otherwise cold skin. She'd been here for the last hour, ever since Pastor Tom and Bobbi left.

As her thoughts attacked her, she wanted nothing more than a glass of wine, but she didn't let herself have one. She was done with trying to numb the pain.

Instead, she let her thoughts travel back to August, when she remembered Marti going through a period of being quieter, more aloof than usual. Marti had blamed it on losing a federal grant for La Tierra Prometida. Then one of her most active volunteers had moved away, heaping more responsibility on Marti. There were so many excuses, so many reasons.

Savannah should have known there was more to it.

Why hadn't she asked more questions? She should have insisted that Marti sit down with her and talk, really talk. Savannah should have looked away from her own problems long enough to truly be a friend.

Maybe Marti had threatened to turn in whoever attacked her. Maybe that person had tried to kill her to keep her quiet.

She tried to remember if Marti's attitude about anyone had changed since August. Savannah searched her memory. She couldn't recall Marti being fearful about her job or about going into the village where the migrant workers lived. Certainly she'd be tense if one of them had attacked her. She'd remained active at her church. No changes there.

What had changed or caused her stress?

Landon.

There was his name, coming up again.

But Marti had never been particularly fond of Landon. She claimed he didn't pay the workers enough and made them work too hard. Landon claimed he gave them a better life here than they had in Mexico. He said they always had a choice about working for him or finding another job. They'd clashed on many occasions.

But Landon wouldn't risk everything he'd worked for by assaulting someone, just as he wouldn't risk everything with attempted murder. He was smarter than that.

So who else?

The bigger questions were: Would Marti ever wake? Would Savannah ever have a chance to mend the fracture in their friendship?

She wished she could turn back time.

She'd been wishing that every day, so fervently that her heart ached.

She stared at the flames, the ache in her heart growing deeper with each question.

What would it be like if Ella were still alive? She'd be three, walking and learning to talk. Would her hair still be curly like

Reid's? She'd had an infectious giggle and beautiful eyes. She had deserved a chance at life.

And how about Reid? Would the two of them still be married? Would they have overcome their differences? Would he have ever stopped blaming her for getting him fired from their church?

Her mind went back in time even further. What if she'd never given up her career? Maybe she would have covered the uprising in Northern Africa. The situation in the Ukraine. Her career seemed more loyal to her than people ever had been.

She shook her head. She'd been so careful not to rely on her heart. She should have stuck to her guns. Then she wouldn't have been so let down by Reid. By the church. By God.

The ringing of Savannah's cell phone jolted her from her thoughts. She pulled it from her belt and answered.

"Good, the phone works," a male voice said.

"Excuse me?"

"It's Clive. I just wanted to check on you. Good to know the cell phone works."

She leaned back into the couch, relieved for the distraction. "Yes, it does. Thank you again. I still haven't been able to find my phone. I've tried calling the old number and listening for the ring. It's nowhere."

"Hopefully it'll turn up soon. How's your friend doing today?"

"No changes."

"There's still hope. Don't forget that."

"Thanks, Clive."

Ask him why he was in the migrant camp. But she couldn't. It wasn't her business, and now wasn't the time. She had other things to think about.

Starting with a visit to Lucia.

CHAPTER 23

Savannah dodged the rain as she ran from her car to Lucia's house. She had always liked the girl—Lucia had been a frequent visitor to La Tierra Prometida headquarters. Whenever Savannah was there working on finances, Lucia seemed to show up, eager to talk.

And according to Marti, she only came when Savannah was there. Savannah had never understood that. The two of them would talk some, but then Lucia always had a reason to go.

Something about Lucia reminded Savannah of herself. Maybe it was the dogged curiosity in the girl's gaze. Maybe it was the hunger for answers. Maybe it was the fact that Lucia always talked about the greater good.

Lucia opened the door before Savannah even finished climbing the porch steps. Savannah was quickly ushered inside and given tea and cookies at an old folding table shoved into the corner of the living room.

Savannah looked around. Two men sat at a table in the kitchen playing cards and smoking cigarettes. Alba was on the porch shelling beans. Two children played soccer in the side yard, despite the dismal conditions outside.

The smells from the night of Señor Lopez's death were still present; maybe they were always here. Every available surface was cluttered with boxes of food, newspapers, clothes, or diapers. A box of produce sat on the kitchen counter, right beside a milk jug full of flowers. Both compliments of Landon, probably.

"How are you?" Savannah asked, taking a sip of her tea.

"We're doing okay," Lucia said in broken English. "How's Señora Marti?"

Savannah frowned. "She's hanging in."

"I pray for her every day. Señora Marti would never try to take her own life."

"I agree." Savannah paused and leaned forward. "Listen, Lucia, I've been thinking about our conversation. About Papa. About Felipe and Jorge."

Lucia nodded, hope filling her gaze. Before Savannah could continue, she shoved something into her hand. "Take these."

Savannah looked down at the bag Lucia had given her. There were three pills inside. "What is this?"

"It's Papa's medication. Can you have it tested?"

"Tested for what, Lucia?"

"It's supposed to be for his cancer, to help ease his pain in his final days. But I wonder if somebody tampered with it."

Savannah didn't want to tell her that this sounded like a long shot. Instead, she nodded and slipped the bag into her purse. "I'll see what I can find out."

Lucia smiled. "Thank you."

Savannah nibbled on a cookie before wiping her mouth with a Christmas napkin. "Lucia, is life really that much better here?" She looked around. "Is living here an improvement on your old life?"

"There were no jobs for me back in Mexico. I don't make much, but it's enough to send home to my brother."

"I thought Jose was your brother?"

"I have a younger brother, too. He wants to be a doctor. I send my paychecks to him so it can help pay for his tuition."

Savannah's heart softened. "That's kind of you, Lucia."

"Anyone would do it. Sacrifice for family. It's just what you do."

Savannah felt pangs of guilt once more. Maybe that's where she'd gone wrong. She hadn't sacrificed enough. If she had, things would be different right now.

She cleared her throat. This wasn't the time to start beating herself up. She had other things to think about.

"Tell me about Felipe and Jorge." Savannah pulled out her old reporter's notebook, ready to take notes. Just feeling the paper in her hands caused adrenaline to surge through her.

"Felipe was nineteen. He came here alone, without a family. He said he wanted to make money so he could send it back to his mama and papa in Mexico. He was quiet, kept to himself."

"When did he disappear?"

"Three weeks ago. He never showed up for work. No one has seen him since then."

"You never told the police?"

She shook her head. "People said he ran from immigration. I don't believe it."

"How well did you know Felipe?"

She blushed a little. "Enough. He liked to go walking on the train tracks with me. He'd find old date nails—you know, the ones with the date engraved on the top. He found some going back to the 1940s. He was trying to collect all the different years."

Railroad tracks?

Savannah remembered the flattened pennies she'd found. Were they somehow connected with Felipe? Had he gone underground, maybe as part of some kind of crime rampage?

"Did he ever put coins on the tracks and come back to see how the trains could flatten them?"

"He talked about it once. Then he said he needed to keep every penny he could and not waste any money." Lucia tilted her head. "He mentioned you once, you know."

Savannah pointed at herself. "Me? I don't ever remember seeing him."

"He saw you coming and going from La Tierra Prometida. He said once that you reminded him of his mother. You weren't old enough to be his mom, of course."

Savannah nodded, a sick feeling in her stomach. "How about Jorge? What do you know about him?"

"He disappeared a week after Felipe. He was a little louder, more gruff. If he drank too much, everyone knew to stay away from him."

"How did he disappear? The same way Felipe did?"

Lucia nodded. "He didn't show up for work, so a couple of people got worried and looked for him. He was gone. No one's heard from him since then."

"Did he live alone?"

"No, he lived with six other guys. The last one to get home had to sleep on the floor." Lucia shrugged. "It's just the way we live around here."

"Do you think I could see where they lived?"

Lucia stood. "Of course."

They stepped outside. Lucia huddled with Savannah under the umbrella as they hurried across the wet ground. They stopped in front of a small wooden structure that reminded Savannah of an old cabin from a rustic summer camp. One of the stories she'd written early in her career had been about a suspected drug ring operating at just such a camp. She'd gone undercover as a counselor and exposed the camp's owner as the culprit. That was the story where the investigative bug had really bitten—and bitten hard.

Lucia twisted the lock and pushed the door open.

"Can we just go inside like this?" Savannah asked.

Lucia nodded. "Everyone's at work right now. This was Jorge's place."

It *was* an old camp building, Savannah realized. The walls were made of cinderblock, painted a dirty white. Three bunk beds were in the two rooms on the end. A bathroom was in the middle. Savannah peered inside. Wads of toilet paper overflowed from the commodes, the trashcans, even the sink. The place smelled of sewage, and urine stained the walls.

She shook her head. Whose fault was this? The residents for not taking care of the property? The landlord for not maintaining things? No one should live like this.

"Who owns this place?" Savannah asked.

"You won't believe me."

"Try me."

"Chief Lockwood."

CHAPTER 24

Savannah found nothing of interest at Jorge's place other than deplorable conditions. Next, Lucia led her to an old camper—Felipe's place. Although propped up on cinderblocks, it was still lopsided.

Savannah reached for the door and was surprised to find it unlocked.

She looked back at Lucia, who shrugged. "We don't lock up things like you do in America."

Savannah peered inside. "Who lived with him?"

"He was looking for a roommate. But this place is tiny."

Savannah scanned the inside. It *was* tiny. There was a small kitchen with a crooked pedestal table to the right. On the left was a couch, an old TV, and a coffee table loaded with half-eaten bags of chips, cookies, and empty soda bottles. An off-center door appeared to lead to a bathroom and another to the closet.

"I'm guessing the couch pulled out into a bed," Savannah said.

Lucia nodded.

"No one's touched this space since he was last seen?"

"As far as I know."

Savannah began wandering the perimeter of the room. There seemed to be absolutely no personal effects here, mostly just remnants of food, though a soccer ball lay in the corner.

"Where are his clothes?"

"Try the closet."

Savannah opened the door and saw a rumpled mess of material on the floor. She looked through a few items but found nothing.

She walked over to the couch and moved the cushions.

Nothing.

She moved some of the junk on the coffee table.

That's when something caught her eye.

It was a penny.

Flattened.

Cold realization burst through her. Whoever was leaving these pennies was doing it on purpose. First at Señor Lopez's. She was certain now that the one she'd found at her place was a new one. Now this one at Felipe's.

This wasn't a coincidence. Someone was leaving a calling card.

A killer, perhaps?

She picked it up, certain this was important, and slipped it into her pocket.

• • •

By the time Savannah got back to her place, it was getting dark outside.

The rain had strengthened, coming down harder, accompanied by occasional thunder and lightning. Her umbrella was useless as the wind whipped underneath and inverted it.

By the time she reached her porch, she was breathless. She unlocked her door—she'd thought twice about leaving it unlocked today—and rushed inside. She shivered as she stripped off her coat and set the umbrella in the corner.

What a day.

Something was stirring inside her. Maybe she couldn't make things right with Marti just yet. She couldn't apologize to her and tell her she was spot-on. But she could look into these disappearances.

Reid's voice slammed into her mind.

"Why do you always feel the need to expose things?" His hands flew in the air in exasperation.

"Shh. You're going to wake Ella. And I expose injustices, not things," Savannah had retorted.

He'd stared at her, looking absolutely flabbergasted. "Even in the church? My own wife?"

"Just because someone goes to church doesn't mean their heart isn't black. I thought I was being very respectful when I raised those questions at the meeting tonight."

"Church should be a safe place."

"Safe for who? You? Me? God doesn't call us to be safe. I think you just said that in one of your sermons." She should have resisted the quip, but she hadn't stopped herself. "Only in America do Christians think that. We want to be in our comfort zone, serve God when it fits our lifestyles."

His mouth had gaped. "You think persecuted Christians have the market on what it means to be real?"

Her hand had gone to her hip. There was no holding back the fight in her. "If you put it that way, then yes, they do. When your life is on the line, the authenticity of your beliefs are solidified a lot more quickly."

Savannah shook her head, snapping back to the present. As she walked toward the kitchen, her back muscles tightened. The feeling was becoming all too familiar.

She paused and glanced around.

Her breath left her lungs when she spotted something on her kitchen counter.

Another flattened penny.

Someone had been here.

The killer had been here.

CHAPTER 25

Without thinking, Savannah ran toward the back door.

If the killer had been here, then maybe he was still here.

She couldn't deny the possibility.

The rain pelted her as she flew out the back door. She didn't know where she was going; she only knew she had to move.

Clive.

Maybe Clive could help.

She started toward the guesthouse, the water blurring her vision. She rubbed her eyes, trying to clear them.

Thunder rumbled overhead, only intensifying her shivers. As lightning flashed across the sky, she saw the silhouette of a man standing at the edge of the woods.

She gasped.

Had she been seeing things?

The sky went dark again, and she lurched to a halt.

She hadn't been seeing things. There was a man out there, a man who was watching her.

As she turned to run back to the house, her foot caught on a root, sending her tumbling to the ground. Stunned, she tried to push herself up.

Her ankle protested.

As lightning flashed again, she looked toward the woods where the man had been.

He was gone.

"Savannah?" someone called.

She stifled a scream, swinging her head wildly toward the voice. It was Clive, she realized.

His arms encircled her and he pulled her to her feet. "Are you okay?"

She shook her head. "No, I'm not okay."

"Let's get you out of the rain."

. . .

Before Clive could second-guess himself, he gathered Savannah in his arms and hurried across the lawn.

He'd been looking outside his window earlier as lightning flashed. That's when he'd spotted Savannah running and then falling. He'd rushed out to make sure she was okay.

She trembled in his arms now, which only made him quicken his steps. He reached his house, pushed the door open, and laid her on the couch. Moving quickly, he found a blanket and tucked it around her shoulders. A fire already crackled in the fireplace in front of them.

He bent down to look at Savannah's face. Her hair clung to her cheeks, her eyes had a wild look about them, and her teeth chattered. "Let me make you some coffee."

She nodded, and he reluctantly left her. The coffee had already been percolating, so he poured a cup and brought it to her. He sat down beside her and watched as she took a sip. "Do you want to tell me what's going on?"

She stared at the fire, almost as if she was in another world.

He wasn't sure she was going to speak. When she finally did, her words stunned him.

"I think something strange is going on here in Cape Thomas. Someone tried to murder Marti, they possibly killed Señor Lopez, kidnapped two migrant workers, and they're leaving me clues."

He blinked, trying to understand everything she'd just said. "What?"

She shook her head slightly, still staring into the fire. "I know it sounds crazy. It sounds crazy to me, too. But I can't deny the evidence anymore." She finally looked at him. "I don't know why I'm telling you this. I guess Marti's in the hospital, and I've isolated myself from everyone else. I didn't exactly plan on being here."

"Okay, let's backtrack a little. Why do you think someone's leaving you clues?"

"I keep finding these." She reached into her pocket and pulled out the penny she'd found at Felipe's. She set it on the table.

"A flattened penny?" He picked it up and examined it.

She nodded. "I found one at Señor Lopez's house after he died. I found one at Felipe's house—he's a missing migrant worker. And I've found two inside my house."

"So you think a killer is leaving these for you?" He stared at the piece of oval copper.

She rubbed her arms. "I know it sounds crazy. But something's off. Something's wrong."

"Why were you running?"

"I'd just found another penny in my house. Then I saw a man watching me from the woods."

Clive stood, his muscles rigid. "Just now?"

She nodded. "There's no need to go after him. He's gone."

"How can you be sure?"

"He doesn't want to be found. I wasn't supposed to see him. The lightning gave him away."

"Let's call the police."

She shook her head. "I've talked to the chief almost every day this week. I'm not sure if he simply doesn't want to acknowledge what's happening here or if he's too lazy to do anything. He doesn't believe me anyway. He's patronizing at best."

"Why would someone target you?" Clive asked, trying to put the pieces together.

"I have no idea. But I can't help but think everything is somehow connected."

"Who's Señor Lopez?"

"He's a migrant worker who died this week."

"Died of . . . ?"

She bit her lip. "Cancer, supposedly. I mean he was diagnosed with cancer, but he called me to his deathbed and told me it was murder."

"You think he's connected with the disappearance of two migrant workers and the possible suicide of your best friend?" He tried to keep the skepticism out of his voice.

"I know it sounds crazy. I know it does. But something's going on." She started to stand. "I should go—"

He grabbed her hand and pulled her back down. "No. Please stay. I don't think you're crazy. I'm just trying to put the pieces together."

Reluctantly she sat back down. She hugged her coffee mug with her fingers and leaned forward.

"You're going to get sick in those wet clothes. Can I get you a sweatshirt at least?" he offered.

She nodded. "Sure."

He returned a moment later with a gray hoodie. She slipped into the bathroom to put it on. When she emerged, Clive's heart leapt into his throat. She was gorgeous anyway. But seeing her with her hair wet and her body wrapped in his oversized sweatshirt made him feel things he hadn't felt in a long time. A long-buried desire burned in him.

When she sat on the couch, he purposely scooted away. He had to keep his distance, especially when all he wanted to do was wrap her in his arms.

"Did you eat, Savannah? I've only known you a few days, and I already think you've lost weight." It was a nice, safe change of subject.

"I haven't eaten yet."

"Let me fix you something."

"Don't go out of your way."

"I'm no chef, so I promise it'll be nothing fancy."

She stood. "I can help."

"No, you stay there. Drink your coffee. I'll be fine." He could put some distance between Savannah and himself this way.

He pulled out some chicken breasts, a box of pasta, and vegetables for a salad. He started working on the meal, keeping one eye on Savannah.

Why was the woman so fascinating to him? He'd been trying to get her out of his mind, but it didn't seem to work. Ever since that day at the hospital when she'd let down some of her walls, Savannah had consumed his thoughts.

He couldn't let that happen. He had to stay focused. He couldn't let anything get him off track.

Yet he had so many questions he wanted to ask her about how she got here. He wanted to know her story. But if he started asking her questions, then she might very well ask him questions in return. That's what he couldn't afford.

Besides, what exactly was going on here in Cape Thomas?

He finished cooking, plated up the food, and brought it over to the coffee table. "It might be warmer to eat it here."

Savannah smiled slightly. "Sounds nice." She lowered herself to the floor and sat cross-legged across from him. "You didn't have to do this, you know."

"I had to eat anyway. Why not with company? So you have all of these theories. What are you going to do about them?" Clive stabbed a piece of chicken as he waited for her answer.

Savannah shook her head. "I wish I knew. I'm meeting with Marti's boyfriend as soon as he can get into town. Maybe he has some answers."

"Why are you frowning?"

She sighed. "She didn't tell me she had a boyfriend. There was a lot of stuff she didn't tell me. I don't know if she thought I was too emotionally fragile or what."

"Why would she think you're emotionally fragile?"

She set down her fork, lines pulling at her eyes, her lips. "I used to be an investigative reporter."

His throat tightened as she said the words. This could be trouble. Or it could be a good thing. Either way, he had to make sure Savannah never got suspicious of him. "What happened?"

"I gave that career up to get married to a pastor. A year later, we had a baby." She drew in a deep breath. "In the meantime, I took a position as a freelancer for the local newspaper and started getting suspicious of the town's sheriff. I'd heard rumors about him being corrupt, but no one had ever been able to bust him. I started doing some digging. I read through tons of old public reports and files and found some inconsistences. I confronted him about it and he just laughed it off. I kept following the leads. I kept pushing."

Clive could tell this wasn't leading anywhere good.

"I pushed hard enough that I started receiving threats on my life. Reid, my husband, begged me to back off. I told him I just had to do one more thing. Just one more." She shook her head. "But it was too late. Reid went out to pick up some ice cream and took Ella with him. They took my car. No one knew the ignition had been rigged. One turn and the whole thing exploded. It was intended for me, of course. But they both died."

He reached across the table and squeezed her hand. "I'm sorry, Savannah."

"Not as sorry as I am. I didn't know when to stop. I was blinded by this need for justice."

"You were doing what you thought was right."

Her tortured gaze met his. "And it got my family killed."

"The only ones to blame are the ones who tampered with your car. Did they ever get caught?"

Savannah nodded. "He's in jail for life now."

"How'd you get here?"

"I had to make some changes. My life had revolved around journalism, but that was over. Then my life revolved around my family. That was over. I was left with nothing."

"Your faith?" Clive questioned. "You were a pastor's wife."

"I was a terrible pastor's wife." She let out a bitter laugh. "I mean I was terrible."

"You don't seem like a terrible person, so I doubt you failed that horrendously."

She leaned back. "You know all those books you read, the ones where a guy and girl meet, they come from two totally different life-styles, but they fall in love, and they believe that love can conquer all? Life isn't like that."

"I can't say those are my type of books, but those stories are an escape. They're not often reality. At least not with the people I know."

She stared at him a moment, and he knew the questions that were coming. Questions he didn't want to answer.

"The people you know? You almost sound like you know that firsthand."

He played with the stem of his glass for a moment. "You could say that."

"How'd your wife die? I mean I know that's personal. If you don't want to answer, I understand."

He decided to tell the truth but choose the details carefully. "She was actually murdered."

CHAPTER 26

Savannah gasped. "What?"

Clive nodded, his expression pensive and uneasy. "It's true. I came home from work. We were supposed to have dinner and talk. I called to her when I walked in. She didn't answer. I went upstairs to look for her. I found her in the bathroom. She'd been shot."

"That's awful, Clive. I'm so sorry."

He glanced down at his hands, a new somberness coming over him. "Me too. I wouldn't wish that on my worst enemy."

"They catch the guy who did it?"

"No, the DA thought they did. But they had the wrong guy, convicted him, sent him to prison."

"That's terrible. Are you sure he was the wrong guy?"

His face looked hard, unyielding. "I was certain of his innocence all along."

"Can you really ever be that certain of someone's innocence?"

"I can."

"Then the real killer is still out there?"

He nodded. "That's right."

"That's gotta make it hard to sleep at night."

"You better believe it."

Somehow, through their tragedies, she felt more bonded with the man, despite her doubts about him. Despite the fact that she felt he was hiding something. Hiding a lot, perhaps. Her kinship with him felt larger than her doubts at the moment.

"Savannah, you said you were an investigative journalist?"

"That's right."

"Then what does your gut tell you to do? Where does it tell you to start?"

She sucked on her bottom lip a moment, trying to ascertain the answer. Finally she nodded. "My training would tell me to start with the inner circle of each of those people involved. See who connects them. See who they have in common."

"Any idea who that might be?"

Faces flashed through her mind until only one remained. She closed her eyes, not wanting to believe the truth. Finally she nodded. "Landon Kavanagh."

. . .

Clive felt something stirring inside him.

There was that name again. Landon Kavanagh. It couldn't be a coincidence. Clive just had to find the evidence to nail him.

"Have you met Landon yet?" Savannah's voice pulled him from his thoughts.

He shook his head. "Not yet."

Savannah pressed her lips together for a moment. "He's a kind man. I can't imagine he'd have anything to do with this."

"People wear all kinds of facades." As soon as the words left his mouth, he wanted to snatch them back. He knew a thing or two about wearing facades and had no right to point his finger at anyone else.

Savannah nodded. "I know, but I think he really wants to look out for the good of the community. He's generous, has a soft spot for animals. He's one of the few employers who gives the migrant workers bonuses at the end of harvest season."

"If he's innocent, then investigating him shouldn't do any harm, right? Any evidence you find will prove that he's not guilty."

"Then it would be a dead end."

"Maybe something else will come up in the process."

She tilted her head. "Why do you sound like you know so much about this?"

He shrugged, reminding himself to look casual. "Too many crime dramas on TV?"

She laughed and leaned back. "Everyone thinks they can be a detective now. I've heard that one before."

"They make it look like so much fun on TV." He shifted. "Actually, one of my odd jobs was working in the prison system for a while. I guess I did learn a few things there."

"I see." She set her empty plate down and stood. "I should be going."

"I'll walk you back."

"You don't have to do that."

"You thought someone was inside your house, and then you saw someone watching you in the woods."

"Now I just sound paranoid."

"I'd feel better if I could check things out for you."

"You want to be a gentleman, so I won't refuse."

Clive grabbed an umbrella, and they stepped outside. The water was still coming down at a steady pace. Clive huddled with her under the umbrella. He enjoyed her warmth, her sweet scent, and her company way too much.

Together they darted across the lawn and through her back door.

"Do you ever lock your doors?" Clive shook his wet jacket in the mudroom.

She shrugged. "Yes, but I don't like to. What's the point of moving to the country if you act like you're living in the city?"

"Considering the fact that you think someone is breaking into your home?"

She raised a hand. "Don't say it. Besides, I actually did lock it earlier. When I ran out after discovering the penny, I just forgot."

"You mind if I check things out?"

"Be my guest." She waved her hand, giving him free rein of the house.

He looked in every room, in every closet, and under every bed. There was no one there.

Not much of Savannah was here either, for that matter. Everything seemed so basic. There were no pictures, no knick-knacks, no anything from her past life.

Only a pink baby rattle on her desk.

At least now he understood her grief some more.

He hadn't intended to make any friends throughout this process. In fact, keeping his distance had its advantages. But now that he'd seen a bit of Savannah's soul, he knew that was going to be harder than ever.

He met her by the back door. "Everything's clear."

She nodded, her arms wrapped over her chest. "Thank you."

"Do me a favor, though? Lock your doors tonight."

A slight smile played on her lips. "It's a deal."

He squeezed her arm and instinctively leaned toward her. He caught himself before he got too close. "Good night."

Her eyes held a strange look. Was she feeling something too? She simply nodded. "Good night."

. . .

The next morning, after a restless night of sleep, one where she'd finally given up and worked on her editing projects, Savannah got dressed and drove to the migrant camp. She went to Lucia's house and pounded on the door, but no one answered.

Savannah guessed Lucia was at work.

As she turned to leave, she saw Bobbi at the La Tierra Prometida office, so she decided to swing by. When she walked in, Bobbi was playing with some of the camp's children. Bobbi smiled, the action bright and full of light, when she spotted Savannah. Good. Savannah had hoped that she hadn't totally offended Bobbi yesterday when she'd refused prayer.

"Savannah. Good to see you."

Just then one of the toddlers spilled his drink. Savannah grabbed some paper towels to help clean up, since Bobbi had her hands full of Play-Doh.

"What brings you by?"

"I wanted to ask you about Felipe and Jorge. Did you know them, Bobbi?"

She shook her head. "Not very well."

"Marti didn't believe they just left. She suspected foul play. Did you hear anything?"

"I haven't heard anything, but if I do, I'll let you know. Some of the workers do disappear when they think immigration might be coming around. Others decide to go back to their families at home. Some take other jobs and never bother to tell anyone."

"In other words, this is a long shot."

"I think it's admirable that you want to help."

"If nothing else, I want to do it for Marti's sake."

Bobbi smiled again, rolling a piece of bright yellow dough on the small table. "I understand."

As Savannah turned to go, Bobbi called her name. Bobbi directed the kids to continue playing before getting up and following Savannah to the door.

"I know this isn't my place, Savannah. But I know you used to be married to a pastor."

Savannah's throat burned. This wasn't what she wanted to talk about. Despite that, she nodded. "It's true."

"Marti told me a little bit about your story. Please don't get mad. She was just worried about you."

Savannah wanted desperately to cross her arms, to form some kind of barrier between herself and Bobbi. Instead, she stood there. She'd simply let Bobbi get this out of her system. Let her say what she needed to say. "It's fine."

Bobbi squeezed her arm. "I just wanted to reiterate that hard times in life can either draw us closer to God or farther away. It's never too late to change the course our lives are taking."

"You seem well suited for your many hats, Bobbi. I admire you. I admire your faith. But I can't understand it."

"Savannah." She lowered her voice. "Six years ago, my best friend was brutally murdered. It rocked my world. Turned it upside down. She was such a beautiful soul, and it seemed so unfair that life was snatched from her so soon. I had a lot of bitterness. I wanted to shake her husband, to say the least."

"Her husband?" Savannah questioned.

Bobbi nodded. "He killed her. Just got out of jail on a technicality. They said some critical procedures were violated during the jury's deliberation and that it seriously prejudiced the jury, depriving him of a fair trial."

"Sounds like legal mumbo jumbo."

"Tell me about it. Anyway, they'd been having some problems, but I never thought he'd go that far. I couldn't sing at church on Sundays for at least six months. I wasn't sure what I believed. It was probably my first real test of faith. I dared not mention it to anyone; I was afraid I'd disappoint them. I realized I was putting too much of my hope into worldly things and that I needed to focus on the eternal. We're only here on this earth for a short time. The world is mixed up, but God isn't."

Savannah's throat felt dry and achy. At times she wished she would have an experience and realization that would turn her life around. That she could have hope again, the kind of hope she'd only had when she'd believed in a higher power.

As she left, she couldn't stop thinking about the story Bobbi told her. Her best friend had been murdered by her husband.

What kind of monster would kill his own wife?

Even worse, he was on the streets now.

Savannah hoped the man didn't dare show his face around here.

CHAPTER 27

Clive took a break after dropping off a shift of workers back at their houses. Dehydrated from being out in the sun all day, he took a long drink of water.

There'd been a time in his life he'd vowed to leave this kind of work behind for good. He'd grown up in a lower-middle-class family in eastern North Carolina. Once he reached his teens, he'd spent summers picking collards from the fields to earn extra cash, which he'd used to pay his way through college.

He remembered the backbreaking work, the way the sun beat down on him, the way his fingers would be rubbed raw.

He'd left that life behind him when he got a scholarship, went to law school, eventually passed the bar, and finally worked as a trial lawyer. His days became defined by the cases he won, the designer suits he wore, the fancy restaurants he patronized. It was amazing how time could change things.

He glanced over at Ernie, Landon Kavanagh's right-hand man.

"You been working here long?" Clive asked.

Ernie grunted. "Eight years."

"Your boss seems like a nice guy." He put down his water and grabbed another crate of produce, hauling it to the trailer.

"He pretty much lets me do my own thing. Never did like micromanagers."

"This is some piece of property here."

Ernie nodded, trying to repair a tractor. "Used to be a plantation. I thought Landon might restore it. Instead, he picked a new location on the land and built a brand-new house. He said it's too hard to heat the old ones. They were drafty."

"Is the original house still here?"

"It's back on the other side of the property. Beautiful place. It's a shame it's not being used."

"Is this a full-time job?" Clive tried to keep him talking, get on his good side.

"I take a couple months off in the winter. It's not a bad deal though, because Landon still pays me."

"Sounds like a good place to be."

"I can't complain."

"The migrant workers do a good job?"

"They're hard workers—unless they want to take a siesta."

Clive remembered talking to Savannah last night, remembered what she told him about the people who'd gone missing. "Any problems with any of them?"

"Nope. Landon treats them well. Gives them their own little plot of land where they can grow whatever vegetables they want to eat. He throws parties for them at the end of the season. I see no reason for them to complain."

"Heard one of the workers died recently."

Ernie shrugged. "Señor Lopez worked for years on the tobacco fields down in Carolina. Now that's a hard life. People working the tobacco fields ingest as much nicotine as if they've smoked two packs of cigarettes a day. They get something like the flu from overexposure to the plant, especially if they have to work in the rain a lot. It's a hard life. My guess is that's one reason he got cancer. Of course, seems like you can get cancer from everything now, even plastic and cell phones."

"Are the workers protected here from those types of occupational hazards?"

"They go through training courses, everything from handling machinery to pesticides to drinking enough water. You ask me, they're their own worst enemies."

"How so?" Clive loaded another crate into the truck.

"Drinking too much, not getting here legally. They quarrel between themselves. I suspect a few do drugs."

"In other words, they have money for what they want to have money for."

"That's the way life works," Ernie muttered, resignation in his voice. "No one realizes every penny is important."

"Every penny, huh?" Clive asked.

Ernie nodded. "Every penny."

. . .

Stifled. Definition: *restrained.*

Savannah hated it when she felt restrained, unable to do the things she needed to do.

Then she realized the only one stifling her was herself.

Savannah's sneakers squeaked across the floor as she hurried down the antiseptic-scented hallway of the hospital, eager to see Marti. She'd gotten dressed quickly this morning, wearing cargo pants and a long-sleeved T-shirt. It had become something of a uniform when she was in the field. On her very first international assignment, she'd shown up in heels. She'd quickly learned heels had no place on the dusty streets of the Middle East.

If her mom saw her now, she would be mortified.

Savannah had been raised to be proper. She wasn't allowed to wear her hair in a ponytail. *A lady never leaves home without looking her best.* There was something she liked about living simply and forgetting those pieces of her upbringing. She'd never wanted her family's money anyway. Money always seemed to bring trouble.

Besides, there were bigger issues at hand than the way Savannah looked at the moment. Questions lingered in her mind, questions she desperately wanted to ask. Would Marti ever be able to answer them?

She paused outside Marti's room when she heard voices on the other side of the door.

"Melinda, I don't want to hear you talking about this again. This discussion is closed." The voice was clearly Dr. Lawson's, and he sounded angry.

"But Richard, I really think—"

"Listen, Melinda, you don't need to stir things up. That's the last thing we need. Just drop it." His tone left no room for argument.

Before Savannah could move, the door flew open. A young blond nurse with red-rimmed eyes rushed past her. Beyond her, Dr. Lawson stood with his hands on his hips, scowling. When he spotted Savannah, his smile instantly appeared. Savannah had always suspected he was good at putting on pretenses.

"Ms. Harris. Good to see you here again." He relaxed his arms and widened his stance, trying hard to look more comfortable.

"How's Marti?" Savannah went to her friend's bedside and took her cold hand.

Dr. Lawson glanced at Marti, his gaze lingering on her face. "She's holding her own. The drugs did a number on her."

"So there's still a possibility she'll come out of this coma?"

"That's always a possibility. You and your friend did her the most good when you found her. Raising her up so her airway wasn't constricted, trying to rouse her, all of those things may have saved her life."

She'd have to thank Clive for that. Savannah had frozen at the sight of Marti. Clive was the one who'd taken action.

Dr. Lawson leaned against the bed. "I do have to tell you there's a chance she'll have some brain damage if she comes out of this coma."

"Brain damage?" Every time Savannah turned around she seemed to be slapped in the face with unexpected news. She had been aware that brain damage was an option, but she just hadn't let her mind go there. She still didn't want to.

"It's a possibility. We hope that's not the case, but we can't rule it out."

Savannah found a chair and sat down hard. What if her friend wasn't able to live on her own? Savannah knew Marti wouldn't want to leave the Eastern Shore. She loved it here.

She could live with Savannah. Savannah could take care of her, even if it meant she'd be able to do nothing else.

Dr. Lawson tapped his clipboard on the tray beside Marti's bed, effectively getting Savannah's attention. "Talk to her. It's good for her. Some people believe coma patients can hear you."

Savannah nodded. Before Dr. Lawson left the room, she called his name and he paused.

"This is the medication that Señor Lopez took for his cancer to help treat the symptoms." She held up the bag Lucia had given her.

Dr. Lawson stared at her.

"I was wondering if you could have it tested," Savannah continued.

"What on earth for?"

Great, someone else who thought she sounded crazy. "It's like this. Señor Lopez's family doesn't think he died from cancer. I just want to assure them that he did. I want to make sure these pills were really the ones he should have been taking, that they weren't replaced with something else."

He continued to stare. "You're serious?"

"I know it sounds crazy, but his family is convinced."

He pushed his glasses higher on his nose. "I'm sure I can send them somewhere to be analyzed. But it's not going to be free. The lab will charge something."

She nodded. "I know. That's okay. I'll pay."

He took the pills and slid them into his pocket. "Okay then."

"How long before I get the results?"

"Hopefully within the week."

She flashed a grateful grin. "Thank you, Doctor."

CHAPTER 28

Savannah waited until Dr. Lawson left the room and then approached Marti, again taking her hand.

She and Marti had so many good memories together. They'd been the maid of honor in each other's weddings. They'd gone to different colleges in the same area and shared an apartment. Taken crazy road trips. Explored Europe for a summer. They'd been there for each other through everything: first kisses, divorce, death, career changes. Now this.

"I feel like I've let you down, Marti," Savannah whispered. "There was so much about your life I didn't know about. I need to make things right." She paused. "And I need to figure out who did this to you."

Someone entered the room behind her. Savannah turned and recognized the same nurse from earlier. The nurse quickly averted her eyes.

"I just need to check her IV and vitals," she mumbled. "I won't disturb you long."

Why hadn't the nurse checked those things when she was in here earlier? Had she been distracted by her conversation with Dr. Lawson?

Savannah attempted to play nice. What had Dr. Lawson called her? *Melinda.* "Thank you for taking care of my friend, Melinda."

Her smile seemed more relaxed. "It's my job. I enjoy helping people."

"It's a noble calling."

"Yeah, I guess it is."

Savannah took a deep breath before plunging in with both feet. "I couldn't help but overhear part of the conversation between you and Dr. Lawson."

Melinda's smile vanished. "It was nothing, just a misunderstanding."

"It didn't sound like nothing. You sounded and looked upset."

"I really can't talk about it."

"Please, Melinda, if it involves my friend, then you need to talk about it."

Melinda shook her head, a little too adamantly. "I wish I could. I really do. Please don't worry about your friend. We're taking good care of her."

Voices sounded from the hallway, and Melinda glanced toward the door. Her hands trembled on the IV bag and she lowered her voice. "Now please, don't ask me any more questions. I can't afford to lose my job. I've got three kids at home, and their lousy father doesn't send us any help."

With that, she hurried from the room.

Why was it that at every turn Savannah only found more questions but no answers? What could Dr. Lawson be hiding?

• • •

Savannah was still sitting at Marti's bedside when a man with black, purple, and red spikes of hair peered cautiously into the room. He was medium height, extremely skinny, and wore tight jeans with a

Def Leppard T-shirt. She'd guess he was in his late twenties. His face was angular and his eyebrows thick.

"Marti." He rushed to her bedside, and Savannah saw tears glistening in his eyes. "Oh, my sweet Marti. What happened?" He bent down and kissed her hand, his gaze lingering on her. "She's beautiful, isn't she?"

Savannah nodded. "Gorgeous."

Savannah stepped back and let them have their moment together. Finally the man glanced at Savannah and stuck his hand out, but there was no hint of a smile on his face. "You must be Savannah."

"And you must be Leonard." They shook hands, and Savannah marveled that her friend had fallen for someone like Leonard. Of course, Marti's type had always come as a surprise to her. "I know you want to spend some time with Marti, but could I have a few minutes of your time? There are some important things I want to share with you."

Leonard nodded. "Totally. I want to know everything. There's no way my girl tried to commit suicide. No way."

So he hadn't seen any signs either. That realization brought Savannah brief comfort. "How about if I get us some coffee and bring it back here so we can talk?"

"Sounds perfect."

Savannah returned ten minutes later with two cups of coffee, some cookies, and an apple. She was drinking coffee so much lately that she was actually starting to enjoy it. She sat down across from Leonard, handing him his cup and setting the snacks on a table behind them.

She took a deep breath before starting. "I have to be honest. She didn't tell me about you, Leonard."

He nodded, as if her revelation didn't surprise him. "She was worried about you."

"But if she'd told me she was in a relationship, I would only be happy for her. I don't understand why she wouldn't tell me."

"I'm sorry, Savannah." He shrugged, his eyes sympathetic. "I don't know what else to say."

"It's okay." Savannah watched the floor as she talked. "Where did you two meet?"

"Online. A website catering to people who like conspiracy theories."

Savannah nodded. That seemed to fit. "Where are you from?"

"Berlin, Maryland—not terribly far away."

Savannah licked her lips, preparing to tell Leonard the truth, no matter how painful that might be. "Leonard, I've obviously been wrapped up in myself. I'm ashamed at the level of my self-involvement. But I'm trying to figure out if I'm missing something else. I just can't believe Marti would try to commit suicide."

"She wouldn't. I know she wouldn't."

"So why would someone do this to her? Was there anything else in her life that I didn't know about, something sinister, dark?"

Leonard leaned back, took a long sip of coffee. "Do you want to know how Marti and I clicked? We started talking about the Madden Society."

That was the name that had been scribbled underneath Leonard's name on Marti's calendar. Savannah had never heard of them. "Who are they, Leonard?"

"It's a secret society."

"Secret society?"

"Yeah, apparently top CEOs, actors, senators, authors are all part of this society. They're said to meet quarterly on the shores of the Chesapeake."

"And what exactly does this society do?"

"That's the big secret. No one ever talks about it. We wanted to find out."

Savannah wasn't sure she wanted to ask the next question. "And how did the two of you plan to do that?"

He shrugged. "We were going to spy on them. Take pictures. I was going to post them on my website."

"You said 'going.' Does that mean you didn't?"

"They haven't had their quarterly meeting yet."

"When is it?"

"It's supposed to be sometime this month."

Savannah shifted. "Did anyone know about your plans?"

"I don't think so."

"Think about it, Leonard. It could be important. No one else knew?"

He leaned forward and lowered his voice. "You really think her life might have been in danger because of the Madden Society?"

Dr. Lawson stepped into the room. Savannah straightened and tried to neutralize her expression.

"Savannah, I figured you'd be gone by now," he said. "I just came by to get my pen. I left it here."

Dr. Lawson picked up the writing instrument from the table beside Marti. His gaze stopped on Leonard. Savannah rushed through possible ways to introduce him. Marti's boyfriend? Friend? Don't introduce them at all?

Leonard settled her dilemma by extending his hand to the doctor. "I'm a friend of Marti's. Leonard."

"Nice to meet you." Dr. Lawson glanced back at Savannah and pushed his glasses farther up on his nose. "I have to be on my way. Take care, both of you."

When he was out of earshot, Leonard leaned toward her. "He's in the society."

"Are you sure?"

"Marti and I have been researching it since we met."

"How do you research something that's a secret?"

"Very carefully. Just by talking to people in town, casually bringing up the society in conversation, by doing Google searches."

"Interesting."

"I'll tell you more about it later. Now I want to spend some time with Marti."

Savannah nodded and rose, picking up her coffee and the apple she'd purchased to silence her growling stomach.

"Make sure you wash that apple before you eat it. The pesticides they use on those things can make you sick. They're one of the dirty dozen of pesticide offenders. It's almost impossible to get all of the chemical residue off of them."

Savannah smiled. Yes, he was a conspiracy theorist, just like Marti.

CHAPTER 29

When Savannah got back home, she hopped on her computer and typed "Madden Society" into Google. Hundreds of results popped up. Conspiracy theorists had made crazy claims about them, everything from the society being associated with the occult to members dictating the future of world policies. Interesting stuff. She kept reading.

Apparently there was a waiting list of five hundred people who wanted to join the society but hadn't yet been granted membership. Only men were allowed to join, and the initial membership fee was ten thousand dollars. An additional $2,500 was expected in annual dues.

This was not a club for just any Joe off the street. This was a club for the wealthy, elite, and powerful. Past US presidents had been members, as well as philanthropists, CEOs, and inventors.

Leonard had made it sound as if he and Marti had discovered the names of some of the current members. Just how had they done that?

The Internet opened up a whole world of opportunities, so why not give it a shot, just for fun? She typed in "Madden Society Members." More results popped up. Her eyes widened as she recognized many names, including Congressman Perkins and Dr. Lawson.

She leaned back in her chair. Even if this society did exist, if it wasn't just a conspiracy theory, why in the world would one of the members try to kill Marti? That didn't make sense. In Savannah's estimation, members of the society were just an upscale version of a Moose Lodge or Rotary Club.

She rubbed her eyes, tired of this online research. She flipped off her computer and rose. Just then her cell phone rang. She recognized Clive's number. Her heart quickened, much to her dismay.

"Hey, what's going on?"

"I've got food to cook and no one to eat it with."

"Sounds like you have problems." She couldn't help but smile.

"Want to come join me? No pressure or expectations. Just two people having dinner together."

Some of the tension left her. Though Landon had extended similar invitations in the past, Clive's, for some reason, captured her. Besides, she could use a listening ear. "No strings attached sounds great."

"See you in an hour?"

"An hour."

She realized she was smiling when she hung up and immediately scolded herself. She wasn't looking for romance. She didn't even want to give romance another shot. That's why this seemed like a bad, bad idea.

Sighing, she stood. She had to clean herself up. She took a quick shower, dried off, and dressed in jeans and a lightweight baby-blue sweater. As she blow-dried her hair, she looked in the mirror and frowned at the light dancing in her eyes. She almost looked excited. And the fact that she cared what she looked like only served to disturb her further. What was wrong with her?

She knew the answer. Deep inside, she found Clive Miller intriguing. And handsome. Mysterious. All the right ingredients for disaster.

She'd just have to be on guard, that was all there was to it. She shrugged her confusion off, brushed on some lip gloss, and went downstairs. Outside, her breath vaporized in the crisp air, and she realized winter might come early this year. She still hadn't enjoyed autumn. Chances were, at this point, she wouldn't.

Finally her foot connected with the first step leading to Clive's porch. Before she even reached the door, Clive appeared at the entryway, a warm light from inside glowing behind him.

He leaned on the doorframe, his arms crossed and a grin across his face. "You came."

"Did you think I wouldn't?" She rubbed her shoes on the doormat.

"The possibility crossed my mind."

As she closed her umbrella and leaned it against the house, the scent of garlic and onions and other unnamable but tantalizing culinary delights drifted out. "Based purely on what I smell right now, I'm glad I didn't bail."

"I'd hoped the company might be the drawing point, but if it's the food, I'll take that." He grinned again before extending his arm to lead her inside. "Please, come in out of the cold. I started a fire to warm the place up. I'm not ready to turn on the heat quite yet."

The warmth inside instantly enveloped her. There was something about this old carriage house that she'd always loved. The place was cozy and filled with character.

"Why don't you have a seat on the couch while I finish dinner?" With a hand on her back, Clive led her across the room to a spot right in front of the fireplace.

Relaxing into the soft cushions sounded like a plan to her. She sank there, her gaze lingering on the fireplace. She got lost in the dancing, flickering flames.

"Can I get you some water? Tea?"

"Water sounds great."

He brought her a goblet of water and then returned to the kitchen, which was separated from the room by a bar. "So how was your day, Savannah?"

She mentally ran through the events, starting with the argument she heard between Dr. Lawson and Nurse Melinda and ending with her meeting with Leonard and the possibility of a connection between Dr. Lawson and the Madden Society.

"It was okay, nothing notable."

"How's your friend? Marti, right?"

"I wish I could say there was a change in her condition, but there isn't. I still have hope she'll come out of this."

"There's always hope, Savannah."

Is there? She cleared her throat. "So what are you cooking over there that smells so good?"

"Lamb chops."

Lamb chops? Who was this man? He never failed to surprise her. "It smells delicious."

"We'll see if it tastes the same. It's been awhile since I've cooked it."

"You mean you don't cook like this for yourself every night?"

He chuckled. "Not quite. You?"

"I usually just stick a frozen dinner in the microwave. Sometimes I'll make soup or a salad. Nothing fancy." Cooking for one person had never appealed to her.

Savannah saw the cell phone attached to Clive's belt and remembered her intention to pay for the one he'd purchased for her.

She reached into her purse and pulled out fifty dollars. She strode across the room and placed it on the breakfast bar.

"This is for the cell phone."

He shook his head, taking a break from chopping tomatoes to slide the money back toward her. "I don't want any money. You didn't ask me to buy it for you. I did it because I wanted to."

But fifty dollars was a lot for someone who worked on a farm a few days a week. The gesture had been too generous. "I think it's only fair that I pay."

"And I think it's only fair that you don't."

The stubborn look in his eyes told her that he wouldn't back down. Finally she nodded and put the money back in her purse. "Fine, have it your way."

"If you insist." He winked and brought two plates to the coffee table in front of the couch. "Let's eat."

Steam rose up and greeted her senses. The meal smelled so yummy that her stomach growled.

"Help yourself. I hope you like it."

"I'm sure I will."

"Don't be too sure. I have had some disasters." His twinkling eyes helped put her at ease.

She smiled. "I like your honesty." She thought a moment before adding, "So how does a handyman know how to cook lamb chops?"

He waggled an eyebrow in exaggerated cockiness. "Impressed, are you?"

"I expected Hamburger Helper and canned green beans tonight."

"O ye of little faith. I'm a man of many hidden talents." His expression sobered, and he wiped the corners of his mouth with a napkin before meeting her gaze again. "This hasn't always been my life, Savannah. I know I told you I used to do odd jobs. The truth is that I also used to be a lawyer up in DC."

Her eyes widened. "What happened?"

He hesitated. "I realized there were more important things at stake than my career. So I'm taking a break."

"Sounds admirable." And it also left her with more questions. Why would someone give up a career like that to work on a farm? Something didn't fit. Certainly there was more to his story, but she'd save those questions for later. She knew what it was like when people probed too deeply into the past. Sometimes it was better to ease into the questions.

"I don't know if I'd say that, but I'm doing what I have to do."

"Can I ask another question?"

"Go right ahead." He twirled his fork until linguine formed circles around the tines.

"Why were you at the migrant worker camp the other day?"

He didn't flinch at the question. "I figured I should be familiar with the roads around here, especially if I'm going to drive the van and pick up the migrant workers for Kavanagh Farms."

Simple explanation. Why had she assumed there was something darker involved? Maybe Marti was wearing off on her. She'd spent the last fifteen years listening to her conspiracy theories, after all.

"Why do you ask, Savannah?"

"I'm . . ." She thought twice about her answer and shook her head. "No reason. I was just curious."

His gaze lingered on her, the look clearly communicating that he knew there was more to the story. Thankfully he didn't ask. Savannah didn't want to lie to him, but she would.

. . .

After dinner, they settled on the couch for a moment. Savannah knew she should use the transition as an excuse to leave. But having someone to talk with, sharing a real conversation, felt like a balm to her heart. She traded her water for coffee and wrapped her hands around the warm mug.

"I like this carriage house. If I'd realized just how much I like it in here, I might never have rented it to you."

"Then I'll count my blessings that you're just realizing it now." His gaze roamed the room. "It's perfect for me. I couldn't have found a better place to stay while I'm here."

She settled back and took a slow sip of coffee. She had so many questions about Clive. She needed a safe place to start. "Tell me about your wife. You said she was a marine biologist. How'd you meet?"

Clive's gaze focused in the distance, as if going back to another period in time. "We met when she was protesting a court decision giving fishermen more freedom to harvest oysters. I was leaving after winning the case. She instantly hated me."

"Then?"

"She asked me to sit down with her, hear her side of things. I did. We still didn't see eye to eye, but we did fall in love. We got married a year later and basically lived the American dream. For a while, at least."

"What happened?"

His gaze cut to hers. "Long version or short version?"

"Long."

He drew in a breath. "Lauren and I never had a perfect marriage, but about two years into it, we started arguing. A lot. We both had demanding jobs that often led us away from each other. I could feel our marriage falling apart. We both could. Despite the way things were between us, I loved her and wanted to do whatever it took to work things out."

Savannah's attention focused fully on his words as she waited to hear more of his story. "What happened?"

He shook his head. "I wanted us to both take some time to work on our relationship. I begged her, actually." He paused, and Savannah could see the pain etched on his features, the sadness in his eyes. He met Savannah's gaze. "She said there were more important things at hand, things bigger than our relationship."

"Ouch."

He rubbed his thumb. "Yeah. Ouch. I had suspicions she was cheating on me."

"I'm sorry."

"She was obsessed with something—or someone. It made her lose sleep at night, even." He drew in another breath, and the look on his face made Savannah think that even his lungs ached. For a moment she wanted to withdraw her questions. At the same time, his answers captivated her.

"How long has it been?"

"Six years in December."

"I'm so sorry." Savannah grabbed his hand, regretting her questions.

Slowly he raised his head. "I never knew what it meant to hurt until that moment. Or to truly be angry, outraged, bitter. All of those emotions. Her death wasn't a freak accident. Someone made a choice to end her life, to turn my world upside down. That's hard to stomach, to say the least."

"Losing someone you love is terribly hard. Even harder when there's violence, when it's senseless." Savannah's voice cracked.

Clive reached for her, pulled her against his chest into a hug. She let him hold her, let herself nestle against him as her tears poured out. And out. And out.

She couldn't remember the last time she'd let herself cry. Or the last time she'd let herself be held.

CHAPTER 30

Anger felt like lava flowing through his veins.

How could she still be with Clive? What were they doing in there? How could she let herself be deceived? She had so much more potential.

He was the one who should be saving her.

It wasn't too late.

He walked to the window, careful to stay concealed by the darkness.

He was good at being a shadow when he needed to. He turned it on and off. Sometimes it felt as if one part of his soul didn't know what the other part was doing. And it was better that way.

He had to separate himself. Separate the part of him that people saw with the side that was true.

He peered in the window. What he saw made his agitation grow. Savannah and Clive sat on the couch in front of the fireplace. Savannah's head rested on Clive's shoulder.

The scene looked so peaceful. The two of them looked so comfortable together.

This wouldn't work.

It wouldn't work at all.

His hands dug into the wood of the windowsill, his fingernails aching with intensity as he continued to stare inside the house.

Clive's eyes were open, and he was staring at the fire. His gaze held a pensive look that not everyone could understand. He could understand it, though.

He had to wait and be careful about how he played his cards. He'd reveal Clive's story when the time was right.

CHAPTER 31

Savannah opened her eyes with a start. She sat up, her gaze darting around the room. Where was she?

Clive's. She was still at Clive's. The fire still roared, the sun had set, and darkness stared at them from black windows. Their dishes from dinner still rested on the table, just as they'd left them. Stillness had settled on the house.

"Hey." Clive offered a soft smile from beside her on the couch. The tenderness in his gaze made her heart lurch.

She must have fallen asleep while he was holding her. How could she have let down her guard that much?

The warmth of Clive's arms must have done her in.

"You should have woken me." She raked a hand through her hair.

"You seemed pretty peaceful. I didn't want to disturb you."

She rubbed her eyes, still groggy. "I can't believe I fell asleep. Wow. I'm sorry."

"Falling asleep is far from a sin."

"I'm just usually so much better at being . . ."

"Guarded?"

She let the word sink in before nodding. He'd nailed it, dead on. "Exactly. Guarded."

He leaned toward her, and the scent of his cologne tantalized her, made her want to cuddle up close and breathe deeply.

Their gazes caught, and Savannah sucked in a breath. Clive's eyes mesmerized her and seemed to pull her into another world or state of consciousness.

She didn't argue as his hand went to her neck, his fingers splaying into her hair. He traced her lips with his thumb.

She closed her eyes, enjoying his touch. Relishing it. Her heart raced.

A ringing cell phone slashed the moment.

Savannah's eyes popped open. She jerked back, coming out of her trancelike state. What had just happened? Was she just about to kiss Clive? Was she out of her mind?

Clive's hand slid from her face down to her hand. With his other hand, he reached for the cell phone at his waist. He glanced at the screen then back at Savannah.

"I have to take this call, Savannah." His voice sounded deep, husky.

She stood and pointed over her shoulder toward her house. "I need to go anyway."

"You could stay." His eyes urged her to.

She backed up, shaking her head probably harder than she needed to. "No, really, I should go."

Before he could say anything else, she ran. All the way back to the house.

CHAPTER 32

Savannah had promised Bobbi she would come and help at La Tierra Prometida for a few hours in the morning. Bobbi had some work to do at the marine center and had been volunteering endlessly since Marti had been admitted to the hospital. Helping out was the least Savannah could do, even if she felt like she'd been run over by a truck as she drove toward the migrant camp.

Last night, while lying in bed at home, she'd begun thinking about Clive. About love. About the future.

Her emotions were getting the best of her, leading her down a path she didn't need to be on. She had no right to be thinking about him. Or about the future. She should stay busy editing miserable textbooks. Isolate herself from the comfort of a relationship. Deprive herself of anything remotely enjoyable. It was the least she deserved.

In between all of her conflicting thoughts, her conversation with Bobbi about God had even interjected itself. Five years ago, as a journalist, she'd finally come to the conclusion—found the proof she needed—that God was real. Like any good investigator, she'd had her sources: people whose lives had been changed, scholarly texts, evidence that Christ wasn't a fable but a real person who'd walked the earth and rose again.

She hadn't limited herself to people who believed. No, she'd read reports from skeptics. She'd talked to educated atheists.

And in the end, she believed in Jesus. She'd made changes in her life, in her thinking. Much to the scorn of her friends in academia and her self-reliant mother, Savannah had chosen faith *and* reason over simply reason.

But over time, she'd questioned her decisions and doubted the changes in her life.

Wouldn't it be nice, no matter how much she didn't deserve it, to find hope again? Hope in the future, in people, in humanity?

Savannah snapped out of her thoughts as she pulled into the migrant camp. She immediately hit her brakes. Something was going on.

A police cruiser was parked haphazardly at the entrance, and a crowd had gathered outside. A sense of urgency stretched through the air.

She threw her car in park and ran toward the crowd. She heard a flurry of Spanish and the chief's voice calling for calm.

She spotted Bobbi in the throng and rushed to meet her. "What's going on?"

Tears rimmed her eyes. "It's Lucia."

"What about her?" Savannah could hardly breathe as she waited for the answer.

"She's gone."

Her heart thudded with dread and apprehension. "No . . ."

Bobbi nodded. "Alba went to wake her this morning, and her bed was empty. It was like she was never there."

. . .

Clive didn't have to drive the van today, but Ernie had called him to come in and act as a supervisor. Apparently something had happened at the migrant camp. Clive wasn't sure about the details, but he knew he'd find out when he arrived at work.

As he pulled up to the farm, he thought about his dinner with Savannah the previous evening. The more he got to know the woman, the more she fascinated him.

And even though he was still obsessed with his wife's death, he'd realized last night that he'd moved on. It had been six years, and things had been rocky between them before that. Of course, he wished he could go back and make things right. He'd do anything for that opportunity. But wishing wasn't reality.

Savannah was the first woman who'd turned his head since Lauren. It felt good to have that spark of attraction, even if he knew nothing would come of it. He couldn't even entertain the idea of a relationship until he had closure on Lauren's death.

Then why had he invited Savannah over last night? He told himself it was just to have some company. That he wanted to find out where she was in her investigation. That he truly did have too much food.

But there was a small part of him that had wanted to see her, no matter how doomed a relationship between them would be.

He put his Jeep in park. Landon Kavanagh stood talking to another supervisor by the fence separating the horse pasture from the rest of the property.

Clive slid on his aviator sunglasses and pulled his hat down low, trying to avoid the man. He started toward the barn to meet Ernie and get his instructions for the day.

"You must be the new supervisor," someone called from across the lawn.

Clive froze, tension spreading across his back. He slowly turned and forced himself to smile. "I am. Clive Miller."

Landon extended his hand. "Nice to have you on board. Ernie has said only good things about you."

"I'm grateful for the job." He kept his voice even.

Landon squinted at him. "Haven't we met before? You look familiar."

Clive shook his head. "No, I don't believe so." He tugged at his hat.

He and Landon *hadn't* met before. Even if they had, Clive looked like a different man now. Back then, he'd been the clean-cut, suit-and-tie type. Now he looked like a blue-collar worker.

He held his breath, hoping that Landon had never seen his picture, had never studied his history too closely.

"Maybe you just have one of those faces," Landon finally said. "I'll be seeing you around."

He turned and walked back toward the house.

Clive let out the breath he'd been holding. Good. Kavanagh hadn't recognized him. Not yet, at least. It wasn't too late.

.   .   .

"Chief, this is the third migrant worker who's disappeared. You can't keep ignoring this," Savannah argued.

The crowd still lingered around them at the migrant camp, watching the American justice system in action. Anger simmered in their gazes, making it clear they had little hope that the law would be on their side.

The chief narrowed his eyes. "I'm not ignoring anything. I'm taking a look at the facts objectively. Until this missing persons case today, I had no reason to believe anything was wrong. Lucia puts a different spin on things."

"What are you going to do about this?" Bobbi demanded.

"I'm going to put my men on it. Bobbi, I may need you to translate. Ms. Harris, do you speak Spanish?"

She shook her head. "Not well, I'm afraid."

"I'm going to get statements from everyone. I want to know when they last saw her. Ms. Harris, you could help with the ones who speak English. They trust you more than they trust law enforcement. I'm going to send one of my guys to shadow you, though."

Savannah nodded. "I'll help in whatever way I can."

"Let's get busy," Bobbi said.

"Ms. Harris. Bobbi."

They both turned and waited for the chief to continue.

"I'm going to work to find answers to this. I promise," he told them.

Savannah and Bobbi split up. Officer Tennyson stayed at Savannah's side as she turned toward the crowd. They'd quieted down and now stared at her with expectant eyes. Savannah tapped into the old part of her, the part that was assertive and pushy when necessary. "Who here speaks English? I need to talk to you."

A few people raised their hands. Savannah pointed to a girl around Lucia's age. She seemed especially eager as she stretched her arm high in the air. "I'll start with you."

Savannah pulled her to the side, glancing back to see Officer Tennyson lingering close. "I'm Savannah."

"I'm Daniela. Lucia was my best friend."

"When did you last see her?"

"Last night." Her jaw flexed, tears spilling down her cheeks. "She was upset about something."

"Do you know what?"

"I just know she kept asking questions about Felipe and Jorge. I told her to stop, that she was going to get herself in trouble. But she wouldn't listen."

"Who was she asking about them?"

"I only have theories."

"What are they?" Savannah nudged.

"I saw her arguing with Señor Kavanagh yesterday."

Heaviness pressed on Savannah's chest. "Oh really? Any idea what they might have been arguing about?"

"Lucia always said he was wicked. She never had any regard for the wealthy."

"So you think the argument was more about social class than Mr. Kavanagh doing something wrong?" Savannah clarified, swatting away a fly.

"I don't know. Some workers are getting sick. She thought it was because of our living conditions."

"Who's been getting sick?"

"Lots of people. Mainly feeling tired and nauseous. Could just be from working so hard out in the sun. It takes a toll on your body."

"Is there anything else you can think of that might be helpful?"

Daniela shook her head. "No, but I need you to find my friend, Señora. Otherwise her mother might literally die of heartbreak."

"I'll do my best," Savannah said and started to walk away.

"Señora," Daniela called.

She paused. "Yes?"

"She wanted to be just like you, you know. A journalist. She thought you could do no wrong."

Savannah's heart panged with sudden realization. No wonder Lucia had hung around so much. She'd done her investigating and figured out who Savannah was. Savannah had never picked up on the fact that Lucia actually admired her.

That only strengthened her resolve to figure this mystery out, once and for all.

• • •

As he paced the fields, Clive turned over what Ernie had told him.

Another migrant worker was missing. Did Savannah know yet? This only served to confirm her theory that something was going on.

He wanted to call her, but he would wait until he had more information first. Besides, he had to do his job here or he'd get fired. He couldn't afford to let that happen.

He walked among the trees, making sure everyone was doing what they were supposed to. He'd been assigned to the apple orchard today. The workers placed their bounty into carts they pulled down the rows.

There were fewer workers out here today. Those people from the migrant camp where Lucia lived were apparently being detained and questioned. It wouldn't surprise Clive if the chief ended up out here, too.

He paced closer to the edge of the woods. This was the same stretch that eventually connected with Savannah's property. Movement caught his eye.

He paused.

Had he seen something?

He didn't think so. But it almost looked as if the sun had reflected off a piece of glass—binoculars maybe?—behind a tree.

Clive moved closer. He didn't see the glare again. But he wasn't giving up yet.

He quickened his steps, dodging trees and carts and workers.

He saw the glare again. He hadn't been imagining things.

"Hey you!" he called.

That's when the man took off at a run. Clive was right behind him.

This guy could be a worker being lazy. Or he could be the man who'd broken into Savannah's house. Who'd watched her from the woods.

Clive skirted around the trees and thick underbrush and some abandoned tires. But the man had too much of a head start.

Finally he disappeared from sight.

Clive had no idea who he was. He only knew that he'd seen a streak of purple hair.

CHAPTER 33

Savannah was exhausted and grimy by the time she returned home. She'd spent almost all day with the migrant workers, not only questioning them but helping them deal with their grief and answering their fearful questions whenever possible. It was a position she hadn't expect to be in, but she couldn't turn her back on them. She couldn't bring herself to deny God to them either, and she had offered reassurances about His love.

Now she knew why Marti loved her ministry so much. There was something deeply satisfying about comforting those who were hurting.

She took a shower and threw on some yoga pants and a T-shirt. She had to finish editing that textbook. Her deadline was quickly approaching.

But just as she sat down at her desk, someone knocked on her door. She had a sudden vision of Clive standing there. Her heart lifted at the thought. She'd like to talk to him about everything that had happened today.

Instead, she blinked in surprise when she saw Landon.

"Sorry to stop by unexpectedly," he started.

"It's no problem." She pulled the door back. "Come on in."

He sauntered inside, taking his hat off and placing it on the hook by the door. Savannah led him over to the couch. "Can I get you some coffee?"

"I'm okay. I mostly wanted to check on you." He sat on the couch, grabbed her wrist, and pulled her down beside him. "I'm going out of town in a couple of days and wanted to make sure we connected before then."

A moment of panic rose in Savannah. She remembered Daniela's words. More and more signs were pointing toward Landon's involvement in this. And based on the feeling of unease she had right now, all of those signs were starting to play with her head.

His grip eased. "How are you?"

"I'm . . . okay."

"How's Marti?"

Was he asking because he was the one who'd harmed her? No, she couldn't think like that. Landon was a good man. "She's doing the same. No real change."

"I know that's got to be hard on you. You guys did everything together."

"Yeah, I really miss talking to her." Savannah's heart panged with grief. Figuring out who did this to Marti was the only way she knew how to make things right.

Which brought her thoughts around to her conversation with Leonard and the Madden Society. Surely someone like Landon would know about the Madden Society. She decided to test the waters.

"What do you think about secret societies, Landon?"

Her question obviously surprised him. He pulled back some, his eyebrows rising. "Secret societies? Where did that come from?"

"You know Marti. She was always talking about hidden motives and secret agendas. I was looking through her desk, and she'd made a notation about something called the Madden Society. Ever hear of it?"

"Certainly you're not giving creditability to her ramblings? She already thinks the government is covering up UFO activities! And that you only need to brush your teeth once a day—that the toothpaste makers are paying off dentists in order to get people to buy more of their products."

Savannah raised her hand. "I know some of her ideas are crazy. Some are amusing. A few are disturbing. But I'm really interested in this one. She wrote it on her calendar, at the top of the page for this month."

"Let's say there is a secret society. You think they have something to do with her current situation?"

"I'm not saying anything. The notation just got me thinking. So . . . have you heard of them?"

He shook his head. "No, I think the idea is ludicrous. What would be the need for groups of people meeting in secret? Let me guess—they're powerful men planning world domination." He let out an amused laugh.

"They could be planning something. Maybe it's not world domination. Maybe it's ways to influence the media, to change public thought, to bring certain issues to the forefront through each of their respective jobs."

"Now you're sounding like Marti."

Savannah felt her hackles rising and knew she needed to cool off. "Okay, no more talking about this."

"But you're so cute when you get fired up."

Savannah ignored him and decided to ask a question that was sure to be sobering. "Let's move on. I'm sure you heard about Lucia. What do you think about her disappearance?"

He sighed and rubbed his chin, all signs of amusement gone. "I don't know what to think. At first I figured those other two workers were just going off the grid, you know? They wanted to make their own way here in America and used their work visas to get into the country. But not Lucia. She was different."

"I don't understand why anyone would want to hurt someone like her."

"Maybe there's a terrible misunderstanding. Maybe Lucia will show back up."

"My gut tells me that's not going to happen."

"Is your gut ever wrong?"

"On occasion."

He grabbed her hand and squeezed. "Then let's hope for the best."

Savannah had to get a grip. She stood and walked to the window, trying to force her thoughts to calm down. "I heard you had an argument with her."

He flinched ever so slightly. "You heard that?"

"Can I ask what it was about?"

He let out an airy laugh. "You don't suspect me, do you?"

"I'm just asking questions."

He nodded, withdrawing from her. "She thought I was working everyone too hard."

"Why would she think that?"

"We have a lot of crops to harvest. I pay overtime. No one is forced to work more than they want to. That's what I told her."

"How did she react?"

"She said she thought the workers deserved better. Then I had to leave for a meeting. That was it."

Savannah nodded, letting the new information sink in. She needed some time to process it. "I heard my new boarder is working for you."

"That's right. I'd forgotten about that. Why'd you take a boarder again?"

"Marti convinced me I should do it a couple of weeks back. I placed an ad, then changed my mind. But it was too late."

"You doing this for money? Because I could help you out."

"You know I wouldn't take your money, Landon. I like to make my own way."

He stood and stepped closer. "Just one more thing I like about you. But I also like to help people, especially people I care about. I wish you would have told me. I would have checked this guy out."

"I think I can handle that myself, Landon." She smiled. "But thank you."

"You have to be careful nowadays. You never know who people really are. What did you say his name was?"

"Clive Miller."

He squinted. "Clive. I met him today, as a matter of fact."

"If you hired him, he couldn't be all that bad, could he?"

He let out a chuckle. "There's a difference between letting someone work on your farm and letting someone live on your property, especially when you're a single woman." He stepped closer. "So what do you know about this Clive Miller?"

Savannah shrugged, inching backward just a touch to increase the space between them. "I don't know. He's from Arlington. I guess his wife used to like coming here."

"She doesn't anymore?"

"No, he's a widower." She started to launch into the story of how his wife was murdered, but stopped herself. She didn't want Landon asking too many questions. Some things were best left private.

"Well, I'll keep my eye on him for you. How's that?"

She smiled. "You always watch out for me, don't you?"

He rubbed her cheek. "I try my best."

•   •   •

Clive stopped in his tracks. In the window he spotted Savannah. Beside her was . . . Landon Kavanagh?

What was he doing here?

Obviously the man felt affection for Savannah. That much was clear by the roses Clive had seen on the hall table that first day he was here. But Savannah never really talked about him. She certainly hadn't seemed to turn to him when troubles arose.

Based on the look in her eyes last night, Clive had thought she returned his feelings—feelings he was determined to put a lid on.

This might just make that easier for him.

He paused, flowers in his hands. He'd known they were a bad idea, but somehow he'd bought them anyway. He'd imagined the way her face might light up when she saw them. He'd pictured the two of them talking about everything that had happened today.

Now as he stood on the sidewalk leading to her porch, he saw Savannah and Landon in the window. Standing close. Landon's hand touched her cheek.

Clive shook his head. He didn't want to see more.

Savannah was a grown woman. She was free to make whatever decisions she wanted. Besides, he wasn't looking for a relationship. At least that's what he told himself.

But of all the people she could have picked, why Landon Kavanagh? Couldn't she see through him? Didn't her gut tell her that he was bad news?

He'd have to wait until later to tell Savannah who he saw on the train tracks today flattening pennies.

CHAPTER 34

The next morning, Savannah decided to stop by the migrant camp before heading to the hospital to see Marti. She figured she'd find out more information from the people there than from the police chief.

As she pulled down the road leading to the community, she frowned. It almost looked like everything had returned to normal. But Savannah was sure that for Lucia's family nothing felt normal. How could it? She remembered those days all too well.

She parked outside of La Tierra Prometida, jammed her keys into her pockets, and paused on the gravel driveway. Where did she even start?

In the distance, a familiar figure caught her eye. Dr. Lawson? What was he doing here?

He walked out of one of the houses and started toward his car. He must have felt Savannah's gaze because he paused before hurrying on without waving.

Savannah ran to meet him, her curiosity piqued. "Dr. Lawson!"

Was it her imagination or did he seem hesitant to turn toward her, almost as if he wanted to pretend not to hear and climb into his car?

But when he smiled, Savannah pushed her doubts away. "Hello, Savannah."

"What brings you this way?"

"I make a visit here about once a week."

"Oh, that's right. I forgot."

He nodded, pushing his glasses up higher. "Marti convinced me to not only hold free clinics on occasion but to stop by for house calls. A lot of the people here don't get the medical care they should. I just check on them, make sure everyone's okay. Especially those with diabetes and other conditions."

"That's really kind of you. I'm about to visit Marti myself. I just wanted to stop by here first."

"I'm afraid you won't find any change in Marti. I keep hoping for a good outcome, but it hasn't happened yet."

Something about the wistfulness in which he said the words made Savannah pause. "You care about her, don't you?"

"Marti has a way of getting to you. She was going to attend the harvest festival with me at Landon's."

Savannah squinted. But where did that leave Leonard? How could she be dating Leonard and going to the harvest festival with Dr. Lawson? That just didn't seem to fit her character.

"You going with Landon?" Dr. Lawson asked.

Savannah snapped back to the present and nodded. "He invited me. It sounds like fun."

"I think you'll enjoy it." He opened his car door. "I hate to cut this short, but I've got other patients to see."

As he pulled away, Savannah thought of Landon. She'd gently pushed him away last night, reminding him that she wasn't ready for a relationship.

Was she crazy? Landon was charismatic, successful, wealthy, and kind. He was interested in her, yet the person who was on her mind was a drifter who was actually a former lawyer named Clive Miller.

Of course she had her doubts about both men. Did Landon have anything to do with the odd happenings around town? And what was Clive not telling her?

Right now she had more pressing matters at hand. She found Bobbi watching the children inside.

"How long do you plan on doing this? Don't you have to work?" Savannah asked as she stepped through the door.

Bobbi looked up from cleaning a spill and frowned. "I can only do it this week, then I've got to get back to my regular schedule. I hate to leave the family in a bind, but what can you do?"

"You're going above and beyond. I wouldn't be too hard on yourself."

Bobbi stood, wincing as she straightened. "These old knees aren't what they used to be."

Savannah leaned against the wall, averting her gaze from baby Penelope. She reminded her so much of Ella.

"Any updates on Lucia?" she asked instead.

"No, I haven't heard a thing. It's a shame. I was here all day yesterday, trying to comfort the families. Tom came and helped. But no one thinks she's going to be found alive."

Savannah went cold at the statement. That couldn't be true. Certainly there was still hope.

"Why do they think that?"

She shrugged. "Look at Felipe and Jorge."

The sentiment didn't settle well with Savannah. She tried to find the right words, to say something that would dispute the claim, but she couldn't. Instead, she glanced at her watch. "Listen, I've got to get to the hospital and check on Marti. Do you need me to swing by here and help out later?"

Bobbi smiled. "Thanks, dear, but I think I'll be fine. I'll holler if I need a hand. How does that sound?"

Savannah nodded. "Just let me know."

• • •

Leonard was sitting at Marti's bedside when Savannah arrived. She wanted to ask if he knew about the harvest festival, but decided not to burst his bubble. The man seemed to truly love Marti. His eyes fluctuated between misting and brightening when he looked at her.

"No change?" Savannah said, sitting beside him, even though she already knew the answer.

He shook his head. "No, still the same. She's beautiful, isn't she?"

Savannah smiled. "Inside and out."

Silence fell between them a moment.

"How's the drive back and forth from home going?" Savannah finally asked. "Do you need a place to stay?"

He waved his hand in the air. "Nah, I'm fine. I don't mind it. I actually feel most comfortable in my own home. I'm a little OCD like that."

"Understood."

They settled back, the uneasy quiet of two people who barely knew each other falling between them.

"I found out something about the Madden Society," Leonard announced.

Savannah raised her eyebrows. "Did you?"

He shrugged bashfully. "I'm pretty good on the computer. Anyway, if rumor is correct, they're meeting tomorrow."

Tomorrow? Didn't Landon say he was going out of town tomorrow? Could he somehow be involved with this?

"Where?"

He shook his head. "I don't know. It's hush-hush."

"You really think they have something to do with Marti? I just find it hard to believe."

"If they're doing something they shouldn't be, they don't want to be caught. I think someone in that group is behind this supposed suicide attempt."

It was a long shot. Savannah knew it was.

But what if Leonard was right?

CHAPTER 35

Clive slowed as he pulled down the driveway, the crushed oyster shells under his tires crinkling and cracking under the weight of his vehicle. In the distance, he spotted Savannah sitting on the porch, a sweater pulled around her shoulders and a steaming mug in her hands.

For a moment she looked like the picture of serenity. Of course, he already knew her well enough to know that she was in turmoil. A lot of turmoil. He understood what that was like.

Thankfully, in his darkest hour, he'd realized that the only thing that could fill the voids in his life was his faith. He would have gone off the deep end without it. After talking to Savannah earlier, he'd learned that she didn't share his views. He hoped she might change her mind.

He braked by the house when he saw Savannah wave to him, rise, and walk toward his car. Memories of her and Landon last night flashed into his mind.

It was better that way, he realized. He needed to forget any chance of having a relationship again. At least until he figured out who had really killed Lauren. Until then, he knew there was something dark in his heart. He prayed to get rid of it. He prayed it would disappear.

But it didn't.

Vengeance still reined, its prickly grasp strong and rooted in ways it shouldn't be.

Savannah smiled and leaned toward him, against the door. "Hey there."

The look in her eyes was different, he realized. Something was changing inside her. Maybe this investigation was reigniting old parts of her. Maybe she was finally moving past the terrible tragedy that had happened in her life.

"I have news," he finally said.

"So do I. You first, though."

"Some of the guys in the van were talking today. My Spanish isn't wonderful, but I made out enough. They said they've seen a suspicious van at the migrant camp at late hours."

"What did it look like?"

"Black, tinted windows. It was a minivan, not full size. The license plate was covered with mud, but one of the back windows had a crack in it. It was an older model."

"No one knows who it belonged to?"

"No. They have no idea."

She nodded. "Good to know. That could be our first real clue."

He draped his hand over the steering wheel, resisting the urge to lean closer to Savannah, to find out if she still smelled like strawberries. "Your turn." He'd caught a whiff of the scent as they'd rescued the cat on the beach that day.

"What are you doing tomorrow?"

He tilted his head in confusion. "I'm off of work. Why?"

"How would you feel about taking a little trip? Following someone, actually."

"Who?"

"Landon Kavanagh."

His eyebrows shot up. "You want to follow your boyfriend?"

She laughed, tight and low. "He's not my boyfriend. He'd like to be."

The relief he felt was a sure sign that he was feeling things he had no business feeling. "That's too bad. I hear he's quite a catch."

She dropped her head toward her shoulder. "Do you want to go or not?"

He didn't have to think about it. He didn't even have to know why at the moment. "I'm in."

Savannah grinned. "Great. Let's meet at seven. You bring breakfast."

If there was one thing he'd always liked, it was a woman who knew what she wanted. And he was beginning to like Savannah more and more.

. . .

Savannah and Clive sat in his Jeep outside a restaurant at the intersection of the main highway into town and the road leading to Landon's house. If the man was leaving and going anywhere other than Cape Thomas, he'd come by here.

Savannah sipped her coffee and nibbled on a pastry, both compliments of Clive. He'd also brought some apples he'd picked up at the farm, including the "Landon."

She was all too aware of his presence beside her. He seemed to fill more than his fair share of space. Being so close to him made her heart race and her skin tingle in a way that it hadn't in a very long time.

They'd agreed to wear dark clothing and tennis shoes as well, just in case they needed to remain hidden. Clive had donned sunglasses and a hat. Savannah wore some old jeans and a long-sleeved black shirt, and she had pulled her hair back into a bun.

Her blood was pumping in a way she hadn't felt since her visits to the Sudan. Since she'd exposed a cult leader in Mexico. It was the feeling she got when she was on the verge of blowing something open, exposing a wrong and making it right.

Clive leaned forward, and Savannah's heart involuntarily quickened.

"You've got a little bit of icing at the corner of your mouth." He reached toward her and wiped it away.

Savannah knew her cheeks were probably flaming. She had to get a grip.

Clive leaned back, obviously unaffected by the whole encounter. Instead, he stared out the window. "Get this. You know I'm working as a supervisor over at the farm, right?"

She nodded.

"I walk the property to keep an eye on all the workers. There are train tracks that basically divide the land in half. I saw someone walking on the tracks the other day. Guess what I caught him doing?"

"What?"

"Flattening pennies."

Savannah's eyes widened. "Who was it?"

"Jose."

Savannah's jaw loosened, nearly dropping open. "Really?"

Clive nodded. "I asked him what he was doing. He said he'd found a penny like that in his sister's room. Now he was flattening the pennies in her honor."

She put her coffee down, suddenly losing her desire to drink it. "I think the killer left his calling card, Clive. I don't think Lucia was the one flattening the pennies."

"The more I learn, the more twisted this gets."

Savannah straightened and pointed down the road. "That's Landon's truck."

She put on her hat and some sunglasses as well. With her hair pulled back, she'd be harder to recognize.

"Here we go then." Clive eased the Jeep out onto the road after him.

Landon was headed north, toward Chincoteague and the Maryland state line. They kept a safe distance behind him, cruising northward up Highway 17.

"You said your wife worked at some Save the Bay events. Did you ever meet Bobbi Matthews? She works at the marine center."

Clive shook his head, his eyes still shielded by his sunglasses. "Can't say I know her."

"She's married to a pastor. They're a really nice couple."

"A pastor, huh?" He ventured a glance her way. "Do you ever miss playing that role?"

"No, on several levels. I don't miss the pressure. I felt so much need to be perfect, like I had to always be on, like I had to know the answers. Everything I'd ever done, I did it well. I was a typical overachiever. But then I became a Christian, got married, and was thrust into a different kind of spotlight—not a major spotlight, but the little spotlight of our congregation—and I felt so ill equipped."

"What did your husband say?"

Those days flooded back to her. Being hit by a semi would've hurt less. "Honestly, I think I disappointed him. He thought I'd step into the role more flawlessly. Instead, I freely gave my opinions when maybe I shouldn't have. I asked why someone could clean the bathrooms at church but weren't holy enough to sing on stage for worship team. I questioned why the teens weren't allowed to have pool parties—bathing suits could cause too much temptation, after all—yet the church sponsored a youth camp with a swimming pool. Those man-made rules really burned me up inside." She looked down at her lap. "Maybe I didn't try hard enough. Maybe I should have kept my mouth shut."

"It sounds like a big life change for you. Anyone would need time to adjust. Besides, it's kind of refreshing when people are honest and point out hypocritical thinking."

His words brought comfort, but only for a moment. "The biggest kicker, however, happened while I was working on an article and discovered that the sheriff was buddies with this defense lawyer named Myron Graves. It turns out Myron was paying off the sheriff in order to let people slide by on lesser convictions."

"Okay . . ."

Her blood started boiling again as she thought about it. "The problem was that Myron was on the leadership team at church. He told me if I didn't drop things, he would make life miserable for us. He told me he could see to it that Reid didn't have a job anymore. He did just that. He made a whole list of reasons why Reid should be fired. He presented them to the board, pleaded his case, and Reid was let go."

"Ouch."

Savannah shook her head. "I didn't think Reid would ever forgive me."

"He actually thought it was your fault?"

"In so many words. I was so used to being my own person. Then I moved into a place where I was Reid's wife. Maybe all of that was my secret way of rebelling. I've thought about it a million times, and I still don't know. Maybe the truth was simply that Reid and I weren't suited for each other."

"Did you ever tell Reid that?" Clive's voice sounded soft, compassionate.

"He never said how he felt outright. He always tried to keep things pleasant, but I could see the anger simmering in him. I felt like a zombie for the first two years of our marriage." At the time, she'd blamed it on the life change. But looking back, there were so many other issues.

"And after Reid lost his job?"

"I still couldn't let it go. I kept asking questions about the sheriff. Every time I found something questionable, I kept digging. You know how the story ends."

He reached over and squeezed her hand. "I'm sorry."

"Not as sorry as I am." She stared out the window. With every crop she saw blur past her window, she couldn't help but reflect on how time marched on, through all the victories, through all the tragedies.

"How'd the two of you meet anyway?"

"Afghanistan." She smiled sadly.

"Love at first sight?"

"Something like that. We connected from the start. He was everything I wasn't—grounded, happy to stay in one place, he thought before speaking, was even-tempered. Of course we had *some* things in common. We were both compassionate. We loved working for the good of other people. We were focused."

"Sounds like you had enough in common."

She shrugged. "I transferred to Raleigh, took classes at church on how to become a Christian. We talked about taking mission trips across the globe. I guess I grew up with the concept that true love could conquer all. It didn't. I'd always suspected as much, but for a moment I'd dared to believe differently."

"I still believe that marriage can be good," Clive insisted. "You just have to be willing to work through the hard times. You have to be willing to stick together even when you don't want to. You have to be open to the possibility that your differences can make you better people. Iron sharpening iron. It can be a painful process, but once you get through it, it's worth it."

"Awfully wise words." Savannah studied his profile for a moment. "Enough about me. Tell me about your wife."

He was quiet for a moment. When he spoke, his voice had a new tone. A softer, sadder one. "What can I say?" he finally said. "She always smelled like the seashore. She made shell necklaces and bracelets using what she found along the beach. You knew she was your friend if she gave you one. She wanted to save marine life, but she secretly loved eating fish and shrimp."

Savannah smiled. People were rarely simple to figure out; they could be so complex, with clashing desires and passions—it was both frustrating and fascinating. "How long were you married?"

"Four years."

"No kids?"

"No kids," Clive said. "We talked about starting a family, but we wanted to do things career-wise first." He sent her a wry glance. "I fluctuate between regretting the decision and feeling relief that there wasn't a child in the middle of the mess after she died."

"The mess after she died?" Savannah questioned.

"The investigation. The lives turned upside down. The heartache."

Savannah nodded, understanding washing through her. "The mess," she whispered. There wasn't a better word to describe it.

"It sounds like our heartaches had the opposite effect on us," Clive said. "I was the biggest skeptic. I grew up going to church every Sunday, but I ran from that kind of lifestyle as soon as I was out of the house. But when my wife died, I was at the lowest point in my life. I cried out to God, and He heard me. He offered me hope I'd never had before. I'm still imperfect. I still struggle with things. But I can finally live with a higher focus than life on this earth."

She crossed her arms and stared out the window a moment, a longing stirring inside her. "I could use some of that hope. I guess I always found it in my job. Then my job was gone, and I had no idea what to do with myself."

"The good news is that it's not too late."

Savannah was about to say that it was too late for her. Before she could, Landon's truck turned. "Maybe we're in business now."

CHAPTER 36

Clive kept his distance behind Landon, hoping they wouldn't set off any alarms as they followed him. Landon headed toward the bay. Thankfully traffic on the rural road seemed heavier than usual, making it easier to stay concealed.

He didn't know if the Madden Society—if that was what this turned out to be—would offer any answers about Lauren's death. But he wanted to know what Landon Kavanagh was up to. Maybe today would hold some answers. Plus, he was intrigued by the prospect of spending more time with Savannah. He'd surprised himself by opening up to her more than he'd planned yesterday. Part of him wanted to share more about his past with Savannah, but he knew it was too risky.

Savannah pointed toward the sky where ribbons of white clouds cut through the blue in a crisscross pattern. "See those?"

"The contrails?"

Savannah nodded. "Some people believe they're actually chemtrails—trails of poison chemicals—that the government is spraying into the atmosphere to make citizens impotent and control the population."

"Another conspiracy theory. Did Marti believe that?"

"No, I don't think so. But she's the one who told me about it." Savannah smiled sadly. "I sure do miss those conversations. Marti was like that, all the way back in college. She was always seeing hidden agendas."

They traveled almost a half-hour until finally Landon pulled down a driveway. He stopped at gates at the front of the property, talked into a little box, and proceeded through once the gates opened.

"I guess this is as far as we're going," Clive said.

"That house is impressive." Savannah stared at the property in the distance. It was sprawling and white, with large columns at the front. The bay sparkled behind it, and woods surrounded it on either side.

"I wonder who lives here."

"Congressman Will Perkins," Clive muttered.

Savannah's gaze shot toward his. "You're sure?"

Clive nodded. He didn't feel like mentioning that he'd been here before for a political fund-raiser. "Come on. I'll find somewhere to hide the Jeep, and then we'll need to do the rest on foot."

"Sounds like a plan."

He pulled farther down the road and found a service road cutting through the dried fields of corn. He drove down the road a half-mile before charging into the crop. The tall plants easily concealed his vehicle.

Savannah turned to him, surprise in her eyes.

He shrugged. "We've got to make sure we're not seen. If this is the Madden Society and there are powerful people here, they'll most likely have security and bodyguards. If they see my Jeep, they'll start searching for us."

"Well done. Almost like you've done this before."

"You don't have to be an investigative reporter to be nosy." He gave her a wry grin. "Okay, let's go."

"Are you thinking the same thing I am? That we should cut through the field and try to reach the woods surrounding the property? From there, we can try to find the best place to get a view of what's going on."

"Sounds like a plan to me."

"What I can't figure out is what to do if everyone's inside the house."

Clive shrugged. "Then I guess we're out of luck, because I don't see any way we're going to get close enough to that house to see inside. It's gated, they have watch dogs, and I have no desire to end up in jail."

Again, he thought to himself. But he didn't dare speak that thought aloud.

He wanted to tell Savannah the whole truth at some point. But right now was definitely not the time.

. . .

Surrounded by acres and acres of corn, Savannah felt claustrophobic. The sky was wide open above her, but the stalks of corn stretched endlessly in all directions, closing in and unnerving her. It was like a prison with no escape.

Finally they reached the woods, but as she surveyed them, they didn't make Savannah feel much better. Forests that were this close to the bay were filled with marshy indentions, tangled vines, and pesky underbrush.

She tucked her hair into her cap.

"So no one will recognize you?" Clive asked.

She shook her head. "So I won't get ticks."

Clive chuckled. "Smart lady."

Savannah began tromping through the woods. She'd done worse for the sake of a good story, so she didn't complain. As long as she could see Clive, she had a sense of security. It had been a long time since she'd felt this comfortable with someone; her ease with him was a mystery, especially considering the questions she still had about the man.

She was certain there were things he wasn't telling her. Like, what had he done in the years since his wife's death? Just how specifically had his wife's death turned his life upside down? Why had he really walked away from his career as a lawyer?

"You doing okay?" Clive asked.

He held her hand—just as a means to stay together, Savannah told herself. "Yeah, I'm fine."

"I think we're almost there."

Honestly, she wasn't used to being the one not taking the lead on something like this. But she'd defaulted to Clive since he seemed to know what he was doing. Nice as it was, it also raised more questions.

Finally the darkness of the woods seemed to break, indicating that the house might be ahead. They slowed their steps and came to a stop at the edge of the property.

Clive had been right. This was the congressman's backyard. His white mansion stood proudly in the distance, and from here they had an eagle-eyed view of his property.

An eight-foot iron fence protected the land, and Savannah spotted two Dobermans patrolling in the distance. The backyard was a true piece of landscaping beauty, featuring a pool with a waterfall, a covered, multilevel patio, flowers overflowing from a stone wall, curvy walkways, and statues.

But what interested Savannah the most was the men who milled around.

She checked the perimeters of the space. Sure enough, she spotted three men in suits wearing sunglasses and, if she had to guess, earpieces.

Security.

"We've got to stay low," Savannah murmured.

She glanced over at Clive and saw that he had binoculars to his eyes.

"You thought ahead," Savannah observed.

"You can't have a stakeout without them."

She frowned, but only because she wished she'd thought of it first. "See anything interesting?"

He twisted the focus knob. "Not yet."

Savannah stared again, trying to make out faces. She was too far away, though. But she had thought of one thing that Clive hadn't. She reached into her backpack and pulled out her camera. She hadn't used this sleek piece of equipment in years. But it had a great zoom.

She skimmed over several people before stopping on Landon.

If this was the Madden Society, then he'd lied to her. Why would he lie to her? What was the purpose of keeping a group like this secret?

Two reasons came to mind: They were hiding something, or they were living out some kind of childish boys-only club fantasy. The latter seemed unlikely, given the caliber of the people involved. Certainly these men had better things to do. Then again, people were complex and surprising.

Maybe Marti had put too many ideas in her mind. Did secret societies really exist? Did a small group of men really come together to make decisions that could affect the masses?

Savannah shook her head. She had a hard time believing that.

But then what was she seeing right now? A social gathering?

"You look deep in thought."

She shook her head. "If Marti and Leonard hadn't thought this was a secret society, then I wonder if that would have ever crossed my mind. They planted the idea in my head, so naturally my thoughts are leaning that way."

"Is a secret society so hard to believe?"

"Not if I see Elvis show up on an alien spaceship," she muttered.

"You're pretty funny."

"I used to be." A sad smile played on her face.

"It's starting to come back. That's a good sign."

"It's when I start believing that the Illuminati are real and the Freemasons are hiding clues in public monuments and currency that you should start to worry about me."

Considering her doubts about Clive just moments before, she mused, perhaps she *was* prone to believing in conspiracies . . . or at least conspiracies that held that no one was who they really claimed to be. Perhaps *not* believing that would be naive. Didn't everyone hide certain parts of themselves? She did. Marti had.

"Do you recognize any of these guys?" Savannah asked. She focused her camera lens, trying to get a better look.

"I see the congressman, of course."

"You know much about him?"

"Off the top of my head? Not really. He chairs some committees. He's been around for long enough that he's pretty powerful."

Savannah panned her camera lens around. "Now that's interesting."

"What?"

She hesitated to even start, knowing how her words would sound. "That's Rupert McDonald. He owns two cable networks and five newspapers—at last count."

"So far we've got a congressman, a media mogul, and one of the richest farmers on the East Coast."

They exchanged a glance.

Savannah drew in an uneasy breath and turned back to her camera. "There's another familiar face. Our local doctor is there—Dr.

Richard Lawson. I have to say, he's kind of out of place among the rest of the crowd. He's not as filthy rich. Some of these groups—if they're real and all—you have to buy your way into."

"But maybe he's still influential."

Savannah snapped some pictures, especially of the faces she didn't recognize. Maybe someone would. She only wished she was close enough to hear their conversations. But she was too recognizable to at least two people there. There was no way to get closer.

"Uh-oh. The security guards are walking this way," Clive whispered. "Stay low."

Savannah crouched down, holding her breath. They were nearer to the fence than they should be, but it was too late to move now without drawing attention to themselves.

The guards were close enough now that Savannah could hear their voices.

"They're talking about making money. What could be more important than that?" one of the guards said.

"Money sounds good to me. Think they'll give us a raise?"

The two men laughed.

"Seems like a pretty pat gig."

"You know how many people would love to know about this meeting? All these guys gathered here in one place? If the wrong person found out, they could do some serious damage here."

"Can't deny that."

They were close enough now that Savannah could hear the grass rustling under their feet, hear the keys on their belts jangle. One wrong move and they could be discovered.

She stole a glance at Clive. Her worry was reflected in his gaze. She hoped the underbrush concealed them enough.

Her backpack, only on one shoulder, began to slide.

She froze, holding her breath, hoping the bag wouldn't move any more.

The footsteps got closer.

Just then her backpack slid faster. She reached to grab it, and her camera smacked onto a root underneath her. The sound cracked through the air.

"What was that?" one of the guards asked.

Savannah squeezed her eyes shut, anticipating disaster.

CHAPTER 37

Clive braced himself for fight or flight.

If they stayed low enough, they wouldn't be spotted. But it was going to be close.

"Probably just a squirrel," one of the guards said. "You know how they are this time of year. Saving up nuts for winter and all."

"I don't see anyone out there."

"Congressman Perkins would probably want us to double-check."

"I'll stay here and keep my eye out. Why don't you get one of the dogs?"

"Sounds like a plan."

One of the dogs? That wouldn't be good. If they were caught, Clive would never figure out who killed his wife. The spotlight would shine on him and ruin any chance he had to investigate. Not to mention that being here was breaking the terms of his agreement. This wasn't good.

"Savannah, we've got to run," he whispered.

Her gaze met his and he saw her nod subtly.

"On the count of three, we've got to take off. Otherwise, as soon as the dogs are out, we're done. Understand?"

"Got it."

"One." He peered through the marsh grass that tickled his nose. The guard had his back turned, probably looking for his partner. If they were going to make a run for it, the time was now.

"Two." The man still had his back to them.

"Three!"

He grabbed Savannah's hand, and they darted through the woods.

"Hey! Stop right there!" the guard yelled.

They kept going. They dodged trees and stumps and roots and underbrush. Marsh water soaked their legs

Just when Clive's breathing grew strained, he heard a dog barking in the distance. Closer than he liked. Getting closer, he realized.

They had no time to slow down.

Finally the cornfield appeared. They darted between the stalks. Leaves slapped their faces. Dry cobs crunched under their feet, nearly rolling their ankles. Bugs buzzed by.

Clive kept his grip on Savannah's hand. He knew if they lost each other out here, they might never find each other again.

The dog's barking still sounded behind them, but not too close. They had to move. Things could change in the blink of an eye.

He knew the direction of the Jeep, but they were moving so fast he barely had time to check. Right now they just had to get far away from the property. If he were caught, it would have a ripple effect on his future. Everything would be ruined, and he couldn't let that happen.

Suddenly Savannah cried out behind him. He turned and saw the expression of pain on her face as she clutched her calf.

"I hit something," she panted.

Her jeans were ripped and blood already soaked the edges.

He wrapped an arm around her waist. "Come on. We've got to keep moving before we can get you some help."

She nodded through gritted teeth and tried to press ahead. They made it several feet, fighting through the dried stalks around them, but Clive finally stopped. He could tell she was struggling.

"Maybe we should rest a minute."

Savannah shook her head. "But the dogs . . ."

"I don't hear them right now. Maybe they think they scared us away and that's enough."

"The way they were acting, they want us caught and tried."

Her face tightened as he lowered her to the ground. "Let's just wait a minute. Finding us out here is like finding a needle in a haystack."

She grimaced and clutched her leg. "Are we going to find our way out of here? That's the other question pounding in my head. We might as well be lost at sea."

He squeezed her shoulder. "We're going to get out of here. I promise."

She sucked in a quick breath and grabbed his knee. "Listen."

The sound of voices crept closer toward them over the fields.

"I think we lost them." It was the voice of the taller guard.

"At least we found the Jeep," the shorter one said. "We'll run the plates. Maybe we can track them down that way. Then we can make sure they stay quiet."

"Not to mention figure out why they're here."

The voices faded. But the alarm sounding in Clive's head only grew louder. He had to think of a way out of this.

"I think they're gone," Savannah whispered.

"Bad news is that we need a ride home."

"Why can't we take your Jeep? It's going to lead back to you anyway."

Clive shook his head. "It won't. It's a friend's. Did you leave any personal effects inside?"

"Only my cup."

"Good. We should be okay." Clive had been careful not to leave anything.

"What about your friend? Will he get in trouble for this?"

"He doesn't live around here. He's been out of town and will just say the Jeep was stolen so he won't be implicated. I can't let them trace the Jeep back to your place. I'm not going to put you in that position."

"What about your friend?"

"He's a Navy SEAL, and he's single. He can take care of himself. I'll give him a heads up." He gestured toward the rip in her jeans. "That's a nasty cut. How are you feeling?"

She squinted. "It hurts. I don't know what I hit."

"We need to get you cleaned up. But first we need to find a way out of here."

"There's someone I can call."

"Please say it's not Landon Kavanagh."

That actually got a small smile out of her, but only for a moment before her face paled. "No, not Landon. It's someone else I know. Her name is Bobbi Matthews. She's dependable and trustworthy, and I think you'll really like her."

Clive felt a rock form in his stomach.

How was this going to play out?

. . .

Savannah stuffed her phone back into her pocket and turned to Clive. First she'd called Bobbi for a ride, and then she'd given Leonard an update on what they'd discovered. She'd made sure not to talk too long. She needed quiet so she could listen for telltale signs they'd been spotted.

They'd hobbled closer to the road where Bobbi would pick them up. They just had to stay concealed until they saw her car. It would take her an hour to get here, and twenty of those minutes had already passed.

"Did your friend have any additional insight?" Clive asked.

She shook her head, ignoring the pain in her leg. "Not really. He seemed thrilled that his theory has some validity."

"You sure he's trustworthy?"

"He was dating Marti. He wants to find out what happened to Marti more than anyone."

Clive squinted against the sun. "What's his name?"

"Leonard Griffith. You ever met him?"

"I don't think so."

"You'd remember him if you did. He has a big purple streak going through his hair."

Something clouded Clive's gaze.

"What?" Savannah studied his face as she waited for him to explain.

He shrugged, noncommittal. "Nothing. I just saw someone in the woods the other day who had purple hair."

The pain in her leg distracted her from dwelling on his statement much longer. Did she need stitches? She wasn't sure. But she definitely needed to get the cut cleaned.

Just then Bobbi's car pulled to a stop in front of the cornfield. Savannah tried not to wince as she hobbled toward it. Her leg hurt more than she wanted to admit.

Clive helped her, offering his arm then finally just picking her up and carrying her to the front seat. He whisked her inside, putting his sweatshirt on the seat so blood wouldn't saturate it. Then he climbed into the backseat.

Savannah looked at the driver. "Tom? What are you doing here?"

"Bobbi was tied up watching the kids. I told her I'd come. It beat being left with a roomful of children. She's much better at that kind of thing than I am."

"I appreciate you coming here." She pulled on her seat belt and shut her eyes as her cut throbbed.

"Are you okay?" Tom asked.

She forced a nod. "Nothing a little antiseptic, bandages, and Tylenol won't make better."

Tom glanced in the back where Clive, who moments earlier had been taut with tension, now seemed more relaxed.

"This is my friend Clive," Savannah explained.

"Nice to meet you, Clive."

"You too," Clive said, his face turned to the window.

"Anyone want to tell me what's going on?" Tom started down the road.

Savannah surveyed the fields. She half expected to see the security guards setting up an ambush down the road. But nothing happened, even as they passed the front gates of the congressman's home.

"It's the least we can do since you went out of your way," Savannah began. "It's kind of a long story. It involves Marti."

"And the congressman?" Tom asked. He sounded casual, as if nothing ever flustered him.

"How'd you know?"

"Everyone knows Congressman Perkins has a place on the bay. I've been to a community fund-raiser at his house before. Based on your condition and secrecy, I'm sensing trouble."

"It's a long story." Savannah rethought telling Tom what they'd been doing. The last thing she wanted was to implicate him. "It's actually better if you don't know."

"You're not going to get yourself in trouble, are you?" Tom asked, his voice compassionate and concerned.

Savannah shook her head. "No, not trouble. I'm just looking for answers. However, sometimes those two things are one and the same."

"I have some answers I could give you."

She let out an airy laugh. "I know. Jesus. God. The Bible."

"I think God loves the doubters, Savannah."

His words left her speechless for a moment. "What?"

He nodded, continuing to drive down the road. "It's true. People who doubt and search for the answers and research for themselves end up coming to the faith with strong convictions once they finally realize the truth. He wants us to be grounded in His Word, to face the questions."

"But faith, by definition, dispels doubts. Faith is believing *despite* the doubts. I don't know that I can ever really have that faith."

"I think you already do."

"No offense, Pastor, but you obviously don't know me that well. Lately Christianity just seems like Greek mythology. I mean what if hell is just some conspiracy to trick the masses into believing in a moral absolute?"

"What if it's not?"

"That's your answer?"

He shrugged. "I think the answers are simple, though we try to make them complex." He glanced at her. "I don't want to give you easy answers, Savannah, but I don't want to give you too much theology either. Jesus intended for Christianity to be simple, to be something that anyone could understand. That's why I don't want to give you an exogenesis about the texts of the Bible. I could offer evidence that Jesus really did come to earth, I can show you documents that prove the miracles of Jesus's time. We make decisions about faith based on fact. We make decisions on life and our beliefs based on probabilities. You're someone who's searched for answers as a career. Are you telling me there's not a part of you that's still searching?"

Savannah ignored her ache, ignored the fact that Clive was being strangely silent in the backseat, and ignored the fact that only minutes earlier she'd been considering the possibilities of a secret society. Now she was considering something even more improbable.

"Sometimes it would be nice to know that there's more to this life than just living and dying," she admitted.

"Don't let yourself become one of those people who, no matter what the proof, still deny the truth. Hurts can let us do that sometimes. Hurts come because we live in a world where God has given men free will. But God is love. A loving father gives his children, once they're of age, the ability to make their own choices. Our Heavenly Father does the same, and because of that, chaos sometimes ensues."

Savannah couldn't reconcile the image of God with a father. Savannah's dad had been the CEO of a Fortune 500 company until he died of a heart attack when Savannah was ten. He'd left her and her mom set for life financially. But Savannah hadn't really known her father. He had worked all the time, even on vacation. In Savannah's family, value was based on net worth, not on relationships.

Just then a siren sounded behind them.

Savannah's stomach sank. Had they been discovered? Did someone know that Pastor Tom had picked them up after they'd trespassed on the congressman's property?

She glanced back at Clive, but his sunglasses concealed his eyes. Why was he being so quiet?

She gripped the armrest as the police car got closer, still behind them. Tom pulled to the side of the road. The officer veered into the left lane and sped past them.

Her heart rate slowed for a moment.

"Wonder what the emergency is?" she asked, finally finding her voice. It sounded strained when she spoke, a sure giveaway of her guilt.

"Every time I see an ambulance or police car, I lift up a prayer," Tom said. "I've been called to too many scenes with police cars and ambulances. They almost always mean someone is hurting, either physically or emotionally."

"That's a nice sentiment." It was. Every time Savannah saw an emergency vehicle from now on, she'd probably remember that Pastor Tom used those opportunities to pray for others.

He slowed as they spotted a cluster of vehicles up ahead.

"Do you mind?" Tom asked. "I just want to make sure they don't need anyone here for spiritual counsel."

Savannah nodded. "Sure, we'll be fine."

Her gut clenched, though. She didn't want to raise any questions. Riding with Clive and the pastor, traveling south, injured—someone could put everything together.

Tom was a saint for not asking too many questions. Any normal person would have. But Tom seemed more concerned with her soul than her circumstances.

He pulled over near the scene. Three state police officers, two ambulances, and a fire truck were there. There were only woods surrounding the area—no stores, houses, or restaurants. Savannah didn't see a car crash, though. What was going on?

After Pastor Tom climbed out of the car and walked toward the scene, Savannah turned to Clive. "You're being quiet."

"Just listening." He still hid his eyes behind those glasses.

Savannah would give anything to know what he was thinking at the moment. "Is something wrong?"

"Just processing. You know how that can be. Your friend seems really nice. And wise."

Savannah glanced back at the scene. Chief Lockwood was out there, too. Pastor Tom stood next to him, his hands on his hips, nodding at something the chief said.

"What do you think's going on?" Clive asked.

"I haven't a clue." She squinted, the sun glaring on the windshield. "There's too much blocking the view."

She sank lower in her seat as the chief glanced at Tom's car. Could he see her through the windshield? Was he asking Pastor Tom questions about their presence now?

What if the congressman had called the cops and there was an APB out for their arrest?

Her heart skipped a beat as the chief walked toward her. She glanced back at Clive, and they exchanged a worried look. Quickly she threw the sweatshirt over her leg, hoping to conceal her injury so he wouldn't ask too many questions.

She forced a smile as she rolled down the window. "Good afternoon, Chief."

"Ms. Harris." He looked in the backseat and nodded at Clive. "Didn't expect to see you here."

She shrugged, maybe a little too big. "Didn't expect to be here."

"Taking a ride with the pastor?"

Savannah licked her lips. "Watching ministry in action. It's the least I can do for Marti—trying to lend a hand whenever I can."

He stared at her another moment. She held the sweatshirt more tightly over her leg. Finally he broke his gaze and stepped back. "Good for you. Take care."

Savannah let out her breath as he disappeared into the crowd. "You think he suspects something?"

"I can't tell what that man is thinking. Mostly about how he can keep his job, if I had to guess."

"The fact that I didn't ask what was going on was probably the biggest red flag of them all." She'd just wanted to keep the conversation as short as possible. But the chief had to know her well enough by now to realize how inquisitive she was.

Finally Pastor Tom walked back to the car. He opened his door but didn't climb inside. Instead, he leaned in to address them. "They found a body."

Savannah sucked in a breath. *Not Lucia. Please, not Lucia.*

She couldn't say anything, just waited for him to finish.

"It's Jorge," he finally said. "And it's not pretty."

CHAPTER 38

Savannah sucked in a deep breath as Clive cleaned the cut on her leg back at her house. She sat on the edge of her bathtub, squeezing a rubber duck—a goofy present Marti had given her—in her hand.

"This is a good one," he mumbled. "You might even need stitches."

She resisted a moan and squeezed her eyes shut. "It could be worse. I could be Jorge."

He dabbed more antiseptic cleanser on her leg, patted it dry with a paper towel, and pulled out some bandages. "What do you think happened to him?"

"That's what I keep thinking about. I don't know. This wasn't some kind of drug-induced accident. There were bruises all over his body. Something bad happened. All that speculation that he simply left wasn't true. That means someone has Felipe and Lucia also. We've got to find them before the same thing happens to them."

"How do you plan on doing that?" He put another butterfly bandage across her cut. It was going to take several to cover the injury.

"I have no idea." She blew out a sigh. "I'll be interested in hearing what Dr. Lawson says. I'm sure there'll be an autopsy on Jorge. The way his body was bloated . . ."

"Dr. Lawson? He's the doctor caring for Marti, right?"

She nodded. "He's also the town's medical examiner. He took over the position when I moved here. I don't think they have to utilize him very often."

"I can't imagine they would."

Her thoughts still churned inside her. "There are just too many strange things going on. Bad ones, too. Are they connected? Am I reading too much into this and becoming paranoid myself? Maybe I just need to accept that Marti did try to take her own life, that Señor Lopez did die of cancer, that Felipe and Lucia were running from immigration, that Jorge's death can be easily explained. If I could rule out just one of those variables, then maybe I'd know where to turn my focus. As it is right now, my thoughts are all over the place."

He secured the last Band-Aid. "Trust your gut, Savannah."

"My gut is out of practice. It's not what it used to be."

She lowered her leg to the floor, flinching at the discomfort.

"If you notice any signs of infection, you need to get right to the doctor." His look of concern was enough to take her breath away. It had been a long time since someone had looked at her the way he did.

"I will." She stood, limping a few steps until Clive took hold of her arm to help her. "Right now, I'm going to send those pictures I took at the congressman's house to a friend of mine. If anyone can identify the people who were at that meeting, it's him. This could be a wild goose chase, but at least I can rule out this whole secret society and move on if that's the case."

"It *is* a bit of a stretch to think that group would be behind these acts."

She bit back her pain as Clive helped her downstairs. Clive's well-defined muscles were a nice distraction. "But it was one of the last things Marti was looking into. That's the only reason I'm giving this a second thought. Well, that and because I don't understand the secrecy of it all. Secrets indicate that people are hiding something, and we usually only hide the bad things in our lives."

All of us, she thought. *We put on masks.*

Clive helped her into her office chair, where she uploaded the files from her camera. Then she started to write an e-mail.

"Who's this guy you're sending the photos to?" Clive leaned against her desk, his arms crossed and a thoughtful look on his face.

"A former colleague. He actually knew my husband, too. They went to high school together. He was the one who introduced us. His name is Stone Michaels."

Clive raised his eyebrows, obviously impressed. "You know Stone?"

She nodded. "Yeah, he's a good guy, a straight shooter. And he owes me one."

"Of all the people who could owe you, he'd be a good one."

Savannah hit "Send," then swiveled in the chair to face Clive. "Why were you so quiet in the car on the ride home?"

His eyes widened, but just for a moment. "I was just thinking. Why?"

"It seemed out of character. When people do things out of character, there's usually a reason. I almost had the feeling you were uncomfortable."

"I'm not very trusting of people I don't know, Savannah."

She nodded, supposing that made sense. Then she reached down and picked up Tiger. She held the little fur ball in her lap and stroked his head as thoughts turned over in her mind.

Clive stood, and Savannah was all too aware of his presence. Something about him made her feel protected. It was a good feeling.

"I should probably go. It's been a long day, and I have to work tomorrow."

She stood, realizing too late how close the two of them would end up. She started to step back when Clive grabbed her arm. She froze. Her heart stopped before rushing into action again, sending blood to stain her cheeks.

She looked up and saw the expression on his face. Saw the smoky look in his eyes. Felt the crackle of electricity between them.

He stepped closer; she didn't move.

His hand went to her neck, and he rubbed the delicate skin there. A longing welled in Savannah, a longing that scared her, that made her feel things she hadn't felt in years.

She craved his touch in a way she shouldn't.

He leaned closer, and she closed her eyes.

Just then something crashed outside the window.

CHAPTER 39

How dare Clive Miller think he could sweep into Savannah's life and steal her heart?

That was a position only he was equipped for. It just wasn't time to reveal that information yet. He had to wait for the right moment, the right timing. Savannah was special; he'd known that from the first time he laid eyes on her.

She needed someone to watch over her. She needed his protection from Clive Miller, only she didn't know it yet.

He crouched in the woods and watched.

Clive stood on the porch, pacing back and forth, looking for a clue as to what had happened. His hands were on his hips, and a look of unease was on his face.

That potted plant had to fall and give away his presence. The clay planter had to shatter into pieces.

It would never have happened if Savannah hadn't almost kissed Clive. He'd been content to watch from his place in the woods. But through that window with the shades open, he'd seen the two of them talking. Getting closer.

They'd been getting closer for a while now.

He had to put a stop to that. Somehow.

He had to figure out a way to discourage Savannah from asking so many questions. Her questions weren't a part of his plan. But how could he make her see that without revealing himself?

He stopped breathing a moment as Clive stepped off the porch and walked toward the woods.

Would he be discovered?

No, he was a shadow. People never saw him. Not this side of him. They only saw the pieces he wanted them to.

That's what made his whole plan so perfect.

CHAPTER 40

First thing in the morning, Savannah went to the hospital. Leonard was sitting at Marti's bedside, and she updated him on what had happened. She thought she saw a touch of admiration in his eyes when she finished.

"Good work." Leonard shook his head. "But I don't like this. Something's going on."

"Do you really think a meeting like that has something to do with Marti's current state?"

"She told me she'd discovered something about one of the members of the Madden Society. That was one of the last things I heard from her. I think there's a good chance there's a correlation."

She studied his face, trying to picture him with Marti. She'd seen Marti's type before. She'd married a mountain biker with a penchant for adventure. The marriage had only lasted a year because he'd been adventurous in other areas besides athletics. Mostly with other women. From there, Marti had moved on to guys who were the opposite of her ex. Responsible. Steady. Reliable.

Like Dr. Lawson.

Not like Leonard, though.

"What happened between the two of you? You said you hadn't spoken in several days. Then I called and told you what had happened to her."

"I was at a conference in Denver. My days were packed from sunrise to sunset."

Yet when Savannah had called, he'd answered. Maybe she'd simply caught him at a good time. "What kind of conference? You never did tell me what line of work you're in."

"I'm in IT."

"IT? Really." That seemed to fit his motif perfectly.

"Believe it or not, I used to be a hacker back in the day. Then I turned my life around."

"Were things going well between you and Marti?"

"We had our differences. Of course. Doesn't every relationship? We were both passionate people. We felt strongly about things."

Savannah stared at Marti's face. Passionate and opinionated definitely described her friend. "Did she seem like herself the last time you saw her?"

"I think she was really struggling with something. She didn't want to talk about it yet, though, so I was giving her some time to work things out. I figured she'd tell me in her own time." He squeezed Marti's hand.

Savannah nodded somberly, realizing just how painful reality could be. "You're probably right."

Silence passed between them for a few minutes.

Leonard turned toward her. "Did you bring those pictures with you, by chance? The ones you took of the Madden Society? I'm anxious to see who's involved."

"They're on my computer at home."

"Could I see them sometime?"

She nodded. "Sure. I'm meeting with someone for lunch, but why don't you stop by around two? I'll show you then."

"I appreciate that." He glanced at his watch. "Listen, I'm going to work for an hour or two. I want to reserve some of my leave time, especially since I don't know how long Marti is going to be in the hospital."

"Makes sense to me."

He offered a half wave and then slipped out the door. Savannah sat there in silence for a moment until the door opened again.

Dr. Lawson walked in. He stopped in his tracks when he saw Savannah. "Wasn't expecting anyone to be in here." He walked to Marti's bedside and checked her chart. "How are you, Savannah?"

"Hanging in. How about you? I heard you were called in for some police work yesterday." *Called away from your little secret society.* She kept that thought silent.

"I'd actually taken the day off and was spending some time at my fishing cabin."

Savannah paused. "Fishing cabin?"

He nodded. "I own a little place on one of the barrier islands."

"Oceanside? Nice."

He nodded again. "It's always been a dream of mine to have my own little island. It's only a couple of acres. But it's my little slice of heaven."

He was lying. Was it because everyone who was involved with the Madden Society had to lie about their whereabouts? Or was there a different reason?

"It sounds nice."

He put the chart back and adjusted Marti's IV. "I'm afraid there's no change. I keep hoping every day there might be."

"You and me both."

He started toward the door, but stopped. "I had Señor Lopez's medication tested. The results were on my desk this morning. There was nothing abnormal about them. I just wanted to let you know."

Disappointment gnawed at her. It had been her one lead, her best chance of finding proof that something really was going on.

She might as well just chase after Bigfoot because it seemed she'd never get anywhere with this new investigation.

"Thank you, Dr. Lawson."

She stood. She had to get to her meeting with Bobbi, then be home in time for Leonard's visit.

.   .   .

"So this mechanism pumps out all the chemicals in this barrel," Ernie explained to Clive. "You won't be operating this, but I need you to make sure the workers stay out of the fields we're spraying."

Clive patted the huge red barrel full of liquid. "This is all pesticide?"

"Only about one percent."

"How often do you spray this?" Clive asked.

"Two or three times a year. You're not one of the organic folks, are you?"

Clive shrugged, his gaze moving beyond Ernie to the workers in the fields in the distance. Could the pesticides be making them sick? "Haven't given it much thought lately."

"Well, this product not only keeps insects away from our produce, it prevents weeds, stops disease, and preserves the product longer. I say it's a miracle."

"I can tell you're a fan."

He chuckled. "I was actually a chemist in my younger days."

"From chemist to farm foreman?"

Ernie nodded. "Yep. Office work wasn't for me. I'm like my dad. I like to use my hands. So, as much as my mom and dad wanted me to be educated, to have a better life than they did, I discovered that the life they had was the best."

"It's good that you discovered it. Some people don't." Clive shifted, trying to make small talk to get in Ernie's good graces so he could ask him more questions.

"I still use my scientific training for the hybrid products Landon creates. I didn't abandon my education completely."

"Smart man." Clive tapped the top of the barrel. "So can this stuff make the workers sick? I mean how long do they have to stay away?"

"No. We put up signs to remind them to stay out of the fields. It depends on the pesticide, but some require twelve, twenty-four, or forty-eight hours of drying before they're deemed safe. We take all the precautions."

"And the pesticides are safe for human consumption?"

Ernie nodded. "Their potency fades with time. That's why we have to reapply. By the time this gets to the people eating it, most of the pesticides are long gone."

"Most?"

"That's why we encourage people to wash their veggies. The EPA tests the produce to make sure the levels are safe." He finished his maintenance check on the machine and turned to Clive. "I've got to start spraying. Listen, keep an eye on Jose. He keeps wandering off. I've given him two warnings already. One more and he's gone."

Clive nodded and started toward the fields. The work out here wasn't easy, but Clive's conversations with the workers suggested that they didn't mind it. They worked hard, grateful for the opportunity. It beat the nothing that many of them had left behind.

Clive had discovered that many sent a good chunk of their earnings to support relatives back home. They had a strong sense of family like that.

That's why Jorge, Felipe, and Lucia's disappearances had such a huge impact on everyone. He could feel it in the air today, a sense of mourning that hadn't been there earlier.

Clive walked the rows of fields for three hours until finally it was time for everyone's lunch break. Clive knew he had a brief window of opportunity.

He remembered Ernie's comment about the original house on the property. He wanted to find it. He'd found a picture on Lauren's phone of an old house, and he'd spent hours driving up and down these roads trying to locate the place, to no avail. Now he wondered if the house could be the one right here on Landon's property. It would be the perfect place to hide something. Maybe even to hide someone. Plus, he'd seen someone in the woods. Leonard, maybe? Savannah had described him as having purple hair . . .

At this point, every lead was worth checking out.

He ducked into the woods. He didn't have time to walk through them all, but he knew that if he did, he'd end up at Savannah's. He also knew from looking at old maps of the area that the old house was closer to Landon's side of the woods than Savannah's.

When he was sure no one was looking, he slipped between the trees. He moved quickly, looking for a sign of what used to be.

Finally he reached a clearing. In the distance he saw an old house, battered and weathered with age. Behind it was an old barn. Overgrown weeds surrounded the structures, and someone had used it as a dumping ground over the years. There was a washer and dryer, an abandoned boat, and more tires. Tires seemed to be plentiful out here.

This was it. The house from Lauren's picture.

He took a step closer and glanced at his watch. He had to get back; half of his break was up. But at least now he knew it was here. And it was the perfect spot to hide something.

When he had the chance, he'd return.

CHAPTER 41

Savannah shifted in her seat at the local diner. Bobbi had called this morning asking to meet her. She had something she wanted to share, but Savannah couldn't imagine what it might be.

Finally Bobbi walked in, cast a weary smile her way, and slid into the booth across from her. The waitress placed a plate in front of Savannah with a cheeseburger and fries. She shrugged at Bobbi.

"I couldn't resist."

Bobbi smiled. "You know, I think I'll have one, too."

The waitress nodded and walked away.

Bobbi leaned across the table toward her. "I heard you had a rough day yesterday. You didn't go cow tipping, did you?"

Savannah didn't try to stop the billowing laugh that escaped from her. She was glad for the unexpected break in tension. "Something like that, only not quite cows." *High-powered national leaders instead.*

"Tom said you had a friend with you?"

Savannah's humor disappeared. Was this about Clive? "That's right. He's my boarder, actually, but we've struck up a friendship."

"That's nice." Bobbi shifted. "That's not why I asked you to meet with me, actually."

In record time, the waitress brought Bobbi her food. She excused herself to pray for a moment.

Bobbi said amen and then nodded toward Savannah's food. "Why don't you dig in? I have a few minutes. You?"

Savannah nodded, trying to squelch her curiosity. Her rumbling stomach made the final decision. "Sure."

"Someone stopped by La Tierra Prometida yesterday. His name was Leonard, and he said he was a friend of Marti's."

"Her boyfriend," Savannah corrected.

Bobbi raised her eyebrows. "I didn't realize . . ."

Savannah shrugged. "I didn't either. I found his name on Marti's calendar and called him."

"I've seen him around before."

Savannah's curiosity was piqued. "Really?"

"In fact, I saw him last week. With that purple streak in his hair, it's hard to miss him, especially in a small town like this."

"Last week? That can't be right. He said he was in Colorado last week."

Bobbi lowered her burger onto the platter. "I'm certain I saw him. He was at the grocery store."

Savannah's instincts went on full alert. If Leonard wasn't in Colorado last week, and if he was in town . . . could he have had something to do with Marti's so-called suicide attempt?

It was a possibility she was going to have to face. That one little piece of information changed everything.

CHAPTER 42

"I know you've been concerned with everything going on over at the migrant camp," Bobbi started. "And there might not be any connection here, but I thought it was worth mentioning."

She pushed her plate away, and Savannah knew that whatever she was about to say would be heavy. Bobbi seemed to be struggling with her words.

"Six years ago, one of my colleagues suspected that something was going on in the bay. Specifically, she thought that chemicals were being dumped there."

"Why did she think that?"

"We were having a high number of fish kills."

Interesting, Savannah thought. But what did this have to do with the migrant camp?

"We took samples and found high levels of some unusual chemicals. But all of our research disappeared."

"Disappeared?"

Bobbi nodded. "It was there one day; the next day it was gone. We contacted authorities, but they didn't take us seriously. They insisted that these things happened simply as a part of nature."

"Bureaucrats questioned the marine biologists?"

Bobbi let out a bitter laugh. "It's true. My friend wouldn't let it go, though. She pushed and pushed. She just knew something corrupt was going on."

"What happened?"

"She's the one who died. Murdered by her husband."

"That's terrible. I remember you mentioning her to me."

"It was a huge loss for the community. She was doing great work. She truly loved her job."

"Did the fish kills continue?"

"No, that's the strange part. They stopped. So I let it drop. Damage had already been done, but at least something changed. Tom didn't want me to push too much."

"Why? Were you making people mad?"

Bobbi drew in a deep breath. "I always suspected Lauren's husband might have been wrongly accused. I always wondered if someone killed her to stop her research and then framed her husband. I don't know. Something about it always bothered me. Even though she and her husband didn't get along great and were working through some things, I never got the impression he was violent or short-tempered."

"You met him?"

She shook her head. "No, we never had the opportunity to get together."

Savannah leaned closer. "That's interesting, Bobbi, but what does it have to do with what's happening now?"

"You're going to think I'm crazy. But I keep wondering if there's something on the farm that's making the migrant workers sick. Their rate of cancer is high. Plus other ailments seem to be constantly cropping up, namely breathing problems and nausea."

"Landon provides lunch for them every day, doesn't he? You think he's putting something in their food?"

Bobbi stared at her hands—her fingers rubbed together nervously on the table—and shook her head. "I don't know. I just think it's strange. Maybe it's nothing. Maybe it's the conditions they're living in. Maybe it's genetic."

"Their water? Could it be their water?"

"I have no idea, Savannah. I just thought it might be worth mentioning. I know Marti noticed, too. She worked hard to get Richard Lawson to come out to the migrant camp to offer free clinics and home visits. She didn't want anyone to suffer."

"I'll see what I can find out, Bobbi."

"Do me the biggest favor of all, though. Be careful."

. . .

Savannah's hand hovered over her computer keys.

Leonard was coming to her house. What if he wasn't who he claimed to be? What if he had something to do with Marti's coma?

Something wasn't adding up, and he had too many connections to lingering questions.

She glanced at her watch. She still had twenty minutes before he was supposed to be here.

Quickly she typed in his name and the Madden Society.

Pages of results popped up.

She read the most recent posting. It was a blog.

"Confirmed: The Madden Society met at Congressman Perkin's house yesterday. Confirmed members in attendance include Landon Kavanagh and Dr. Richard Lawson."

Savannah gasped.

Leonard had used the information she gave him to run what was the beginning of an exposé.

Maybe this wasn't about Marti at all. Maybe Leonard had had hidden motives this whole time.

She closed her eyes as facts began colliding inside her head.

Marti hadn't told anyone about her boyfriend. Savannah had thought the whole time that Marti liked Richard Lawson anyway.

Marti also hadn't told Savannah about being attacked. The only reason she'd told Bobbi was because Bobbi had seen a bruise.

What if Marti hadn't been trying to hide everything from Savannah?

What if . . . ?

"I'm sorry you had to see that, Savannah," said a voice from behind her.

She gasped and whirled around.

Leonard stood there, his hands shoved into his pockets.

"The back door was unlocked. I didn't mean to scare you."

She stood and backed against the wall. "I didn't hear your car."

"I got here earlier. I parked out back and explored the property a little bit. I didn't think you'd mind."

"I do. I do mind."

He stepped closer. "It's not what you think."

She glanced at her desk, looking for something to defend herself with. In this case, the pen wasn't mightier than the sword. "Then why don't you explain? You weren't really Marti's boyfriend. You beat her up, didn't you?"

"It's not like it sounds." He inched closer, his face twisted.

"Stay where you are. Don't come any closer."

His shoulders sagged. "Please, let me explain."

"Please do." She pressed herself into the window.

"We did meet online. We both had a love for conspiracy theories. Eventually we met in person. We both were obsessed with the Madden Society. We thought it would be fun to bust them, to make those rich guys realize they weren't untouchable."

"But . . ." Savannah knew there was more coming.

"Marti got distracted. She had other things to do, she said. But we were so close."

"So you beat her up? Caused her to fall into depression?"

"No! It wasn't like that. We had a disagreement. I grabbed her, trying to get her to listen. I knew I could convince her. We were so close to discovering the truth. But she said she had other matters to attend to. Things that were more important."

He ran a hand through his hair and sighed, his body tight and his breathing heavy.

"I told her fine, and I pushed her away, trying to show I didn't care. I pushed too hard, and she stumbled back into a table. She cracked her head. I knew I'd hurt her, but I didn't mean to. You've got to believe me."

"And then you wouldn't leave her alone? Did you stalk her?"

"No, I just tried to apologize. She didn't want anything to do with me. I think her secret project was really bothering her."

"Maybe you were the one bothering her." Savannah's fingers inched closer to the phone in her pocket. If Leonard attacked, she wouldn't have enough time to pull it out and dial.

But she did have scissors on her desk. If she could only grab them . . .

"I don't know. I just know she changed."

"When you hurt someone, that's what happens."

"It was an accident!" His nostrils flared.

Words, Savannah. You have a way with words. Use them now. "What are you doing here right now, Leonard?"

"I just want to bust these guys."

"You lied to me, Leonard. I don't trust people who lie to me."

"Please."

Savannah could see the touch of crazy in his eyes. Talking was doing no good right now. Quickly she snatched the scissors from the cup holder on her desk. She aimed them at him. "Stay back, Leonard."

"I only want answers. Like any good journalist. You understand that."

"I wouldn't hurt someone I cared about to get a story." As soon as the words left her lips, she realized the lie in them. She'd hurt her husband and baby in the ultimate way. They'd been killed because of her.

Before she could explore the thought further, Leonard darted toward the back door.

Then he was gone.

•   •   •

Savannah considered calling the police. But she wasn't sure what good that would do, and aside from being creepy, he hadn't done anything to her. Still, she couldn't stop looking out the window, watching for him.

Where was his car? She didn't see it anywhere, even though he'd said he parked at the back of her property.

And where was Clive? She knew he was working today, but she really wanted to share all of this with him.

What if there was something to what Bobbi had said? What if somehow the migrant workers' food or water was being contaminated or, even worse, poisoned? But wouldn't Dr. Lawson see the connection if that was the case? And what purpose would it serve? And who would be behind something like that?

The most likely person who came to mind was Landon. His name was coming up way too often for her comfort.

She glanced at her watch. She didn't want to stay in the house any longer. She had too much on her mind.

She found herself driving back to the hospital. Maybe she would run into Dr. Lawson there, and she'd be able to ask him a few questions. Maybe he'd seen some symptoms of contamination or poisoning in the workers he examined.

She stopped in front of his office as voices drifted out. He was talking to the nurse. What was her name again? Melinda. That was it.

"I don't like all of these secrets," Melinda whispered.

"We don't have any choice," Dr. Lawson responded. "There's a lot at risk here."

"It just seems so wrong."

"Not much longer. Just remember that."

Savannah ducked around the corner when she heard the door opening. Her heart was pounding. What were they talking about?

She needed to corner the nurse and ask her. She was more likely to talk than Dr. Lawson.

She waited behind a vending machine until she saw Dr. Lawson walk past. As soon as he was out of sight, she composed herself and headed toward Marti's room. Melinda was inside.

The nurse looked up in surprise. "Savannah. Wasn't expecting to see you again today."

"Marti's been on my mind. I just wanted to see her."

"She's hanging in. Her brain activity is still good, which is a positive sign. I really think she's going to pull through this."

Savannah shifted in the doorway. "Melinda, I have to ask you something."

The nurse paused, her skin paling. "Okay."

"What's going on between you and Dr. Lawson? And don't tell me nothing. I've nearly walked in on two conversations now that indicate something is wrong."

She shook her head. "It's not what you think."

"You have no idea what I'm thinking. I'm thinking about Jorge."

Melinda's eyebrows knit together. "Jorge? Who's Jorge?"

"The man who was found dead on the side of the road yesterday."

She gasped. "Dead?"

"Murdered, most likely."

"No. I think you've got this all wrong." Her voice sounded brittle.

"Then correct me. Please. Because I'm not one to give up. If you don't let me know, I'm just going to dig on my own. And I might not use as much discretion."

Melinda stared beyond Savannah, into the hallway. "Close the door."

Savannah clicked it shut behind her, anxiety creeping in. "Closed."

Still, Melinda lowered her voice. "Dr. Lawson and I have been seeing each other."

"That's it? What's so secretive about that?"

"My husband and I are in the middle of a divorce. If he found out about Richard and me, he'd claim we've been seeing each other for longer than we actually have. The judge could rule in his favor, and I can't let that happen."

"How long have you been seeing each other?"

"Three months."

So Dr. Lawson had been leading Marti on? He was obviously keeping secrets, and they reflected poorly on his character. But not murderously so.

"Please don't tell anyone."

Savannah nodded. "I won't."

"I've got to check on my other patients."

Savannah watched her walk away, her head pounding.

She wasn't ready to give up yet, though. If Dr. Lawson was just hiding an affair, if that's all he was guilty of, maybe he'd be willing to talk about the migrant workers and their health. It was worth a shot.

She kissed Marti's forehead and then slipped back into the hallway. A moment later, she knocked at his door, and he called for her to come in.

"Savannah. Fancy seeing you here again."

Her opinion of the doctor had gone down some, especially in light of the fact that he'd been leading Marti on. She pushed those thoughts aside and put on a pleasant facade. For the greater good, she told herself.

"I have a question for you. Do you have a minute?"

He glanced at his watch. "Only a minute."

"Have you noticed any of the migrant workers getting sick? I mean like a common theme, a lot of the residents coming down with the same ailments?"

His eyes narrowed with thought. "I can't say I have. Why would you ask?"

"I received a tip that something is going on."

"That's pretty vague, Savannah."

She leaned forward, making the decision to share more than she'd planned. "I think someone is sabotaging the workers' food or water supply."

"That's a big accusation, Savannah."

"I know it sounds crazy. But you're over there once a week. Have you seen anything?"

He tapped his fingers together. "I have noticed a trend of stomach problems. Do you think that's related?"

"It could be. I also heard there's been a high number of cancer diagnoses. The disease crosses all barriers—gender, race, economic, cultural."

"There's a huge number of cancer diagnoses everywhere, not just in the migrant camp."

She couldn't argue with that. "I was wondering if you might want to check into the other ailments. I don't know who else to ask."

He nodded. "I'm not sure there's anything to it. But I'll see what I can find out when I go to the migrant camp again. I'll check for similar symptoms."

"I appreciate that. And if you could keep this quiet, that'd be great. I'm not sure who to trust yet."

"Understood."

Savannah stood to leave when Dr. Lawson called her name. She paused.

"I think it's honorable what you're doing, just to let you know. Marti would be proud."

Savannah smiled. "Thank you."

CHAPTER 43

Back at home, Savannah spent a while on the shore, reflecting on everything she'd learned, until the sun started to sink low. It was useless to try to make sense of it all. If there were dots to be connected, she felt incapable of the task. She needed a good night's rest to settle her mind. Maybe in the morning she'd see things more clearly.

Up in her dimly lit bedroom, Savannah changed into a white T-shirt and her pajama pants. She couldn't wait to fall into bed.

Tiger! she remembered.

Had she fed Tiger today? She'd check and then go to bed. She already knew the next day would be a long one.

She padded downstairs. Where was Tiger? Usually he was at her feet every moment. Perhaps he'd found a nice little niche somewhere and was curled up sleeping. She added food to his bowl, clicked off the kitchen light, and climbed the staircase. He was probably just asleep.

The house felt so big at night, as if it had much more space than she needed, with too many dark corners and empty rooms. She should have thought of that before she purchased it, but she'd given in to whimsy. It was funny, the things people tried to fill themselves with, hoping to feel better.

She'd realized some time ago that her dream of a big house meant nothing without a family to fill it. Clive's image briefly flashed through her mind. What would it be like to have a family with him? He was willing to take risks. He wasn't willing to leave well enough alone. Yet guilt still gnawed at her, a prison in its own right. She didn't deserve happiness. The reminders were coming with less frequency lately, but they still rang true.

She sighed and turned off the hall light. As she stepped into her bedroom, she paused. Why did something feel different?

She scanned the room. Everything appeared in place. She must just be paranoid.

As she moved toward her bed, something leapt at her. She gasped and flew back. Tiger stared at her from the bed, his fur raised, hissing. He must have jumped out of the closet.

"Tiger!" An airy laugh escaped as she picked him up. "You shouldn't do that to me."

As she cuddled him to her chest, she sensed movement behind her. Before she could turn, a hand clamped over her mouth. An arm locked around her midsection, paralyzing her. She struggled, to no avail. The intruder—a male, she was sure—had a grip of steel. He pinned her against him, and she felt something sharp at her neck. A knife. She stopped struggling, fearing the blade would pierce her skin if she made the wrong movement.

Electrified silence surrounded her.

Savannah was keenly aware of the man's heart beating calmly against her back, as if being in her home was just another day at the office.

"I've got a message for you," he whispered, his unfamiliar voice hoarse but measured.

The feel of his breath through her hair made Savannah's stomach churn.

"If you don't want to get hurt, you'll stop asking questions and mind your own business. I won't warn you again. Understand?"

When she didn't respond quickly enough, he repeated, "Understand?"

She nodded, fear trickling into every bone, her very breath.

A knock came from downstairs. Savannah tensed. Who could be here?

"Expecting someone?"

She shook her head.

The knock sounded again. "Savannah? It's me, Clive. The light's on inside your car. I don't want your battery to die."

Savannah's heart raced even faster, if that was possible. She hoped he wouldn't be hurt, that this intruder wouldn't go after him.

"Pretend you're not here," he ordered.

But Clive knew she was home. He'd seen her car. Was he the nosy type who would try to find her, make sure she was okay? Or would he go away when she didn't come to the door?

"Savannah?" The knob on her back door jingled.

"Go downstairs and give him the car keys. Mention anything about me, and I'll finish off your friend Marti. Got it?"

Savannah's head spun.

"Got it?" He pressed the knife into her throat until she nodded.

"Go down the back stairs so he can't see us."

The back stairs? This man knew a lot about her life. He'd done research to know the layout of her home. Chills raced down her spine.

"Savannah?" Clive called.

Slowly they moved down the stairs. One wrong move and that knife would slice her skin. It could destroy even more than her flesh—her bones, her organs, her life.

She walked carefully, terrified of making a wrong move.

"Tell him you're coming," the intruder demanded.

"Coming!" Her voice was just above a whisper. She cleared her throat. "Coming!" That time it sounded louder.

"Remember, one wrong move and—" The knife pressed harder.

Savannah nodded. He released her, and she tried to compose herself as she walked to the door, but her hip bumped into an end table. Ella's rattle fell onto the floor.

She gasped, wanting to pick it up. But she couldn't. Not now.

At the back door, her hands fumbled with the lock. Finally the knob twisted. She cracked open the door and saw Clive standing on the other side, peering in at her.

He grinned devilishly. "I just got home and saw the light on inside your car. I didn't want your battery to die."

Savannah nodded and tried to keep her voice even. "I appreciate it. I'll turn it off in a minute, as soon as I finish what I'm doing."

"Don't be ridiculous. Hand me your keys, and I'll do it for you." He shrugged. "Plus, I have to admit that I wanted to see you again."

She was keenly aware that the intruder was watching. "That— that would be . . . great. Thank you." She reached for the keys, but her hand trembled so much that she could barely hold them. She slipped them through the crack, hoping Clive hadn't noticed.

His eyes narrowed, all sparkle gone. "Are you okay, Savannah?"

She nodded. "Just tired."

The slits became even narrower. "Are you sure?"

"It's been a long day. I'm headed to bed. I'll just pick up my car keys from you tomorrow. Is that okay?"

He swung her key ring around his finger, studying her with thoughtful eyes. "Sure thing. Whatever's easiest for you."

His gaze lingered another moment before he turned and headed down the back porch steps. Slowly she closed the door and turned, expecting to see the intruder with his knife.

No one. Nothing.

She backed against the door. Fear pricked her. Where had he gone?

Her eyes scanned the room. She didn't dare move for fear he'd be on her again. Where was he waiting, trying to make sure Clive was gone before he reappeared? Was he planning what else he'd do to her before he left? Maybe pop a few pills into her, just as he had with Marti?

Run. She could run. Open the back door and go as fast as her legs would take her.

But he'd threatened her best friend . . .

"Savannah?" Clive's voice came from the front of her house now. Based on the volume of his voice, he was inside. A moment later he appeared in the opening to the kitchen. His gaze stopped on her. "Why's your front door open?"

The intruder must have left while she talked. Relief flushed through her.

"Savannah?"

She propelled herself from the doorway into Clive's arms.

"What's going on, Savannah? Are you okay?" His voice sounded urgent.

She started to share and thought twice about it. First she needed to take another look around. Make sure they were alone.

Her gaze wandered the crevices of the house, the shadows. She saw no one.

"Savannah?"

Her gaze snapped back to Clive. "I . . . there's . . ." A picture of Marti flashed in her head. Dear, sweet Marti.

"You look like you've seen a ghost."

"There was . . ." She sucked in a deep breath and squeezed her arms more tightly around her chest. "There was a man in my house. In my bedroom." She remembered the feel of his gloved hand over her mouth. The smell of the outdoors on his clothing. "Oh my gosh."

At that instant, her gaze was drawn to the floor. Ella's rattle.

It had been crushed into uncountable pieces. The intruder must have stomped on it when he left. Tears rushed from her eyes, spilling down her cheeks.

She sank to the floor as reality hit. Clive caught her, pulled her back up with a firm grip on her arms.

"When was he here?" he demanded.

She tried to get the rattle out of her mind. "He was here when you came to the door. He must have snuck out the front while we talked."

Something flashed in his eyes. Anger maybe. "You need to call the police, Savannah."

She shook her head. "No! I can't. I can't. He said he'll kill Marti if I do."

"Savannah . . ."

"Marti . . ."

"What about Marti?"

"He said he'd finish her off."

.   .   .

Savannah closed the door after Chief Lockwood left. She'd given him the full report, Clive staying by her side the entire time. His presence was an immense comfort. If she believed God cared, she would think He'd sent Clive as a boarder.

Clive stepped close to her and rubbed her arm. "You did great. It was the right thing to tell the chief."

Savannah nodded, running a hand through her hair. "Thanks." She stepped back, her head pounding. "Let me put some tea on. Tea makes everything better."

Clive's hand remained on her back as they walked into the kitchen. He leaned against the counter while she filled a kettle and put it on the stove. "Thank you, Clive, for everything. I'm really glad you're in the guesthouse."

"So am I." He took a step closer, his eyes dead serious, concerned. "I don't like this, Savannah."

"I don't like it either."

One minute they were staring at each other, the next minute, she was in Clive's arms. Her head nestled under his chin. Being so close to him felt way too easy, too natural.

And for the first time in years, she felt protected, sheltered, grounded. She drank in each inch of his strength, savoring the moment, soaking in the scent of his leathery cologne, the vague yet strangely compelling odor of sawdust.

She still couldn't be sure how it happened, but his lips touched hers. Gently they mingled. Savannah's body came alive as some kind of longing she didn't realize she had surfaced. Passion stirred inside fiercely. She wrapped her arms around his neck as the kiss deepened. He responded with equal passion, longing.

What was she doing?

As quickly as the kiss began, it ended. Savannah pulled away and scooted back until she hit the kitchen counter behind her. She had to look away from Clive, away from the smokiness of his gaze.

"I shouldn't have done that," she mumbled. Her finger clamped over her mouth. She could still feel the excitement of his lips rushing over hers.

He stepped toward her. "Why not?"

Some unseen connection seemed to pull her toward him, as if it were out of her control. "A million reasons," she whispered.

"Because you're afraid."

"Afraid of what?" Her heart raced.

"Afraid you might actually start believing in something again." He stopped in front of her, trapping her against the counter.

"I'm not afraid of believing. I'm more afraid of never believing again."

He stooped down until their lips met again, unrestrained, hungry.

The teakettle whistled. Savannah let it.

CHAPTER 44

Savannah awoke the next morning to the sound of someone's fist slamming repeatedly on the door. She glanced at her alarm clock. 6:30. Who could possibly be here at this hour?

She swung her legs out of bed, slipped on her robe, and hurried downstairs. As she rounded the bottom of the staircase, she spotted Clive sitting up on the couch and pulling on his shirt. She didn't let her gaze linger, no matter how much she wanted to.

The rap at the door came more quickly. She glanced out of the window and spotted a familiar pickup truck.

Pulling her robe more tightly around her, she opened the door. Landon Kavanagh stood on the other side.

"Savannah, are you okay? I heard about what happened last night—" He stopped, his gaze locked on something—or someone—behind her.

Savannah gripped the door handle and squeezed her lips together. Landon's gaze came back to hers, accusation—or was it concern?—written there.

"What's going on?"

"This is . . ." She glanced behind her at Clive with his tousled hair, his hands on his hips. Instantly she remembered the feel of his lips on hers and felt blood rush to her cheeks. More so, she knew exactly how this looked. "This is . . . the boarder I was telling you about."

"Landon." Clive nodded.

Landon scowled. "When you said boarder, I assumed you meant he was staying in the guesthouse, not with you."

Clive moved closer behind her, and Savannah knew she had to act fast.

"He's not staying with me."

The tension between the two men was palpable. She knew she had to get away from Clive, from that magnetic pull she felt toward him.

She cleared her throat. "Excuse us, Clive." She slipped through the door and closed it behind her, ready to face Landon alone on the porch.

Landon's eyes remained on the front door, as if he could still see Clive on the other side. Finally he looked at her again, the disapproval on his face softening. "The chief told me what happened last night. Are you okay?"

She folded her arms over her chest and nodded. "I'm fine now. It was a rough night, though."

Landon's gaze flicked to the front door again, no doubt to where he assumed Clive stood on the other side. "Yeah, I bet it was."

"It wasn't like that, Landon. He slept on the couch. Understandably, as I was frightened."

"You should have called me. You could have stayed at my place. You know my house is plenty big."

"I appreciate that, Landon. I do know that I can always count on you."

Silence stood between them.

Landon shifted. "Do they have any idea how the intruder broke in?"

"No idea."

"Any signed of forced entry?"

"No."

His look of concern was quickly replaced by anger. "Why would someone threaten you? Do you know who it was? What happened?"

"Landon, I don't think Marti tried to commit suicide. I think someone tried to kill her and make it look like suicide."

"That doesn't make sense, Savannah. You know Marti. She's—"

"Don't say it. She's spirited. She'd never try to end her own life."

"Who would try to kill her? She helps people for a living. You think this goes back to the migrant workers getting sick?"

Savannah kept her features even. But she'd never mentioned that theory to Landon before. So where had he heard it? Lucia, maybe?

"How do you know about the workers getting sick?"

He frowned. "I own the farm, Savannah. I try to keep up with these things. I've heard the scuttlebutt. I've upped our safety procedures, encouraged them to wash their hands and take more breaks and drink more water."

She forced a smile. "Good. I'm glad you're watching out for them."

He grimaced. "I don't like this. I don't like you staying here."

"I'll be careful."

"You know I care about you, Savannah." His voice softened, and he rubbed her arm with his thumb.

"I know, Landon. I'm just not ready for a relationship yet." As the words left her lips, she remembered the kiss from last night. Her lips tingled at the thought, but she quickly dismissed the mental replay. Last night had meant nothing. It was nothing more than a kiss shared by two grieving people.

"I'll wait for you until you are, you know. I've always known, from the moment I met you, that there was something special about you."

·   ·   ·

By the time Savannah stepped back inside, Clive was gone. She wished the realization didn't cause her heart to feel a little cooler. She walked to the dining room and shoved the curtains aside in time to see an old F150 rumbling down the driveway. Without asking any questions, Tom had let Clive borrow the vehicle to get to and from work. The truck was probably twenty years old, had terrible shocks and faded blue paint, but at least Clive had something to drive.

Just where was he going? There was still so much she didn't know about him.

She dropped the curtain. She had more important things to do today than ponder Clive's life. In a few months, he'd be gone. She couldn't afford to get involved, even in a fling. She had to put some distance between them. And she had more important things to occupy her thoughts, such as figuring out who'd tried to kill Marti, who'd threatened her, and why.

She was determined to get to the bottom of it.

Savannah shivered. Her house felt cold. She glanced around her office. Would she ever feel safe in her house again?

Last night flashed back into her mind, and her throat tightened. Fear rose, just as real as it had been hours earlier.

Calm down, Savannah. Calm down. Take a deep breath. There's no one in your house now.

She closed her eyes, tried to calm herself down. When her heart started beating at a steadier rhythm, she allowed herself to ask the hard questions. How exactly had the intruder gotten in? How long had he been hiding in her closet? And what would have happened if Clive hadn't come to the door when he did?

She shuddered. She couldn't think about it. Maybe the police would have some answers for her soon.

She must have hit on a nerve for someone to feel threatened enough to come into her house and warn her to be quiet. So that meant she was getting close to some of those elusive answers, right? But what exactly had been the magic area that caused someone to react this way?

As she replayed the events from the last several days in her head, one stood out. The Madden Society.

She started upstairs to her room when something caught her eye. She paused by her desk.

It was Ella's baby rattle. The pieces had been glued back together. Clive. *Clive* had done this for her.

She smiled.

She closed her eyes and held the rattle to her chest a moment, thankful that he'd attempted such a task. But deep inside, she knew it would never be the same.

"Ella, your momma loved you," she whispered. "I'm so sorry I couldn't protect you like I should have."

She looked at it again through bleary eyes, shaking it back and forth. Then she stopped.

There was no longer the sound of a lone bead circling the inside. It must have fallen out when the rattle was smashed. Her heart thudded in her ears. If she believed in symbolism, she would see this as a sign. Maybe it was time to stop isolating herself in a prison of her doing.

Carefully she placed the rattle back on the desk. It was time to move on, as hard as that would be.

She got dressed. She came back downstairs and found her car keys in the kitchen. Since the morning was chilly, she pointed the keys toward the back porch door and hit the remote start button.

That's when an explosion sounded outside.

She ran to the window and saw that her car was on fire.

CHAPTER 45

The chief came to her house for the second time in twelve hours, along with a fire truck and an ambulance. They spent the first hour putting out the flames and investigating both the car and the area surrounding it. Finally the police chief stomped onto her porch to get an official statement.

"Any idea why someone is targeting you?" he asked.

She shook her head, wishing more than anything that she had the answer to that question. She felt numb, in shock, dazed. "Not really."

He asked a few more questions, took some notes. Finally his eyes met hers again. "I promise to make this a priority."

She sensed he was wrapping up the conversation, and something ignited inside her. What good were the police if they couldn't protect her? They needed to do more than make this a priority—they needed to figure this out, and they needed to figure it out now.

With every act of indecency, her anger—righteous, in her eyes—began to grow. Maybe this was the time to ask the chief about her suspicions, to stop holding back. Really, she had nothing to lose.

"Did you ever get the results back on that blood found in my guesthouse?"

He puckered his lips thoughtfully. "I haven't heard back yet. I'll follow up on that."

"What about the paper Marti's note was written on? Did you check to see if it was printed at her house, on her printer?"

He nodded slowly. "I did send it in to be tested. We haven't gotten the results back yet. I'm afraid this may not be a priority at the state crime lab, especially since all signs point to Marti as an attempted suicide."

"If it's not attempted suicide, then you're letting a killer walk the streets right now."

"I think you're getting ahead of yourself now, Ms. Harris."

She swallowed hard, trying to keep her emotions in check. "Chief, is it true you own some of the property where the migrant workers live?"

He nodded slowly, something flickering in his gaze. "I do."

"Have you been inside and seen the conditions?"

He remained silent a moment, amazingly nonplused. "I haven't been inside for a while. Why? Is everything okay?"

"There are too many people living there and in squalid conditions." She remembered how Señor Lopez's house had looked, recalled the smell, the sense of hopelessness that seemed to permeate the very walls of the place.

"Well, Ms. Harris, I set the ground rules, and I expect my tenants to obey them. They don't always stick to them."

"So you turn a blind eye to it? Would you do that if the property wasn't your own?"

He stared at her another moment. "I try to cut them some slack. I know their lives aren't easy. Affordable housing is a necessity."

"So are sanitary conditions."

He sighed. "If it makes you feel better, I'll look into it."

Just then Clive's truck squealed to a stop, and he ran to the porch, concern on his face. "What happened?"

Before Savannah could answer, the chief excused himself, insisting he'd be in touch. Had he just used Clive's arrival as a reason to avoid her questions? Was he hiding something as well?

"Savannah?" Clive asked.

Savannah snapped back to the present. "I used my remote start to warm up my car. As soon as the ignition turned, the car . . . blew up." She shuddered.

"They must have left the light on. It was the only reason I stopped by last night."

She nodded. "Thankfully you didn't have to start my car to turn the light off."

Clive pulled her into a hug. "I'm sorry, Savannah. You're handling all of this extremely well, I have to say."

"I don't know if I'd say 'well.' But thanks for the vote of confidence. Honestly, this whole thing has shaken me up. It's brought back too many memories of . . ."

"Of Ella?"

He'd remembered her name. Something about that comforted Savannah immensely. She nodded.

"Yes, Ella. I'll never forget that night." It flashed back to her, each detail painful and real. "I was still fuming over a disagreement with Reid, my mind was racing over whether or not the FBI would press charges against the sheriff, and I was trying to figure out if I could find a sitter for Ella so I could track down one more lead." She shook her head. "There was always one more lead."

Clive squeezed her arm.

"That's when I heard the explosion. I ran to the window, and the car was in flames. I ran outside and tried to pull Ella out. It was no use. I couldn't get close enough to the car. So I lay there in my front yard in shock as I watched the car burn. It was one of the first times in my life I felt totally helpless."

He pulled her into a tight hug. "I'm so sorry, Savannah."

"Whoever did this knew about that night."

"You think it's connected?"

She shook her head. "No, I don't. But I think someone's done their research. I don't actually think he wanted to kill me. I think he knows my routine, knows that I always use remote start. This is just one more way to send me a message, to tell me to back off."

"Are you going to?"

"I've come too far. I'm not giving up now. Not when Lucia could still be out there. Not when more people could be getting hurt."

He kissed her forehead. "Good for you. I think you're brave, Savannah."

Warmth spread through her heart at his affirmation. "Thank you."

She stepped back, their talk giving her the strength to continue with her day. Her heart still felt heavy, but she was ready to dig in, to get dirty.

She stared at the heap that used to be her car. "I guess I need to rethink my plans for the day."

"What do you need? I can help you out."

"I don't even know what I need. My insurance company will probably get me a rental, but they haven't cleared it yet."

"I actually had an idea for today. Something I wanted to check out. Will you go with me?"

She looked up at the glorious features of his face, thinking about how she could look into those green eyes forever. "Will it bring me any closer to the answers?"

"I'm hoping. But to be honest, this could be a red herring."

"We'll never know unless we check it out, right?"

"You're going to want to tuck your hair into a hat again." He smiled slightly. "Ticks."

Twenty minutes later, Savannah was ready. She held back her surprise when Clive took her hand and pulled her toward the woods. "Really?"

"You'll see. But it's going to be a hike."

"I've always wanted to explore the woods by my property."

"You're about to get your chance."

They stepped into the trees, and Savannah pointed. "Looks like a trail. Someone's walked through here before."

Clive squatted, examining the trampled underbrush. "Savannah, it almost looks like someone's been using this trail recently."

"Why would you say that?"

"These weeds are new, yet they're crushed."

Savannah shivered. "Who'd be going to and from these woods?"

He looked up at her, dead serious. "That's an excellent question." He stood and took her hand again. "Let's see where this trail leads."

They'd only taken several steps when Savannah spotted something that made her blood go cold. She pulled Clive to a stop and pointed to a tree.

"What is it?"

"There. On the ground. Flattened pennies."

CHAPTER 46

"Are you sure you want to keep going?" Clive asked Savannah. Her skin had gone pale, and he could feel the trembling of her hand.

She nodded, climbing over a fallen tree. "Yeah, I'm sure. I want to know what's going on."

He admired the determination in her gaze. Most people would have run and hidden by now. "Okay. Let's go then."

They continued to tramp through the woods. Clive held her hand as they maneuvered around trees and puddles and underbrush.

"You weren't kidding when you said this was going to be quite the hike," Savannah muttered.

"Not much farther." If he was right, they were maybe ten minutes from the house.

"You're not taking me to Landon's property, are you?"

"Officially, yes. But not the cultivated portion."

"You've got me curious."

"Speaking of Landon's farm, it seems like a lot of the things going on lead back to his place. What's his most valuable resource there?"

"His workers?" Savannah asked.

He smiled. The fact that she'd thought first of people said a lot about her character. "Not in this case. It's the new hybrid apple he developed. He's spent hundreds of thousands to develop it."

"Okay . . ."

"If someone got their hands on his formula, he could lose all that money."

"You think all of this is because of an apple?"

Clive shrugged. "Not necessarily. But the money involved in that one crop might be enough for some people to want to murder to keep the formula safe. What if the migrant workers who disappeared are the ones who walked into the middle of something? Some kind of backhanded deal that no one was supposed to see?"

"It's something I haven't thought about before."

"I'm not saying I'm right. But maybe this is a start."

"Does it have anything to do with this little hike?"

"Maybe. There are some secluded buildings on Landon's property. They're not in use anymore, but I saw some boats going to and from them one night."

"Is that really what you were doing on the bay?"

He smiled. "Partly. I'm just wondering if something's happening out there."

"It's worth looking into."

The forest looked lighter ahead, and Clive wondered if this was where the clearing was. He hoped so. They quickened their steps until they reached the area where the trees thinned.

"Wow." Savannah stood on the edge of the woods, staring at what was before her. "It's like something that time left behind."

Clive nodded. "This used to be the original home of the property owner."

"From the street, you can't even tell anything was ever here."

"The woods have overgrown the area in front of the house. There used to be a street, but it was plowed under and became part of the fields."

"How do you know all that?"

"I went to the library."

Savannah let out a small chuckle. "Good for you."

"Want to check it out?"

"Do I ever."

Though the trees had cleared, the underbrush grew thicker as they walked toward the house. Clive noted that he didn't see any signs that people had been here recently, and he frowned. That didn't fit with his theory that someone was using this property.

"Let me check out the porch first. This place is rickety." Clive climbed the wooden steps, noting the give of each board. This place was a pit. It had been beautiful at one time, probably a place full of love and laughter.

Look at it now.

Look at *Clive* now.

It was amazing how time could batter both structures and lives and turn them into something unrecognizable. Of course, with the proper care and attention, he supposed even old and storm-weathered properties could become beautiful again.

He turned to Savannah. "Come on up. Just watch that middle step."

He reached out to give her a hand as she climbed onto the porch.

He never thought he'd be at the place in his life again where he'd feel as if he might want to give love a chance. But when he was with Savannah, it felt right. They felt right together.

But he still had to tell her the whole truth. Only he knew how the whole truth would sound and how anyone normal would react when hearing it. He wanted to know she trusted him before he shared the events of the past six years.

"I can't believe *anyone* knows this is here," Savannah mumbled, stepping over a missing plank.

"It's more visible from the bay."

"I've always worried that the close proximity to the bay would set my property up to be used in some kind of smuggling operation. Drugs, mostly, but with all the military organizations in the area, it could even be weapons or who knows what else? Seafood, for all I know."

"That would be a new one."

They walked toward a window and peered inside. Time and wildlife had obviously taken advantage of the property. Even a tree had begun growing up through the floorboards.

"It looks like no one's been inside this death trap in years," Savannah said.

Clive couldn't argue. "It looks about as abandoned as abandoned can be. I'm not even sure we should go inside. There's no evidence anyone's been here at all."

"Where's that leave us?"

"Back to square one?" He rubbed his chin and let out a sigh. "Something's happening out on the bay, and I feel certain it's tied to this property."

"There's the old barn," Savannah suggested.

"Let's see if it's in any better shape." From a distance, the barn looked like a dilapidated mess. One half had collapsed, and vines traveled up the other half, practically claiming it.

They traipsed across the overgrown lawn until they reached it. They skirted the front and went around to the exposed side. Inside, it looked like a black abyss.

Disappointment bit down on Clive. "Looks like this was all for nothing."

Savannah bent down and squinted. "I don't know about that."

Clive, curiosity piqued, walked toward her. "What is it?"

She followed something toward a large, overgrown fig tree against the barn and moved aside some of the branches. "I'm not an expert on these things, but that looks like a generator to me."

. . .

Clive peered over Savannah's shoulder. "You're right. That's a generator, and it's new. Someone has been using this property."

"Let's go around to the other side, see what we can find."

He followed Savannah, liking the change in her personality. He had a feeling this was the real Savannah, the person she'd been before life had battered her.

She paused in front of the old barn doors. "Do you think we can get these open?"

"Let me try." He braced himself against the edge. The door slid open more easily than he anticipated. Almost as if it was well greased.

What he saw inside made his pulse race.

He hadn't been wrong. Someone *was* using this property.

"Oh my goodness." Savannah stepped closer, her eyes as wide as the full moon. "What in the world?"

Clive walked inside. This section of the barn had been totally rebuilt with fresh lumber supporting the walls and ceiling. He reached toward the wall and found a switch. Light filled the space.

"What is this?" Savannah whispered, her eyes still big with wonder.

Huge metal cylinders stood against one wall. Measuring cups and bags of unknown substances were scattered everywhere.

"Maybe someone's making synthetic drugs," Savannah offered. "I've heard they're all the rage."

"That might explain why some of the migrant workers are getting sick."

"Maybe they're testing the drugs on them?" Savannah asked.

He bent toward some of the supplies. Dish soap. Kerosene. Baking soda. Lemon extract. There were also several unmarked containers, some with powder, some with liquid.

What Clive didn't see was any kind of finished product.

Savannah reached down and picked up an apple. "I don't suppose this would be the way someone steals the secret formula for a new designer apple?"

"I have no idea."

There were several buckets of apples at a workstation in the corner. Some were sliced, others were whole. They seemed to be placed in a certain order, as if someone was observing the results of some kind of experiment.

"This is creepy," Savannah said.

"We'd better leave before someone finds us here."

Savannah nodded.

Clive grabbed one of the apples. Could Lauren have had anything to do with this? Or was he looking in the totally wrong direction for answers concerning her death?

"What are you doing?"

"Trying to get to the bottom of this." He grabbed her hand. "Now come on. Let's get out of here."

He turned off the lights, slid the door shut again, and took off toward the woods. When they were safely out of sight, Clive ventured a look back. Someone was coming.

He tugged Savannah down behind some thickets.

"What?" she whispered.

He nodded to the opposite side of the clearing. "Look. It's Jose. And he's going right for the shed."

CHAPTER 47

Savannah watched as Jose walked toward the barn doors. "Should we stop him? Confront him?"

Clive shook his head. "Not until we know more. Let's watch him for a minute."

Jose walked around the outside of the barn, peering this way and that. When he finished his perusal, he started back to the woods on the other side of the property.

"Strange," Savannah whispered. "What was he doing?"

"I have no idea. Maybe he sensed someone was watching him and didn't want to give too much away."

"I keep trying to put the pieces together. They're almost fitting, but it's like we're missing the one piece that connects all of them."

"Let's talk as we walk," Clive said.

When he took her hand again, she didn't argue. She liked feeling that they were a team. She felt more of the ice around her heart breaking away.

"We have a secret lab where someone may be (a) trying to copy a hybrid apple formula or (b) trying to develop a synthetic drug," Savannah started. "We have one dead migrant worker who was beaten. Two missing migrant workers. One migrant worker who died of cancer. We also have Marti, who I think was forced by someone to overdose and make it look like suicide."

"Put that all together and what do you have?"

"A mess?" She rubbed her temples. "Someone's trying to cover up something. They're either killing off the people who find out about it or . . . ?"

"This may not be likely, but maybe this isn't connected. Maybe our finding today and the issues with the migrant workers are separate."

"It could be. Then we have the Madden Society. We have the break-ins around town lately. Boats mysteriously coming and going at night along the bay."

Savannah's phone beeped. She pulled it from her pocket. "I must have just gotten back into range. It says I have a voice mail message."

She dialed in her code and listened.

It was her friend Stone.

"Look, I found out some interesting things from those photos you sent me. I e-mailed you all of the names. I'm curious as to what's going on. You want to keep me in the loop?"

She told Clive about the message, and they hurried back to Savannah's place. Their excursion had taken longer than Savannah expected, and the sun was already beginning to set.

They got back just in time because Savannah's leg was beginning to ache. Her cut still hadn't healed, and the long hike had made her sore.

She had visions of taking a long, hot bath. Then she remembered the man who'd snuck into her house. Would she ever be able to relax in her own place again? Or would she always jump at every creak now?

She unlocked her door, and she and Clive went inside.

"How about if I get us some water while you pull up the e-mail?" Clive offered.

"Sounds great." She plopped into her office chair, her body thanking her for the break. She turned her computer on and waited for it to boot up. Finally the home screen flashed on, just as Clive pulled a dining room chair up beside her.

"Let's take a look at what we have here." She could hardly to wait to see what Stone had found out.

But when she clicked on her e-mail, nothing came up.

"That's strange," she mumbled.

She tried again and had the same results. Her inbox was empty.

Finally she realized what she was looking at. "Someone wiped my e-mail out. All of it."

"Who would do something like that?"

Only one person came to mind. Leonard, the former hacker and all-around liar.

CHAPTER 48

He paced the area, the space hidden from everyone's eyes but his.

What a perfect setup. No one suspected a thing. No one suspected him.

And hopefully after that nasty little encounter he'd set up with Savannah, she would leave well enough alone.

She was supposed to help him, but all she'd been doing lately was hindering; asking too many questions; probing a little too deeply for her own good. He'd had to take desperate measures. At first he was just going to rig her car. He knew she started it with her key chain and wouldn't be hurt. He also knew the message it would send about her family. It would have been enough to sufficiently shake her up.

Not only that, but not having a car anymore should help keep her in one place.

He'd gotten nosy while she was gone and broken into her house. Then she'd returned unexpectedly. He'd had to revert to plan B. But it had ended up being much more fun than he'd anticipated. Too bad Clive had to ruin everything. Again.

He knew his threats wouldn't last for long. And he wasn't nearly finished with his experiment. There was so much more work to be done.

Which meant that he needed a scapegoat. He needed to find someone else to take the fall until he had everything in order.

He had the perfect person.

He walked across the room to where the woman lay. Her eyes widened when she saw him. She squirmed, trying to get away, but it was no use. Her hands were restrained on the gurney, just like someone at a mental hospital might be.

He had experience at mental hospitals. That's where his mom was now. In a nice facility where the doctors could control her many problems without fear of her hurting herself or anyone else. Good thing diseases like that didn't run in the family.

He brushed her dark hair back from her face. "There, there. It will be okay," he murmured.

He didn't like to think of her by name. No, he liked to think of her as a test subject. It made it so much easier.

If she hadn't been snooping, she would have never been chosen. The two men could disappear and no one really knew them well enough to confirm they'd been taken.

But this young woman was different. She was loved. She was missed.

He had to take care of her before she ever, ever had a chance to talk.

He pulled out a needle and filled it with the sample he was developing. Her eyes widened even more when she realized what he was doing.

When would she learn that there was no need to fight it? There was nothing she could do, and no one was coming to help.

He injected the substance into her arm.

Now it was wait and see.

He wondered how Savannah would like being his next test subject.

CHAPTER 49

Insanity. Definition: *Doing the same thing over and over and expecting different results.*

While Clive used her shower to clean up, Savannah tried to reach Stone again. His phone kept going to voice mail, so she kept trying, all the while questioning her own sanity for foolishly repeating the process, knowing she'd get the same results.

But then the unexpected happened. The sixth time she tried, he answered.

"I was in an interview," he explained. "Based on how many times you've called, you're anxious to talk."

"My computer has been wiped clean. I didn't get any of those names."

"A few I'm still trying to place. But the head of the FDA was there. There were also a couple of other congressmen, the CEO of a consumer products company, and one of the largest distributors of produce on the East Coast."

The apples. Did this all have something to do with those apples? Certainly a hybrid method wouldn't be worth murdering over . . . would it?

"I appreciate your help."

"Sounds like an interesting story. You going to cover it?"

Savannah stared at her computer a moment. "I don't know about that."

"You were one of the best, Savannah. It's a shame you're not out there fighting in the trenches anymore. The world needs more people like you."

Her heart twisted at his words. "I'm surprised you'd say that, especially after everything that happened."

"It was horrible what happened. But it wasn't your fault."

Her heart went from twisting and aching to pounding in her ears. "How can you say that? You were Reid's friend."

"I'm your friend, too. I knew both of you. Look, maybe I should have said this years ago. I just try not to ever make assumptions. But in case you didn't know, Reid loved you."

"You didn't see what went on behind closed doors."

"You're right. I didn't. But I know he fell in love with you because you had spunk, drive, and a good heart. He knew you'd probably have a hard time adjusting to life being married to him. He felt guilty for putting you in that position. That guilt may have come out as anger, but it was anger toward himself, not you."

Her throat felt tight and achy. "Really?"

"It's hard living in a fish bowl, Savannah. Sometimes we think we've overcome issues in our lives only to realize we've stuffed them deeper inside us. We've hidden our sins instead of destroying them."

"What are you saying?"

"I'm just saying that Reid struggled with his anger. He wanted things to be one way and denied they were actually quite the opposite. He thought the way you spoke the truth about the church was refreshing, but he also wanted to play it safe. He couldn't have it both ways. He knew better."

"I guess I should have, too."

"That's called a relationship, Savannah. You became accustomed to short-term friendships as a journalist. The long ones are the hard ones. You two would have worked things out. I know you would have. God's going to teach you something through all of this. He always does."

When Savannah hung up, her head was pounding. Had Stone spoken the truth? Had Reid's anger with himself been behind some of their marital strife?

Clive came back downstairs, and Savannah forced a smile.

One thing was for sure: she had a lot to think about tonight.

. . .

Clive left Savannah's place reluctantly. Part of him wanted to stay on the couch again, but he sensed that Savannah liked her independence. For that reason, he simply checked the house for her. No one was there.

He waited downstairs while she took a shower and cleaned up. He fixed sandwiches for them. Then he'd kissed her forehead and returned to his little cottage in the back. Though he was exhausted, he wasn't sure how much sleep he would be getting tonight. He had too much on his mind. There were too many answers he still needed to discover.

He reflected on what Savannah had told him about her phone call with Stone. The head of the FDA? The largest produce distributor on the East Coast?

He reached into his pocket and pulled out the apple. Was this the answer to all of their questions? Good and evil had begun in a garden. Could this forbidden fruit be the beginning of the evil in this area?

He needed to find an answer to that question. There was only one person he could think of to ask, and seeing him would be a big risk. But was the risk worth it? It could mean protecting Savannah. But would it lead him any closer to finding his wife's killer?

He sighed and went to grab a change of clothes.

But something on the couch caught his eye. It was a shell necklace. One that had belonged to Lauren.

The blood drained from his face.

Someone knew who he was. Was it the same person behind the acts of violence around town?

CHAPTER 50

The pounding on Savannah's door woke her up the next morning. With a sigh, she pulled her robe on and went downstairs. Landon Kavanagh stood at her front door.

Again.

Fire flashed in his eyes. Then she saw the stack of papers in his hands and how tense his shoulders looked.

"Landon . . ."

He held up the papers. "I would have called, but you still haven't given me your new phone number."

"I intended to. It slipped my mind."

He nodded to the inside of her house. "Do you mind?"

She opened the door wider. "Not at all. Come on in."

Landon stepped in, wiping his dew-damp boots on the rug at the entryway. When he stopped, his gaze locked on Savannah. "I think we should sit down."

The tension that had begun in Savannah's shoulders at the sight of him spread to her neck and all the way down her spine. She said nothing, just walked into the kitchen and took a seat at the table. Landon sat across from her, gripping the papers and looking at her with that all-too-serious gaze.

"Savannah, did you ever do a background check on your boarder?"

Irritation pinched her spine. "Clive, his name is Clive. And yes, I checked his references."

Landon shoved the pile of papers across the table. "Well, I did a full-fledged check for you. His real name isn't Clive. It's Jack. Jack Simmons."

Savannah nearly reeled but stopped herself. "Is that right?"

"Did he tell you about his wife?"

Savannah didn't let her gaze linger on the papers. Instead, she nodded, glad to prove to Landon that she wasn't totally naive. "Yes, I know she was murdered. It sounds awful."

Landon leaned across the table toward her. "Did he tell you he went to jail for her murder?"

Savannah sucked in a quick breath, her gaze fluttered to the pile of papers before her. "What? No. You're making that up. Why would you say that?"

He pushed the papers into her hands. "Check it out yourself. The only reason he got out of prison on a lifetime sentence was a technicality. Most people still think he's guilty. He'll be retried for the crime. They're collecting more evidence now."

Savannah couldn't focus on the words. Everything seemed to blur. A few phrases from a photocopied newspaper article jumped out at her.

Prominent attorney . . . Guilty of brutally murdering wife . . . Neighbors heard them screaming at each other the night before . . . Lifetime sentence for his crime . . .

She shook her head in disbelief. No . . .

She looked up and saw Landon watching her carefully.

"I knew he was trouble, Savannah. You need to evict him. Now."

Her head spun. She stood, knowing she needed some time to herself to process everything. "I need to let this sink in. I need to think." She picked up the papers. "Can I keep these?"

"Of course. Do you want me to get rid of him for you? He's dangerous, Savannah."

"No, I'll be okay." Would she? "I just need a moment alone to process this."

"I can call the chief. He can handle this."

She placed her hand on his arm. "He's not going to hurt me, Landon."

"I bet his wife said the same thing."

Savannah squeezed her eyes shut, a sick feeling roiling in her gut.

.   .   .

Clive glanced at Savannah's house as he left for work later that morning. He had the persistent urge to check on her, to see how she was doing. But he didn't want to smother her.

Instead, he drove to Landon Kavanagh's farm and went through his regular routine of driving the van and picking up the migrant workers. After he dropped them off, he went to find Ernie and get his assignment.

When he walked into the barn, he realized no one was there. Where was Ernie? He was almost always here, doling out instructions for the day.

"How dare you come on my property!"

Clive turned at the sound of the unexpected voice. Landon Kavanagh stood there, veins bulging at his neck and his expression crazed.

Clive knew there was no need to deny anything; Landon had discovered the truth, as Clive had known he would eventually.

Was he the one who'd left the necklace at his house? The timing fit . . .

Landon charged him, his face red and his fists balled. This wasn't the calm, cool, collected man everyone else saw.

Just as Clive expected.

Landon threw a punch, and his fist collided with Clive's jaw. Clive rubbed the tender area, letting the man get the first punch in. Clive needed to be in control.

He tried to swing again, but Clive blocked him.

"Beating me up isn't going to help anything," Clive told him through clenched teeth.

"You think you're sly, don't you? Coming on my farm, working for me, right under my nose." His face reddened as he pulled free of Clive's grasp.

"I wasn't hiding from you, Landon."

"You don't look anything like the lawyer you used to be. I guess prison toughened you up." Landon backed up, his chest heaving in deep breaths.

"Some would say that."

The two began circling each other like a pair of dogs pitted against one another.

"I heard you got out," Landon continued. "I figured you might try to come after me. You going to kill me now, too?"

"I didn't kill Lauren. I think you know that." Clive reminded himself to keep his voice even.

"You think the real killer is still at large?" Landon huffed out a laugh. "I don't think so. The right person was behind bars. You know you were a raging fool. Mad with jealousy."

"Because you were having an affair with my wife? You're right. I was mad. But I wouldn't have killed her. I would have killed you, if anyone."

"She loved me," Landon insisted, jabbing a finger into his chest. "We saw eye to eye on things. She was going to leave you."

Clive continued to breathe steadily, to not let his emotions get the best of him.

"Then why did you kill her?"

Landon's eyes widened. "I never would have hurt her."

"You would. And you set it up for me to take the fall."

"You're crazy." He lunged at Clive again.

The two fell on the ground. Clive blocked Landon's fist before it collided with his face again.

He managed to flip Landon over, to pin him on the ground. But only for a moment. Landon kneed him in the gut.

In the brief moment Clive tried to catch his breath, Landon was on his feet. He lunged at him again.

The two struggled until suddenly Ernie was there, pulling Clive back.

"What's going on here?" he demanded.

Landon spit blood, seething. He cast an angry look at Clive as he took a step back. His whole body was tensed, ready to fight.

"Nothing," Landon muttered. "Please escort him off my property. I never want to see him here again."

． ． ．

"Thanks for coming by, Chief," Savannah started. "Can I get you some coffee?"

"No thank you." He shook his head and lowered himself into the chair across from her at the kitchen table. "What can I do for you?"

She reached into her pocket and pulled out the pennies. She dropped them on the table in front of Chief Lockwood, listening as they clinked together. The sound sent a shiver up her spine.

He glanced up at her as if she were crazy.

"Whoever is behind the crimes going on in this area is leaving behind flattened pennies." She explained how she'd found all of them.

"And you're just now choosing to tell me?"

She could see the gears turning in his mind as he stared at the coins. He knew something.

"No offense, Chief, but you don't seem to take me very seriously."

He twisted his head, his eyes widening. "Maybe I've underestimated you."

Underestimated her craziness. That's probably what the chief meant, Savannah thought. That didn't deter her.

"What other crime scenes have pennies been found at?"

He pressed his lips together. "There was one on a homeless man we pulled out of the bay. We figured he'd gotten drunk, fallen off the bay bridge tunnel, and hit some rebar on the way down. He was found not far from where some bridge construction was going on. We're rethinking that scenario now and testing his wounds."

"Sounds like a good idea."

"You mind if I take these?"

"I'd be concerned if you didn't," Savannah told him.

He stood, wiping them all into an evidence bag he pulled from his pocket. She swallowed, her throat dry. Should she tell him about Clive?

"One more thing, Savannah. I thought you'd want to know that we arrested someone for the break-ins in the area."

She held her breath. "Who?"

"Jose Lopez."

She gasped. "What? Señor Lopez's son?"

He nodded. "Apparently he was stealing food to feed his family."

CHAPTER 51

He needed another test subject. The young woman and the man had run their course. Soon it would be time to dispose of them. He had the perfect plan, one which people would never suspect involved him.

Except half of the thrill was having people actually know his name.

He'd first killed six years ago, and it had been easier than he'd thought possible. No one had suspected him.

No, Jack Simmons had taken the fall. He'd gone away to prison, supposedly for life. Until that technicality had released him.

Poor guy. Everyone had been so quick to believe he was guilty. He'd hardly had to do a thing.

Lauren had been just as nosy as Savannah. She'd just kept pushing, kept trying. She wouldn't let things go.

She'd had to die.

Taking that first life had been so easy. The more practice he got, the easier it became. The more excited he became. The more of a thrill he got.

Soon it would be time to get more practice.

Savannah was supposed to help him. He was going to reveal his brilliant plan to her. She could add authenticity to it by writing one of her articles. People trusted a name like Savannah Harris. She was a defender of common people. If she could see the light, she could make other people see the light as well.

But no more.

Now she was useless. He hadn't had time to convince her before she started forming her own opinions.

He rubbed the coin in his hand.

It was time to destroy the value of someone else.

CHAPTER 52

Savannah heard a truck rumbling up the driveway. Clive. What was he doing back from work so early?

Her stomach had been in knots all morning. How could he have betrayed her like this? She'd looked up the details of his trial. Read the details of his life. Realized that he'd gotten out of prison on a mere technicality. Clive Miller was Jack Simmons, no doubt about it.

What if he was guilty?

Her gut told her that he wasn't capable of murder. But passion could cause people to do crazy things. She'd started her career as a crime reporter and had seen her fair share of brutality against spouses and loved ones. A moment of rage could cause seemingly kind people to become monsters.

He stopped in front of her house and hopped out.

She dropped the curtain and straightened her shirt, trying to figure out the best way to handle this situation.

If there was one thing she didn't take kindly to, it was being lied to. She'd had enough of that in her life. Yet here she was again.

His heavy footsteps pounded up the front steps, and he knocked at the door. "Savannah, it's me. Clive. We need to talk."

She crossed her arms and stayed where she was. "I'm not sure I have anything to say to you."

"Please, Savannah. Let me explain."

"What's there to say?"

"A lot. If you'd just let me talk . . ."

"I'd say you've already had plenty of opportunities."

"Please. Just five minutes. That's all I want."

She stared at the door, at the ugly yellow plaid curtain hanging there. Finally she pulled the safety lock off and twisted the handle. But she didn't wait around to greet Clive. She marched into the kitchen and stood against the counter, sure to keep the table between them.

She looked up and saw Clive on the other side of the kitchen. He had a busted lip and a cut on his forehead. Fear washed through her. "What happened to you?"

"Landon Kavanagh."

She raised her eyebrows. Landon had never seemed like a violent, temperamental man.

Clive stepped closer, but when Savannah raised her hand, he took his place back on the other side of the kitchen.

"My wife worked here on the Eastern Shore at the marine center. The job was her life. We were having problems. I don't deny that. But I was framed. Someone set me up to make it look like I killed her." He reached into his pocket and pulled out the shell necklace. "And whoever killed her is gloating. They left this on my couch. Lauren made it."

Savannah stared at the necklace, ignoring the goose bumps racing down her skin, trying to remain calm and logical.

"You're out of jail, yet you come back here. Why?" she asked.

"To find my wife's killer."

"Have you been successful?"

"I've had suspicions all along."

Doubts collided inside her. "Who?"

"Landon Kavanagh."

She gasped, her hand flying to her mouth. "Why would you think that?"

"He was having an affair with my wife. She tried to break it off with him, but he liked getting his way."

Her mind reeled. Landon? An affair? It was a lot to process. "Did you have any evidence?"

"He was unaccounted for the day of her death, but there was nothing to prove anything."

"You got out on a technicality. You could be guilty."

His eyes implored her. "You know me, Savannah. What does your gut tell you?"

"I don't know anymore, Clive—or is it Jack?" She had to look away before she broke, before she gave in to emotions instead of logic and reason. She'd gotten herself in trouble that way one too many times already.

Someone knocked on the door. Relief washed through her. She needed some space right now.

"I've got to go," she started. "Bobbi is giving me a ride to pick up my rental. I . . . I need time."

He nodded, though regret filled his gaze and he seemed hesitant to step back.

"Understood," he finally said.

. . .

"You seem distracted," Bobbi said as they traveled down the road.

Even in October, the woman smelled like sunscreen and salt water. She was totally immersed in doing what she loved.

A moment of envy shot through Savannah.

"I have a lot on my mind," she finally admitted.

Bobbi glanced at her compassionately. "I'm here with a listening ear, if you need it."

Savannah pictured the conversation playing out and cringed. "You probably wouldn't believe me if I told you."

"Try me. I've heard a lot."

Savannah turned toward Bobbi. At this point, she had nothing to lose. Nothing at all. "Your best friend Lauren? You'll never believe this, but her husband is staying in my guesthouse."

Bobbi flinched, her foot temporarily hitting the brakes. "Jack? What?"

Savannah nodded, realizing how unbelievable all of it sounded. "It's true. You heard me correctly. He goes by Clive now. He said he came back to figure out what really happened to his wife."

"I see." Bobbi nodded, but the motion looked tight and forced.

"He told me that Lauren was seeing Landon. Is that true?" Savannah's words rushed out before she lost her courage. Of all the things she feared hearing the answer to, Jack's character—or lack of it—was at the top of her list right now.

Bobbi pressed her lips together for a moment. She remained silent, her hands gripping the wheel and her eyes focusing on the road. "Yes, it's true."

Savannah's heart stammered a moment. At least he'd told the truth about that. It was a step in the right direction. "He also said that Lauren wanted to break it off."

"That's also true. She realized she needed to work on her marriage instead of looking for greener pastures."

Savannah hardly wanted to ask the next question. "Do you really think Clive—Jack—killed her?"

She held her breath, her heart pounding in her ears.

Please don't let me be wrong about someone else. Please. I can see through shady politicians, but am I blinded by my heart? If so, I'm a joke to the profession of journalism.

Bobbi glanced at Savannah, her gaze softening as a sad smiled played lightly across her lips. "I never met her husband, Savannah. Lauren always said he was a good man. A little too dedicated to his job, perhaps. But he was a lawyer. He wanted to fight for justice. Lauren was a marine biologist. Her passion was the ocean. They were going in different directions, but they were both good people."

"You still didn't answer my question."

She let out a breath. "I don't know. At first I just wanted to see him go to prison. To pay for what he'd done. But time has softened me. My emotions aren't as strong. When it all died down, I began to wonder if they'd maybe put the wrong person behind bars. The police were desperate to put a lid on this case. Jack was an easy scapegoat."

"I don't know what to do. About anything right now, really."

"You're a smart girl. You'll figure it out. I have faith in you."

Savannah shook her head, staring out the window. "I don't know, Bobbi. I'm not sure how it's all going to end."

Her cell phone beeped. She looked down and saw an unfamiliar number. She answered anyway. "Hello?"

Static crackled on the bad connection. "Savannah, this is Nurse . . . Marti is stirring . . . I thought you'd want to know."

Her heart rate quickened, and she sat up straighter, adrenaline bursting through her. "Marti? I do want to know. Who is this?"

She couldn't understand the reply. There was too much static. But it was a woman. A nurse at the hospital, if she'd heard correctly.

Then the line went dead.

Savannah hung up and told Bobbi.

"That's great news," Bobbi said.

"Forget the rental car. I'll get it later. Can you swing me by the hospital?"

"Absolutely. I can't stay myself. I've got a meeting with the food bank. Marti wouldn't want me to miss it. Besides, you're the one she'll want to see."

They reached the hospital, and Savannah started to climb out.

"Savannah?"

She paused. "Yes?"

"I'll be praying for you."

For some reason, that thought didn't bother her as much as it once did. "I appreciate it, Bobbi."

"Remember, God is there in the middle of your doubts and questions. You just have to open your eyes to see Him."

Savannah smiled and hurried from the car. She skipped the elevator, opting to run up the flight of stairs. She couldn't wait to see Marti. They had so much to talk about.

As she rushed down the hallway, she passed a woman eating an apple.

An apple.

Her mind flashed back to the fruit she and Jack had found.

She remembered that a member of the FDA had been at the Madden Society. The FDA, which approved the safety of food and drugs. The ones the public trusted to verify that their food was okay to consume.

There were huge vats of some kind of chemical in the barn on Landon's property.

Leonard's words from that first day she'd met him in the hospital returned to her. Don't forget to wash that apple. *They're one of the dirty dozen of pesticide offenders.*

Could all of this be about . . . pesticides?

But what sense did that make? She'd have to think about it more in a moment. Right now she had to visit her friend. Besides, if Marti woke up, she could shed some light on this whole situation.

She ran down the hall and into Marti's room. She paused when she walked inside. Marti lay there, her eyes closed.

Where were the nurses? The doctor?

She'd pictured Marti's eyes being open. Her friend being alert. Conscious.

But from where Savannah stood, she simply looked the same. Unchanged.

She took a step closer and suddenly sensed someone behind her.

Then she felt a sharp pain in her neck, and everything went black.

CHAPTER 53

Someone knocked on Jack's door. He strode across the room and found his friend Wheaton there. In his cowboy boots. In Virginia, a far cry from the cattle ranches of Texas where Wheaton had grown up.

Jack smiled. Some things never changed.

They shook hands and did a half hug.

"Thanks for coming," Jack told him. He glanced outside, checking to see if anyone else was around. "I couldn't exactly leave the state."

"The DA is looking for anything he can find to put you back in prison."

Jack nodded. "I know. I'm afraid he might get his wish."

Wheaton stepped inside, and his hands went to his hips. "What's going on?"

Jack held out an apple.

Wheaton raised an eyebrow. "Do you want me to take a bite and fall into a deep sleep?"

"You're no Snow White." Jack's smile slipped. "No, I wonder if there's something special about it. Could you check? I know the woman you've been dating works for a lab."

"Bethany, you mean."

Jack nodded. "Yeah, Bethany."

Wheaton took the apple from him. "I'll see what I can find out. It seems like a long shot."

"A long shot is better than no shot."

Wheaton shifted. "I can't argue with that. In the meantime, what else is going on? Nice place here."

Jack filled him in, sharing everything that had happened. It felt good to talk to someone who knew him, who believed in his innocence, who'd stood by him through everything. People said that you don't know who your friends are until you face hard times. They were right. Nearly everyone else in his life had fled as quickly as possible.

"I can see it in your eyes," Wheaton said after Jack finished.

"See what?" He crossed his arms.

"Vengeance."

Jack looked away. "Someone killed my wife. They framed me. I wasted five years of my life in prison."

"Aim for redemption, not revenge, my friend. There is a difference. One you will regret, the other you won't."

Jack raised his chin, contemplating his words. No one could possibly understand everything he was going through. No one.

"Someone has to pay for what happened to my wife."

"Let the justice system do its job."

"You saw how well that worked for me," Jack muttered.

"Retribution only feels good for a moment, then you live the rest of your life with regret. Don't put yourself in that position. Don't lower yourself to that level."

Wheaton's words burned in Jack's ears. He didn't know if he could be the bigger person, not when payback was all he'd thought about. For years, it was one of the only things that kept him going. Was it possible to change his philosophy now?

. . .

Savannah opened her eyes and sucked in a deep breath. Her gaze flew wildly about the room.

Where was she? What had happened?

Everything came back to her.

The hospital. Marti. Blacking out.

Who had brought her here? And where was *here*, exactly?

She tried to sit up, but her hands wouldn't move. She jerked them, trying to free herself, but it was hopeless.

Finally she pulled her head up. She was on some kind of table. Like an operating table. Her hands and feet were restrained with leather straps.

Panic raced through her. What was going on?

She swung her head to the side.

It was some kind of run-down house, she realized. It was dark and dingy with no real furniture, only a cabinet and a table against the wall.

She looked in the other direction and gasped. A young woman lay there, wearing a yellow shirt that matched Savannah's kitchen.

Lucia. Her hands and legs were strapped as well. But she wasn't moving.

Beside her, on another table, was a man. Felipe, maybe?

She closed her eyes and tried to suck in some deep breaths. Facts began melding together inside her head.

Only it was too late. All of the answers would do her no good now.

Right now her only priority was to survive.

CHAPTER 54

Jack waited for Savannah to return home. He wanted the chance to explain things to her again. But her house remained dark. Something was wrong.

After pacing for nearly an hour, he finally gave in. He retrieved his father's old gun, one he'd kept stashed away after he'd been released from prison, just in case he needed it. He hoped he wouldn't have to use it, but there were too many lives on the line to not take every necessary precaution. He hopped on the motorcycle Wheaton had brought with him in the bed of his truck.

Right now there was only one person who could help Jack. Bobbi Matthews.

He dreaded seeing her. Seeing the accusation in her eyes. But he'd face Bobbi if it meant protecting Savannah.

He pulled to a stop in front of her house, a small white cottage located off the main highway. He knew where it was. He'd sat outside watching the property before, hoping to see a sign of Lauren emerging. Bobbi's house was where she'd always claimed she stayed while in town, though Jack had suspicions otherwise.

Bobbi answered the door right away. Her face didn't show the shock or dismay he'd expected. Instead, her expression was neutral as she pushed the storm door open. "Come in."

Jack stayed where he was, remaining on the cheerful porch. "Bobbi, I wish I had time to explain. I really do. But right now, I need to know where Savannah is."

Sadness welled in Bobbi's eyes, mixed with a glimpse of wisdom and compassion. "I dropped her off at the hospital. Someone left a message saying Marti was awake."

It was a start, at least. Still, his mind wouldn't rest. "Have you talked to her since then?"

Bobbi shook her head. "No. Why? Is everything okay? I was just about to go down there and check on her, see how Marti was doing."

"She's still not home."

Bobbi's eyes widened. "Maybe she's staying with Marti."

"I've got to double-check." He sprinted from the porch.

"Jack?" Bobbi called.

He slowed for a moment, not used to hearing his real name.

"I hope you find the person who really murdered Lauren."

He nodded, gratitude filling him. Bobbi believed he was innocent. She'd never know what a balm that was to his heart.

"Thank you," he called.

That was all the time he had to show his appreciation. He had to find Savannah and make sure she was okay.

. . .

Serendipity. Definition: *events that happen by chance.*

Savannah didn't believe in chance. She believed that things happened as a result of cause and effect.

Maybe this was the way it was all supposed to end. Savannah being beaten in her own game. There was no one else to pay the price except for Savannah. Her snooping had gotten her here. At least in death there'd be no more guilt about Ella. About Reid.

But then again, there would be no chance to make things right with Jack either. She couldn't deny that they had something special.

She pulled against the restraints again, one minute ready to face death and the next ready to fight it with every last breath. She still needed more time to make things right in the world. Looking at life through the lens of impending death, Savannah realized that seclusion was never the answer. The best way she could make things right was by continuing to fight. By letting the bad guys know they couldn't win.

Besides, if she wanted to save Lucia, she had to first save herself.

God, are you there? It's me, Savannah.

I had the start of a realization the other day. I tried to ignore it, not to think about it too much. But I think my problem was that when I married Reid, I approached You as a belief. I did believe in You. I had all the evidence I needed.

But I didn't have a relationship with You. I didn't allow myself to become transformed through You. I didn't have faith.

Even the demons believe in You and shudder.

What You're looking for are disciples.

That's what I want to be.

I know You love justice, too. Before, I was fighting for justice for the greater good. Now I want to fight for justice for You.

CHAPTER 55

Jack hurried up to Marti's room at the hospital. When he pushed inside, he saw a nurse standing over Marti. He stopped in his tracks, his gaze falling on the bed.

Marti was unmoving. Still. Her eyes closed.

"Can I help you?" the young nurse asked.

"I thought she was awake." He pointed at Marti, knowing he sounded rude.

"Why would you think that? I'm sorry, but nothing's changed." A knot formed between the nurse's eyebrows.

"But . . . my friend got a call from the hospital."

"No one here has called. To my knowledge, at least. I've been here with Marti all day."

Realization rushed through him. Had someone lured Savannah here? Who would have done that?

•   •   •

Lucia finally opened her eyes.

Savannah wanted to jump off the exam table, rush over, and ask how she was doing. But she couldn't move.

"Lucia!" Savannah called.

The girl flopped her head to the side. Her eyes widened when she spotted Savannah. "Señora Harris! No . . . not you. You were my only hope of getting out of here."

"It's not too late, Lucia."

"I've tried everything. There's no escape."

Savannah stared at the ceiling a minute. "There's got to be something." She nodded toward the wall. "What's in those cabinets?"

"Needles. Some kind of medicine."

"Medicine?"

"He keeps injecting us."

"Who?"

"I'm not sure. His face is covered."

"Someone's been injecting you with something?" Her mind raced.

"He said we're like lab rats and that we should be proud that we're a part of his experiment. Sacrifice a few to save hundreds. That's his motto."

Savannah had to get to the cabinet. Maybe there were scissors. Something that could cut through these restraints.

She didn't have much time.

CHAPTER 56

Jack knew it was a risk to drive onto Landon's property, but he didn't have a choice.

Whatever was going on, he didn't like it.

He slowed his motorcycle as he got closer to the farm.

In the distance, where Landon's truck was normally parked, the lawn was empty.

Maybe he had caught a break.

He parked his motorcycle in the cornfield, hidden from sight. Then he approached the barn, staying on the edge of the property.

He walked in and saw Jose taking a water break.

"What are you doing here? I heard you were in jail."

Jose stared at Jack a moment, defiance in his gaze. *"Se retiraron los cargoes contra mi."*

They dropped the charges against me, Jack translated.

"Donde está Ernie?" Jack asked.

He shrugged. *"Él dejó."* He left.

"Where?"

"El bosque." The woods.

Jack stepped closer. "To the house back there? Where you were snooping the other day?"

"Me buscando mi hermana." Looking for my sister. Jose raised his chin.

"Jose, if anything happens to me, call Bobbi Matthews. I'm going back to the house."

"Yo voy contigo."

Jack raised a hand. "No, I need to go by myself. *Solo.* I need you here in case something happens."

Defiance flared in Jose's eyes.

Jack grabbed his arm, determined to make him listen. "I'm trying to find your sister, Jose. Please help me."

Finally some of the fire died, and Jose took a step back. *"Bien."*

With that, Jack darted into the woods.

· · ·

Savannah swung back and forth on the table. She had to somehow become mobile. She had to get out of here and take Lucia and Felipe with her.

"Señora?" Lucia asked.

Savannah kept rocking from side to side. "Yes?"

"What are you doing?"

"I can't just lie here." Savannah tried to get some momentum going.

"It's no use. We've tried everything."

Savannah nodded across the room. "How's Felipe over there?"

"He's weak," Lucia said. "It's just a matter of time. The man said his experiment is over, and he's ready to dispose of us. We served our purpose."

"You know you're worth more than this, don't you?"

Lucia's eyes filled with tears, but she said nothing.

"God loves those who society may not see. He loves the poor, the brokenhearted, the oppressed. He loves those who are hurting. The fatherless. He loves you, Lucia."

More tears flowed.

"I know you've been treated poorly, both as a migrant worker and by whoever brought you here," Savannah continued. "I can only imagine how that must make you feel. You're not a lab rat, though. You're not second class. Don't ever let someone make you feel that way. You're going to rise above all of this and go on to do great things, Lucia."

"Thank you, Señora." A small sob escaped. "I didn't think anyone would care enough to find me. Anyone but you."

Savannah's heart ached at the young woman's words. They were two different people, but Savannah understood where she was coming from. "When we get out of here, I'm going to teach you everything I can about journalism."

"You would do that?"

Savannah nodded, her neck muscles tight and sore from jerking back and forth. "Of course. You were the one who left that note at my house, weren't you? The one saying it wasn't cancer."

"I needed someone to believe me."

"You have someone, Lucia." Savannah offered a smile. "Now we've just got to get out of here."

She rocked back and forth again, trying to get some momentum going. Finally the table gave.

Savannah crashed to the floor. She moaned as her shoulder hit the hard concrete.

"Señora, are you okay?"

Savannah tried to nod, but her neck hurt too much. "I'll be fine."

What now?

She shifted her weight, trying to move the table. It was lighter than she expected, almost like a gurney. If she could just reach that cabinet . . .

She threw her weight forward. The table moved less than an inch. This was going to take a long time.

And a long time was something she didn't have.

. . .

Jack reached the barn just in time to see a figure emerging. He ducked behind a tree, watching. It was Ernie.

He was hauling one of the vats outside in a wheelbarrow, headed toward the bay. Was he going to dump the contents there?

Jack gripped his gun. He'd be back in jail if the wrong person saw him with the weapon, but it was a risk he was willing to take. It was time to figure out what was going on.

"Stop right there," Jack ordered.

Ernie froze.

"Put your hands in the air or I'll shoot. Don't test me."

Ernie raised his hands and stepped back.

Jack slowly approached. "What exactly are you doing?"

"It's not what you think," the man insisted.

"Start explaining." Jack aimed the gun at him.

"It's complicated."

"Start with this. Where's Savannah?"

His eyes widened. "Savannah? Who's Savannah?"

"The pretty woman Landon gives all his attention to."

"I don't know who you're talking about."

"Then what do you know?"

"I'm just following orders," Ernie insisted.

Jack stepped closer, until the gun was only inches from Ernie's chest. "You're wasting my time."

Sweat bubbled on Ernie's upper lip. "I was developing a new pesticide. That's it. No people involved."

"Why are you dumping it?"

"My formula didn't work. Apparently the migrant workers were getting sick. My project failed." His chest rose and fell rapidly.

"You were putting it on their crops?" Jack stared at Ernie for a long minute, replaying their conversations. "That's the real reason you let them have their own garden, isn't it?"

"I did spray it as a test sample. It works great. No weeds. No disease. No bugs. But something in the formula is making them sick."

Everything started to make sense, to come together like an interlocking puzzle. "This isn't the first time you've tried, is it? You dumped chemicals before, and that's why there were all those fish kills in the area."

"It was unfortunate. I really thought it would work this time. I've spent my whole life trying to develop this formula. I'm close. So close."

"Are you the one who killed my wife? Lauren Simmons. She must have caught on to your scheme."

"Lauren was your wife?"

"That's right." The gun shook in Jack's hand. His finger twitched on the trigger.

Justice. Lauren needed justice.

Or did Jack just want revenge for all of his heartache? For all of the things that had been taken away from him, things he'd never get back? He thought of Wheaton's warnings. The line between revenge and redemption seemed awfully blurred at the moment.

"No, I didn't murder her."

"Then who's calling the shots here?"

Ernie shook his sweat-drenched head. "You won't believe me if I tell you."

. . .

Savannah jerked forward, and suddenly her wrist came free. She glanced down and saw the metal piece holding the leather restraining strap on the floor. It must have broken off in the fall.

Wasting no more time, she tugged at the other strap. Finally her other arm broke free. She scrambled to untie her feet as well.

When she finally stood, her knees felt wobbly. Had she been given some kind of drug? She didn't have time to think about it now.

She rushed over to Lucia and undid her straps. Then she slipped an arm around her waist and helped her to her feet.

Lucia sagged against her, moaning.

"Come on. I need to free Felipe, and we've got to get out of here."

Lucia nodded, her face pale, her lips dry and cracked, her hair matted. On a good day, the girl weighed less than a ream of paper; now she was practically a feather.

Savannah left her leaning against the wall and went to free Felipe. He wouldn't wake up, though, and there was no way to carry him.

Savannah shook him again, desperate to wake him up. It was no use. He was breathing, though. That was good news.

"We'll send back help for him. I don't want to leave him, but if we stay, all three of us will end up dead."

Lucia nodded, looking too spent to argue.

Savannah hurried toward the cabinet. She searched through the supplies inside, looking for something—anything—to protect herself with. Finally she put a syringe in her pocket and a bottle in her sweatshirt. Then she slipped her arm around Lucia again.

"Let's go."

She stepped out of the room and surveyed their surroundings. There was a short hallway with a closed door across from them. Everything was dark, making it hard to see. Were there no windows?

She helped Lucia down the hall. At the end of it was a kitchenette. On the opposite side of the room was a desk. Pictures of Savannah, articles she'd written, and articles about Reid's death were all over the wall.

The blood drained from her face.

Then she spotted the pile of flattened pennies atop the desk.

It didn't matter at the moment. The only thing that mattered was that they hurried.

They stepped out of the building, sunlight blinding them for a moment.

Then someone stepped in front of them.

Savannah sucked in a deep breath at the familiar figure standing there.

CHAPTER 57

Jack jumped on his motorcycle and took off down the road. It had taken some persuading, but Ernie had finally told him where the mastermind behind the scheme had a second piece of property.

At the stoplight, he called Bobbi and explained what was going on. She promised to call the police and send help.

Jack only hoped the police were trustworthy. He still wasn't exactly sure who else was involved with this, what the entire scope was.

He got tired of waiting for the light and pulled onto the side of the road. He sped past the waiting cars and turned down a country lane. The miles wouldn't go by fast enough. He pushed the motorcycle as hard as he could. There was no time to waste. Every second that passed was another second that Savannah could be hurt. Killed. He didn't want to think about the possibility.

That's when he heard the sirens behind him.

If he broke the terms of his probation, he'd be sent back to jail.

Breaking and entering.

Assault.

Carrying a gun.

The list of reasons was becoming longer and longer.

He couldn't let that stop him now.

He had to help Savannah first.

He hit the throttle.

Turning sharply, he headed down a road that cut through the corn. The police cruiser would have a hard time getting through here. At least that's what he was counting on.

The road was bumpy. His motorcycle slid, but he righted himself before wiping out.

He glanced in his mirror. The cop car was behind him, plowing through the cornstalks.

Jack turned hard.

He cut through the field, leaves slapping him in the face.

He had no other choice.

Ernie better have been telling him the truth. If this wasn't where Savannah was, he had no idea where else to look, especially not while eluding the police.

Finally he broke through the field and was back on the highway. He sped down the road, thankful that the police hadn't found him again.

Not yet, at least.

He knew it was only a matter of time.

The cornfields started to disappear, replaced with marsh grass and reeds. He was getting closer. The ocean should be appearing any second now.

Finally the road came to an end at an old boat launch. A sandy parking lot, big enough for maybe two cars, was beside it. A black van was parked there.

This was it! Across the water, he spotted a barrier island. A lone building stood there, partially concealed by the trees.

Now Jack just had to figure out how to get across.

• • •

"Dr. Lawson?" Savannah asked.

She pulled Lucia back, tried to place herself between the doctor and the girl.

"Savannah. You're here." He pushed his glasses up on his nose and took a step back.

She stared at the doctor, trying to get a read on him.

"One of the nurses reported someone suspicious transporting a patient from the hospital," he explained. "Then Bobbi called the hospital looking for you. I started putting things together."

She gripped Lucia's arm. "How'd you get here?"

"A black van I'd never seen before was leaving the parking lot. I followed it here."

"You mean there's someone else here?" Savannah tried to keep her voice even.

He nodded. "I saw him go to the other side of the building." He waved his arm, motioning for her to follow. "Come on. Let me get you out of here."

Savannah stepped outside, all of her senses still on alert. She glanced around, quickly assessing where they were.

An island, she realized. A barrier island, most likely.

"My boat is right over there," Dr. Lawson said.

They stumbled through the sand toward it.

"I was trying to find you anyway," Dr. Lawson said. "I looked over my cases as you requested and found some questionable symptoms in some of the migrant workers. I think Ernie is behind this."

"Behind what?"

"He used to be a chemist," Dr. Lawson explained. "He tried to develop a pesticide a decade ago, but it never got approved by the EPA. I think he started experimenting again, using his new product on the vegetable plot given to the migrant workers."

"Then what's going on here?" Savannah asked.

"My guess is that his experiments weren't seeing results fast enough. I have suspicions that he was injecting the pesticide into migrant workers, trying to speed up the process. He knew the product would never be approved if there were any signs it was harmful to people."

Savannah's throat went dry.

She hadn't said anything about needles or more migrant workers being inside.

Dr. Lawson was the one behind this.

"Here's my boat. Come on. I'll get you to the police station, and we can report all of this."

"Can't you call the police now?" Savannah asked.

"I don't have my phone on me."

Savannah didn't believe that for one minute. She froze, her arms straining to hold up Lucia. "I'm not getting on that boat with you."

He narrowed his eyes. "Why not? I want to help you."

"I think Ernie is involved in the scheme." She pushed Lucia farther behind her. "But I think you invested in it. I think you were getting desperate to see a return on your money. You even talked your friends with the Madden Society into investing, hoping that in the future they might turn a blind eye to the dangers of the product. Everyone knows the pesticide market is huge. It could make you rich."

Suddenly his eyes darkened. He stood up straighter, his chin raised. His nice guy persona disappeared. "You think you're so smart. You were supposed to help me."

A chill raced through her. His voice even sounded different. His eyes looked blacker.

"Why would I help you make people sick?"

"Once Ernie got it perfected, your endorsement would have helped it become a smashing success. But then you got too nosy and ruined everything."

"You're crazy," Savannah muttered. "You're not making any sense."

"You don't understand. Developing a safer pesticide would increase the crop yields, feed more people, and bring down prices of food. Do you know how much produce is wasted every year because it's diseased, eaten up by insects, strangled by weeds? There's an alternative to the poison some people are putting on their fields. There's a way to merge my technique with safety. I just needed more time, more tests."

"That's the real reason you offered to volunteer for Marti," Savannah said.

"Yes! I had to be sure their sickness was directly tied in with our product." He scowled. "When I began to see some of the workers getting sick, I developed a powder and gave it to a few of them in pill form. Just to be sure."

"Señor Lopez?"

"He was one of them. The pills worked faster than I thought they would."

Savannah took a step back, seeing the madness in his eyes with every spoken word. "Why'd you try to kill Marti?"

"She saw some labels in my car, she saw the pills, and she got suspicious. She confronted me about it, and things got heated. That's when I knew I had to take action."

"Is she really in a coma?" Savannah dared to ask.

He grabbed a rope from the boat and began twisting it in his hands. "A coma I induced. I couldn't let her die yet. I was afraid it might raise too many questions."

"How could you experiment on people without their consent?"

"I had to!" His voice rose. "It had so much potential. The initial results were astounding."

His eyes lost all emotion. They looked vacant. Drool pooled on his lips. He kept twisting the rope in his hands, most likely envisioning it around Savannah's neck.

Fear ricocheted through her.

He'd lost it, she realized. There was absolutely no reasoning with a madman.

Savannah glanced around. How was she going to get out of this? They were stuck on an island. She might—might—be able to swim to shore, but it would mean leaving Lucia behind. She couldn't do that, not with Lawson here. He'd kill Lucia and Felipe to destroy any evidence.

"I think we should all go back inside now." Dr. Lawson glowered at them. "I'm not sure how you got away. You're just as smart as I thought you were. We would have been so good together. You, the successful journalist. Me, the dashing doctor. I had plans for us, you know."

Savannah shook her head. "I'm not going back inside with you."

Something evil glimmered in his eyes. "Yes, you are."

"No, I'm not." How was she going to get away with Lucia? The girl hung on her arm, practically pulling her down. There was no way.

Lord, help me. What should I do?

Dr. Lawson lunged for her. She ducked, sending Lucia toppling to the ground.

The doctor sprang toward her again, this time catching her arm. Before she could get away, he put the rope around her neck and pulled.

The air left Savannah's lungs. She clawed at the rope. Kicked. Thrashed back and forth.

She looked over at Lucia. Saw her eyes wide with fear.

Something about seeing her caused a surge of adrenaline to explode inside her.

She let go of the rope, reached into her pocket, and unscrewed the top of the bottle. Just as Dr. Lawson tightened the rope, she flung the bottle behind her. The liquid hit his eyes, and he howled with pain.

That gave her just enough time to scramble across the sand. She gulped in deep breaths of air and tried to control her panic.

She grabbed Lucia and pulled her toward the boat. It was their only hope.

Yet such a long shot.

But at the moment they had no other choice.

CHAPTER 58

Savannah pushed Lucia into the boat before climbing in herself.

On the shore, Dr. Lawson cried out in pain and muttered threats. He rubbed at his eyes, bent over in agony.

Savannah quickly looked at the boat's small motor. She wasn't sure how to operate one, but how hard could it be?

The boat was small, the kind used for fishing. She grabbed the string at the motor and tugged.

Nothing happened.

She looked over at Dr. Lawson. He'd straightened and was now lumbering toward them.

Her pulse quickened. Not much time.

They had to get out of here. Had to get help for Felipe. Lucia needed medical care. Fluid. Food. Who knew what else?

She tugged again. The engine sputtered. She didn't have time to look back. She continued pulling.

Finally the engine roared to life.

She grabbed the handle and jerked it to the left, trying to figure out how to get the boat moving.

Just as they began to putter backward, Dr. Lawson lunged at them. He caught the bow of the boat.

Lucia screamed.

Savannah abandoned the engine, stomping on the doctor's fingers. It was no use. His adrenaline seemed to have taken over, and with what appeared to be almost superhuman strength, he clawed his way into the boat.

Savannah clambered back to the engine. She pulled the handle hard, and the boat spun around.

Still Dr. Lawson hung on. His legs were inside the boat now.

And Savannah had no idea what her next move would be.

. . .

Jack treaded water, trying to plan his moves carefully. He'd made the swim from the boat ramp to the island.

He kept himself hidden, waiting for the right opportunity. Now he swam closer and closer to the boat.

If he wasn't careful, the boat's propeller would slice off part of his face.

Dr. Lawson lunged at Savannah, and Jack knew he had no time to waste. He inched to the edge of the boat and remained low as the watercraft jerked in the water.

When he heard Savannah gasp, he struck.

He burst from the water and grabbed the doctor's arm. It afforded Savannah the chance to back away, her eyes wide.

"Jack?" she gasped.

Jack used his grip on Dr. Lawson to pull him into the water. The boat rocked precariously but stayed afloat. The doctor disappeared underwater.

Where had he gone?

"Are you okay?" Jack asked Savannah, climbing aboard.

She nodded, gripping Lucia's hand. "Yeah, I'm fine. I've got to get Lucia some help, though."

Just then the boat swayed.

He braced himself, knowing what was coming.

Dr. Lawson was under the boat.

And he was trying to tip them over.

·   ·   ·

Savannah gasped as she felt the movement of the boat. Suddenly the whole vessel flipped. Water surrounded her.

Lucia. Where was Lucia?

Savannah found her footing and stood. The water wasn't that deep here. Maybe a sandbar.

A few feet away, she saw a flash of yellow.

She dove into the water and grabbed Lucia, pulling her from the water. The girl sputtered before drawing in a deep breath.

"It's going to be okay," Savannah told her. "I'm going to get you help."

On the other side of the boat, she spotted Dr. Lawson and Jack. They tumbled into the water, fists flying.

She had to help.

"Can you stay here for a moment? Can you stand up?" The waves weren't strong and the water only reached her waist.

Lucia nodded.

Reluctantly Savannah left her, praying she would be okay.

She approached the two men from behind. In the flurry of their struggle, neither noticed her.

She reached into her pocket and pulled out the needle. Slipping the protective cap off, she gripped the syringe like a knife.

Just as Dr. Lawson forced Jack's head under the water, Savannah lunged at the doctor. She plunged the needle into his neck.

He cried out with pain and flung her off of him.

His face twisted with agony.

Jack shot to the surface, gulping in mad breaths of air. He grabbed Dr. Lawson and pushed him down. The doctor struggled, flailing and clawing Jack's arm in desperation to regain control.

Jack didn't let up. He held Dr. Lawson under the water. The muscles bulged at Jack's neck and temples.

Dr. Lawson was going to drown, Savannah realized.

"Jack!" she screamed.

His eyes connected with her and something flashed there. Was it guilt? Retribution? Anger?

Dr. Lawson's movements were becoming slower, more lethargic. He didn't have much time before the water filled his lungs and claimed his life.

"You'll create a new prison for yourself if you take a life, Jack," Savannah pleaded.

Jack looked down, and the hardness dropped from his eyes. His shoulders slumped for a moment—not in defeat, but in resignation.

He released his grip on Dr. Lawson, and the man shot to the surface. He sputtered before gulping in deep breaths. He grabbed his throat. His body was bent over, his eyes bloodshot.

"I didn't stop to save you," Jack muttered. "I stopped to save myself."

A voice from a bullhorn cut through the air.

"This is Chief Lockwood. Put your hands up."

Savannah looked back and saw three police boats surrounding them.

Finally help was here.

CHAPTER 59

As Lucia and Felipe were wheeled into a waiting ambulance to be taken to the hospital for proper treatment, Savannah hopped down from the back of the other ambulance where she'd been evaluated. She searched for Jack.

In the background, she could hear the sirens, and she remembered Pastor Tom's words.

Whenever I hear a siren, I pray.

She lifted up a prayer of thankfulness for safety, of gratefulness for second chances, of protection for those who'd be affected by all of this.

Then she spotted Jack. He had wrapped up his conversation with Chief Lockwood and now turned toward her.

She flinched when she saw the beginnings of a bruise on the side of his eye, a slash across his bicep, and a swollen jaw. He'd been willing to risk his life for her. There weren't many people she could say that about.

"Thank you," she said, shoving her hands into her pockets as she stared up at him.

He stepped closer and lowered his voice. "I'm glad you're okay, Savannah."

A lump lodged in her throat. "Jack, I know you didn't kill your wife. I knew even before I figured out Dr. Lawson was behind all of this. I think I knew all along. I just had to make sure."

"I'm sorry I didn't tell you earlier. I wanted to, but I knew how it would sound."

"Really, that's understandable. Any logical person would have run in the other direction," Savannah admitted.

Before he could say anything else, Savannah threw her arms around his neck and pulled him close. She was grateful that he'd come into her life. Grateful that he was beside her now. Grateful for all they'd been through together.

Sometimes all a person had to hold on to was the moment.

His strong arms wrapped around her waist, and they held each other.

Savannah knew one thing: she never wanted to let go.

EPILOGUE

Savannah helped Marti from her car. Jack raced around to join her on the other side.

"I'm perfectly capable of—" Marti started.

"I'm helping," Savannah insisted, taking her arm.

"I can see it's two against one here, so I'll stop arguing," she muttered.

They helped her into Savannah's house, not stopping until they reached the couch, where they gently deposited her. Marti would be staying with Savannah until her life evened out.

"Can I get you some water?" Jack asked.

"What a gentleman. But no, I'm fine," Marti insisted. "Savannah, I knew you should take in a boarder. I'm glad you finally listened to me. He's a keeper."

Savannah and Jack exchanged a smile.

"I agree," Savannah said.

Marti propped her feet up on the table and leaned back. "So catch me up. I already know I have terrible taste in men."

"You heard about Leonard, right?" Savannah straightened the pillows around Marti, wanting to make sure she was comfortable.

Marti nodded. "Yeah, he was afraid you were going to scoop him on the secret society article, so he cleaned out your e-mail account to buy himself more time. He obviously didn't understand your style."

"Seems like he was desperate to make a name for himself," Savannah added. Leonard had been arrested after snooping around on the congressman's property, and he'd spilled everything to the police. He'd even been at Landon's house looking for some kind of clue, some evidence, to prove his secret society theories were true.

Marti rubbed her hands on her jeans. "Maybe I should say that aside from Leonard, I haven't been able to keep up with all the news."

"I don't think anyone in town has been able to," Jack said. He sat down in an overstuffed chair, and Savannah leaned against one of the cushy arms.

Her heart raced when Jack's arm snaked around her waist. Every time he touched her, her heart fluttered and flipped. Best of all, those feelings didn't scare her anymore.

"To sum it up, Dr. Lawson thought he'd hit the jackpot when Ernie approached him about a new pesticide that was having incredible results on the crops," Savannah said. "He wanted to do a five-year study on the new product, but apparently that wasn't fast enough for Dr. Lawson, so he started doing some experiments himself to speed up the results. The police are looking into other mysterious deaths the doctor has connections to."

Savannah picked up the newspaper on the coffee table and held it up. The headlines screamed the truth—about Dr. Lawson and about Jack. She glanced at Jack, knowing just how life-changing this new information was. "Most importantly, Dr. Lawson admitted to the murder of Jack's wife."

"The right person will finally pay the price. It's six years in the making." Jack smiled. He was finally a free man. Truly free.

"And don't forget about that apple you grabbed and had tested," Savannah reminded him. "It was covered with pesticides. The new formula was carcinogenic. The migrant workers were basically used as guinea pigs."

Savannah opened the newspaper. On the second page was an article detailing Dr. Lawson's history, including facts about his upbringing, bullying, coming from the wrong side of the tracks. By all appearances, Dr. Lawson had been the one who called Savannah and lured her to the hospital. He'd disguised his voice like a woman's, making sure the connection was so bad that Savannah hadn't been able to tell.

"I guess Landon wasn't the bad guy after all," Marti said. "He's just an evil corporate farmer who—"

"—pays his workers virtually nothing while making a hefty profit himself," Savannah finished grimly. "He was surprisingly clueless about all of this."

"And I still don't like him," Jack added. "For more than one reason."

Marti smiled at them. "You two are so cute together. One day when you're married, you'll be able to tell your kids how you saved each other's lives and all that."

"I think you're jumping a little too far ahead," Savannah said.

Marti's grin widened. "We'll see." She stood and stretched. "I'm going upstairs to rest for a while."

Savannah also stood, ready to help her, but Marti raised a hand.

"I've got this," she insisted. "Please, let me maintain some of my dignity."

Savannah watched as Marti slowly made her way up the stairs. When she paused halfway up, she started to go after her, but Jack pulled her back down.

"She's got this," he insisted.

Savannah nodded, still not taking her eyes from Marti until she reached the top. Then she turned to Jack. They hadn't had a chance to talk since everything had exploded. There had been police interviews, meetings with Jack's lawyers, one-on-one talks with news stations. Everything seemed like a blur.

He took her hand and kissed it.

"Could this really be over for you?" she asked.

"That's what it looks like."

"I'm sorry for everything, but I'm glad you'll be able to finally move on."

"There are still some technicalities we'll have to work out, but I think this is really coming to a close."

Her throat tightened. She'd avoided asking this question, telling herself she needed resolution in other areas of her life first, areas like Lucia and Dr. Lawson and Marti. Now that Lucia was recovering, Dr. Lawson was in jail, and Marti was out of the hospital, Savannah had no excuses. She had to face reality with Jack, and that reality included the fact that his time in her life could just be temporary. "What will you do now?"

"I'm hoping you might let me stay in the guesthouse."

She playfully raised an eyebrow. "How will you pay rent?"

"I was hoping you might want someone to fix up this place." He looked around her house. "Some paint would work wonders. So would stripping this floor and sanding it down."

"That's an idea. But don't you want to practice law again?" He couldn't give up his career to be a handyman. He was too talented, and his talents would be wasted in a place like Cape Thomas. There weren't enough people to warrant a law practice.

He nodded. "Eventually. But first I have to start feeling normal again. I need time to breathe. Make sense?"

Savannah nodded, some of the tension leaving her. "Absolutely. Sometimes these things take much longer than we anticipate. It's important not to rush things."

He kissed her forehead before picking up the newspaper from the coffee table where Marti had left it. He smiled when he read the headline. It was great to see him smiling so much. He'd regained not only his reputation but his life. He'd proven himself to be stronger than his impulses for vengeance.

"Speaking of careers, wasn't today the day the newspaper wanted an answer from you? Are you the town's new editor in chief? I've got to admit that your eyes light up when you see this newspaper."

"That has a lot to do with the content of the articles." The local newspaper had offered her a position with them, but she was still considering her options. "I'm going back to journalism. I just don't know if I'll keep it local or not."

"Good for you."

She placed her hand on the side of his face, soaking in all of the intricacies of his features. "I like the idea of fixing up the house, though."

He caught her wrist in his hand. "I can't imagine leaving here, Savannah. I can't imagine leaving you."

Her heart stuttered a moment before speeding again. "I can't tell you how incredibly happy that makes me."

He pulled her toward him, his lips covering hers.

When they pulled away, Jack still held her. She nestled her head in the curve of his neck, relishing the feel of Jack's arms around her waist.

Jack wasn't the only one who felt redemption. God had somehow also redeemed her life. He'd taken her messes. He'd taken her doubts. He'd taken someone who felt like a lone bead in an old rattle. He'd somehow made her whole again.

Satisfied. Definition: *content*.

The very thing that Savannah felt at the moment.

ACKNOWLEDGEMENTS

I'd like to thank my husband and children for cheering me on and supporting me. I couldn't do it without you all.

I'd like to thank Kathy Applebee for her input. You have a gift for story, and I'm so honored to know you.

I'd like to thank all of my Facebook friends for pointing me in the right direction for research. If in doubt, I always know one of you will have an answer or can guide me to someone who does. A special thanks to Tamara Davis for helping me name the non-profit The Promised Land and for my Spanish-speaking friends who guided me in translation.

Thanks to everyone I ever interviewed in my nearly ten years as a newspaper reporter. You changed how I viewed life by allowing me into your lives. I'm better for it.

ABOUT THE AUTHOR

USA Today calls Christy Barritt's writing "scary, funny, passionate, and quirky." Her mystery and romantic suspense novels have sold half a million copies, won the Daphne du Maurier Award for Excellence in Suspense and Mystery, and were twice nominated for the *Romantic Times* Reviewers' Choice Award. Christy was born in Virginia, and while she has been writing since she was very young, she's also sung at local coffeehouses and was a newspaper journalist for ten years. Her husband is a children's pastor, and together they have two adorably handsome sons.

Christy is best known for her Love Inspired Suspense novels, as well as her Squeaky Clean Mystery series. She currently has more than two dozen books published.